Author photo © Scott Kershaw

Louise Leverett graduated from Mountview Academy of Theatre Arts in London on a full scholarship before moving to study at the Lee Strasberg Institute of Film in New York. Since establishing her own business 'Rock the Tribes' she is now working on a collection of writings that will eventually be turned into adaptions for screen.

Love and Other Things to Live For

Louise Leverett

ONE PLACE. MANY STORIES

HQ
An imprint of HarperCollins*Publishers* Ltd
1 London Bridge Street
London SE1 9GF

This edition 2019

1

First published in Great Britain by
HQ, an imprint of HarperCollins*Publishers* Ltd 2019

ISBN PB: 978-0-00-823703-5

MIX
Paper from
responsible sources
FSC™ C007454

This book is produced from independently certified FSC™ paper
to ensure responsible forest management.

For more information visit: www.harpercollins.co.uk/green

This book is set in 11.4/16 pt. Adobe Caslon Pro

Printed and bound in Great Britain by
CPI Group (UK) Ltd, Croydon, CR0 4YY

for mum, dad
and alex…

Chapter One – The Curse of a Burning Flame

I awoke to the sound of a clock.

Tick.
  Tock.
    Tick.
      Tock.

Opening my eyes to the beginnings of a new day.

I don't smoke, barely drink, have never experienced casual sex and so this was the tasting menu of new discoveries. I had decided to dip my toe in the final waters of youth as an almost goodbye to my carefree years, complete with late nights and a series of events that had caused my heart to pound and my head to spin. What began with a plethora of shots and inappropriate dancing with a man I barely knew but had worked with my friend, so not a total stranger; perhaps emotionally but certainly not geographically, had now ended with the realisation that the answer to my predicament did not lie at the bottom of a bottle. I had persuaded myself I would see him again, clinging onto the slim thread that last night meant something. But it didn't. And to be totally honest, lashing out at the world as redemption for a broken heart just wasn't as fun as I had imagined it would be.

I was getting over someone. Charlie. Perhaps not going the right way about it but trying all the same. And although my appearance suggested I was carefree, inside I was hurting. Slowly seeping through the cracks of my show, my life, was the added complication of a career low. On a whim that was no longer whimsical, I had left university and a path to study law, exchanging it for the butterflies-in-your-tummy notion that you should chase what sets your heart on fire. I'd lit the match only for it to fizzle into charcoal once the reality hit that photography jobs aren't exactly easy to come by. My dreams had been dowsed cold by stress and financial burden. And now, adding the salt to my wounds, having made the somewhat optimistic decision to move in with a man I'd just met and barely knew, I was back in my old bedroom and back in the flat I'd shared for years with my best friend, Amber. Despite many a raised eyebrow, I'd ridden the wave of infatuation all the way to the shores of his flat overlooking the Thames and now I'd slunk back, just three months later, humiliated and alone.

As I sat on the edge of the bed waiting for my head to stop spinning, sipping on a glass of stagnant water filled with stale, iridescent bubbles, images from the previous night cascaded through my mind. There was wine, spirits, more wine… more spirits… and dancing. Lots of dancing. Crazy moves, big moves, bold moves, total abandonment of body, mind and self-control. Dancing with friends, dancing alone, dancing with the man now lying next to me. I slowly massaged my brow in a belated attempt to melt the thought away.

Looking over at him, the semi-stranger sleeping beside me, I slowly shuffled my way out of the bed and across the corridor to the bathroom. I glanced in the mirror at my reflection: tousled hair with last night's make-up, a squiggly smear of mascara underlining each eye like a spelling mistake. If this was being young and free it certainly wasn't as enjoyable as my friends had suggested. It was all their fault, obviously.

I crouched above the strange, cold toilet pan, the back of my thighs skimming the bowl, my mouth stinging as if stripped by a razor blade. I wasn't about to play the blame game. It was all my own choice, a mess that I had gotten myself into in a moment of panic – a searing fear that I might be getting left behind. But falling behind whom? Myself? As I spun the empty cardboard toilet roll hoping to magic a stream of paper, it seemed as if I'd forgotten to learn the rules to a game that I was now, apparently, an expert at playing.

It was late December, and waking up was beginning to hurt. I made my way across the pavement, halfway between streetlights and sunlight, and turned onto the street that was familiar. I started the day carrying make-up in my handbag, using a public toilet as my vanity: a wanderer, a nomad in between places. And that's exactly where I was, in between places.

I longed for my early twenties: the days of the invincible and raw misconception of youth. It was all fun and games back then. If you don't invest fully then no one gets hurt. But unfortunately, my recent experience with one particular man – the only man, in fact – had become a harsh lesson that

I was wrong. We'd met, feelings were felt and it was now over. I'd been hurt.

In my mind the cause of these relationship problems is that men and women don't understand one another; that, as the well-known book says, we literally are on different planets when it comes to matters of the heart and relationships. Of course, what transpired, in human form, was a cosmic connection that no amount of textbook knowledge could account for. My friend Sean assures me that when it comes to the formidable topic of that four-letter word beginning with 'l' ending with 'e', both on the outskirts of 'o' and 'v', there is no distinct correlation between the sexes. It's just quite hard, for all of us.

We live in the digital age of a steady stream of information right there on our computer screens, influencing our relationship to commerce, the food we eat and now, even our love lives. We can flick through the online catalogue of human faces, swiping left or right depending whether we like what we see, in exactly the same way our grandmothers picked out a cut of meat at the butcher's. It's safe, sterile even, but not quite real. Before we've even met them we know a person's age, occupation, habits, likes, dislikes – basically all the information our ancestors would have found out across a table in the romantic haze of candlelight and that second bottle of wine. We look to our ancestors with a smug confidence that we know better. We live safe in the knowledge that while the notches on the bedpost rack up, no one ever has to get bored with each other.

But through the bright lights and heavy laughter of a fun night out, a little voice of truth inside knew this wasn't for me. I couldn't even handle a man not texting me back, never mind flicking past my face amidst the scores of other women, ten or even twenty at a time. In this twenty-first-century world, I'm almost embarrassed to say that I have remained tied to the notion of monogamy, or old-fashioned love, as it's now known. A stagnant belief that I should probably keep to myself, not exactly like the love we see in the movies but in my heart of hearts, not far off either. I bet Tom Hanks didn't have to ask Meg Ryan if she was still seeing other people as they made their way down from the top of the Empire State Building.

For both sexes, it's certainly been a transition. Although every generation will say they were witness to an epic change in cultural climate – the Thirties' prohibition, the world war of the Forties, the sexual revolution of the Sixties and Seventies – I still maintain that the biggest change, both in the cultural and social climate, was the dawn of the digital age. The invention of the Internet brought along with it a speed of living beyond anybody's imagination. We have the ability to remain in touch with lost friends, lost colleagues... even past loves. But I can't help but think that there are some people who were just meant to be left behind.

As we look around amidst the sea of fast culture, our minds and hearts are expected to keep up with an ever-changing, ever-evolving landscape. Fast love turns to fast disappointment – a speedy turnover in a global economy piling pressure on those struggling to keep up. Me being one of them. We've lost the element of fear that drives us to do the unimaginable, the senseless. We must focus on those spectacular and rare moments when our hearts overrule our heads and swiping a screen is revealed to be just that, a perfunctory movement completely separate from the glimmer of excitement that the sound of a voice brings or the way the heart beats when a certain person is near.

Instead, we keep ourselves at a distance through computer screens, safe inside the trenches, afraid to advance towards enemy lines. But within this battle of dating warfare it is sometimes hard to work out who the real winners even are. It certainly wasn't me and it certainly wasn't now.

And where else do we set this tale of the digital age but in the vast, diverse, empowering city of London. She is the modern-day metropolis inhabiting a wilderness of magic, mystery and intrigue. To me, London is the only permanent fixture within the landscape of movement, bright lights and imagination, a heady mix of corporate business and artistic dreaming: an odyssey of restaurants, bars and nightlife and people... oh so many people, all collectively inhabiting as a bottleneck of strangers, roommates, bedmates and friends. It is the man-made land where the lonely find company and the unemployed find jobs amidst part-time renters and full-time problems.

And it isn't so bad: except the overcrowding, the pollution and the house prices because here, anything is possible, and as much as I wanted to stay under the duvet and come out once the storm had passed, I knew that I had no other option but to set sail. I had a career to find, a love to forget and a future to behold.

So as I stand on the precipice of a year so unpredicted, I'm going to ask a small question to the universe and see what I get offered back: why do I feel so unshakeably restless and what will inevitably be *enough*? And if, as I anticipate, the road gets a little bumpy, my armour will come in the form of my friends. The collection of people whom you choose to ride the wave with: the truth-tellers, the heart-menders, my people to live for.

I met Amber at an after-hours course on corporate law. I was failing my second term quite badly by then and had embarked on some extra-curricular activity in a desperate attempt to boost both my grades and my passion for the subject. Amongst the rows and rows of twenty-year-olds in suits, Amber sat perched on a stool diligently scribbling into a hot pink notebook. She smiled and waved me over.

'Weren't you here last week?' she said. 'Bit dry, wasn't it…'

'A bit,' I said, looking around at the huddles of people talking confidently about shareholder's rights.

'I've got a party later – correction – I'm working at a party later, it's this launch for a cosmetics line. They're going to use my face as a guinea pig. Fancy it?'

She asked me in a way that left me feeling as if I had no option.

'There's a free bar?'

And that wasn't a question.

'Sure, sounds good,' I said.

She smiled. 'Great. I'll see you outside at nine.'

I learned on the way to the party that her name was Amber. She was funny and sharply clever – the type of clever that scared you into not talking, knowing you'd only come off worse in a discussion. Since she couldn't afford law school, she'd been forced to undertake night school as a sideline to her modelling – a part-time arrangement that wasn't going to be forever, she said.

I followed her black ponytail through the crowds and soon found myself sandwiched between the trays of complimentary champagne and a group of shoppers eagerly awaiting the tutorial. I watched Amber, seated on a high stool, her long black hair swept clean off her face, as the make-up artist demonstrated contouring for the less attractive people who believed they needed far more make-up than she did. To my surprise they actually looked interested. I still didn't know who she was, but I'd been able to find a seat next to a real palm tree, shipped in specially for the launch, and I was already three glasses down of the free champers. Gradually, our eyes kept meeting in the midst of face priming and bronzer application and a shared look of disdain proved instantly that we could be friends.

'Where in God's name did I put my phone?' she yelled once the crowds had dispersed, demonstrating the feistiness that she would inevitably need to become a lawyer. As we both began lifting coats and scarfs she emptied out her handbag onto the counter, sorting through the contents, with strips of white tissue paper still clipped in her hair.

'I think it's next to your coat.' I nodded as I downed the rest of my champagne.

'Thanks,' she said, pulling it free. 'I'm supposed to be at another night class but skipped it to be here. Do you think that's bad? They offered me fifty quid an hour so I couldn't say no, really.'

She smiled at me, a smile so full and disarming that it is rarely seen between two women – especially in a big city.

'What are you studying?' I asked, looking at her large black leather bag, bulging with a ring binder and textbooks.

'I want to work in e-commerce,' she said, pulling out a hair tie and wrapping it around her wrist. 'It's retail, essentially, but covering trade laws. Apparently in five years we'll only be buying online and since I won't be able to model forever I thought I might need a Plan B before my face sags. Do you smoke?'

I shook my head.

'Shame. I like your bag,' she said, referring to my pink rucksack, spinning the conversation on its head.

'Thanks,' I said. 'I like your shoes.'

Since that night, we've both stuck around. It's not that she's a good friend per se, it's that we've become a firm fixture in each other's lives. First we created memories and then memories created a history and with that came the foundations of a friendship. Solid but low maintenance.

I wish I had her brains. I think she even surprises herself with her razor-sharp intelligence at times. She's a pro-choice, pro-women ball-buster, blazing the path, charging ahead so that the less confident ones, like me, can trot along behind. She's the one who will convince you that just one more tequila shot won't kill you, knowing that she'll also be there to hold your hair back when you're hanging over the toilet bowl slowly coming to the realisation that it might. For the record: she can hold her drink, I can't. She is also the friend who will read every text he ever sent you and piece together the scenario like the Robin to your Batman, sharing the burden so you feel like less of a sociopath. She can spot a liar from forty paces, she'll defend you but never judges, and beneath the attractive exterior she is actually pretty tough – a lot tougher than me – and life is a little less scary knowing she is on my side.

Sean is a different kettle of fish: a jester in a cashmere cardigan. A New Yorker living in London who I'd met at a farmer's market while embarking on a celebrity-endorsed, high-intensity juice detox. We decided that we would go for sober dinners together and talk about sensible topics like our careers and world affairs. The detox lasted one month, our friendship somewhat longer. On the inside, half an inch beneath the funny, confident exterior, lies a quiet determination, an unyielding passion which leads him to still be in the design studio at eleven thirty, long after his team have gone home. He won't think twice about spending a month's rent on a jumper and will somehow convince you to do the same. He is the friend who will sit and listen to your problems without so much as mentioning his own: there's a resilient enamel that coats a sensitive soul, a soul you have to keep your eye on because deep down you know he isn't keeping an eye on himself. For years he dated Paul, a man almost twice his age, who would do spontaneously romantic things, like arrange a weekend for two in Europe for a birthday celebration. I remember these fine details, as I was the one roped into hiking up Regent Street looking for a pair of brown-leather ankle boots specifically for the occasion.

'I never thought I'd be jealous of my best friend, his older lover and a pair of gloriously soft ankle boots,' I said, pressing my hand firmly inside one. Far from the perfect audience, I watched him walk up and down the carpeted floor of Russell and Bromley one Saturday afternoon as he looked at me for encouragement.

'Just take them,' I said, in desperation, perched on the seats designated for customers to try on the shop's wares, 'and then you can take me for a cocktail.'

There's one memory that will last beyond the drunken nights, the cinema trips, the endless stream of gossiping phone calls – the time I got a different kind of phone call one cold, rainy night in November. It was 2.30 a.m. and I was fast asleep when my phone rang loudly on the bedside table. Seeing it was Sean I assumed he'd been partying and had locked himself out again and needed a place to stay. I almost ignored it.

'What do you want, Sean?' I snapped. 'It's the middle of the night.'

There was a silence. I could hear talking in the background as my eyes slowly opened and I came to my senses.

'Sean, what's wrong? Are you okay?'

'It's Paul,' I heard, quietly but clearly. 'He's been in an accident. I'm at the hospital.'

Thirty minutes later I walked down the long, squeaky corridor that seemed endless and sterile. I turned into the waiting room and saw Sean seated wearing a pale blue jumper and jeans. The sort of outfit you put on in a hurry, I thought to myself. I crouched down and put my arm on his back. 'I'm so sorry,' I whispered.

He lifted his head, his face reddened and swollen from the tears. 'He was driving back from work and a lorry clipped the wheel arch. You know how fast he drives.'

I sat there and held him until sunrise.

Paul's funeral was on a sunny Tuesday morning. It was a small affair, there were no hymns and two readings, and it was over by midday.

Last but not least is Marlowe: graceful swan, mother earth incarnate, encyclopaedia of heaven-sent advice from the sane and grown-up world. She is perfect and I am a mess. We'd met as teenagers – two cocky, know-it-all dreamers, whose backsides were about to be spanked by life right into next Tuesday. While I'd continued this behaviour well beyond its sell-by date, she'd been forced to grow up far quicker than the rest of us. Marlowe is a class act who is seemingly unshakable navigating obstacles that would leave others screaming into their pillow. There's an apologetic air about her, as with those who have spent their life subject to the jealousy of their peers. It's as if they need to make it up to those around them for not being clumsy, or slightly chubby or keeping a coat on when they've spilled soup down their jumper. Or for being born into success, for that matter. Marlowe is constantly under the watch of her parents who seem to guide the trajectory of her life from the conservatory of their conservative city townhouse. Her dad was a famous journalist and now deep into writing his memoirs, and her mum was an English socialite, whose glamour and impeccable sense of style has been retained well into her sixties.

Marlowe was always going to succeed in whichever field she chose to pursue so you can imagine our surprise when things took a turn for the unexpected, a few years ago, one summer afternoon in July. It was the hottest day of the year and London had quite literally come to a standstill. The smell of Hendrick's gin filled the air, and for the first time in a long while a drought had threatened to take hold across Britain.

We'd been invited to one of her parents' infamous bar-becues. They owned a townhouse in West London and for one afternoon a year it became home to the who's who of the slightly elder, more intellectual social scene. At that time, we used these occasions as an opportunity to stock up on free booze before going to a club later that night, but this time things unfolded rather differently. I arrived late, as usual, and expected Marlowe to be in the garden barefoot in jeans amidst a sea of Panama hats and beige summer suits, but this time she was nowhere to be seen. I made my way through the bodies cluttering the house, loud in idle chitchat, and arrived at the bottom of the stairs where I pulled out my phone to text her. As I began to type, I looked up towards the top of the dark staircase to see her seated in a crisp white T-shirt and denim skirt, a distinct shine on her bare shins gleaming through the shadows.

'Jess, up here,' she said, signalling me into the bathroom.

I followed her across the marble tiled floor and there it was, lying on the sink, lodged sideways between the hot and cold taps, the end of the future as we knew it and a building block of a dilemma for Marlowe. A pregnancy test that read *positive*.

'Jesus,' I whispered. 'Is it yours?'

'Of course it's mine,' she snapped, grabbing it to shake it.

'I don't think shaking it is going to help, Mars.'

She sat down gently on the bathroom floor and drew her legs towards her. I took hold of the test to double-check its result and took a deep breath to replace the ones I'd since lost. She looked up at me with glassy eyes.

'What am I going to do?' she said.

And what do you say to the perfect girl, the girl who irons her underwear, who wears white and doesn't spill, the girl now pregnant and crying. I didn't say anything. Instead I just sat down on the cold floor tiles next to her.

'I can't have a baby, Jess. I'm twenty-three years old,' she whispered.

I noticed her hands were trembling, her chipped orange nail polish rubbing against her two front teeth. Girls like Marlowe weren't supposed to get pregnant. She was supposed to spend her days practising law, not the alphabet. I squeezed her warm hand that was still damp from tears. At that point there was a knock at the door, one of the other partygoers, oblivious and persistent, who clearly needed use of the bathroom.

'Just a minute, please,' I shouted politely.

There was a brief pause before they knocked again.

'In a fucking minute!' Marlowe shouted through her tears.

Together we sat side by side on the cold, tiled floor, knowing that in just one afternoon, everything had changed.

In the modern world, there are many options open to women in the wake of an unplanned pregnancy but for Marlowe it seemed the most preferable answer would be marriage. The carefully arranged wedding was six months later and after much debate, they had promised as a family that she would have the baby first and start her career later. But as with most things in life, it didn't really work out that way. Now George was travelling all over the world while Marlowe stays at home. That little blue line we had once gathered around with baited breath is now called Elsa.

Before Marlowe's parents had led her down the road of commitment and common decency, she was a permanent fixture on our nights out. She drank like a trooper, never danced but always turned up in an eclectic mix of designer and vintage clothes, accompanied by a desperate claim that she had purchased them all in the sale. We still see her, usually for relationship or career advice or when we need a sensible opinion and a healthy meal. And despite her newfound love of the quiet life she still comes out to the big celebrations: birthdays, new jobs, new hairstyles. To put it bluntly, Marlowe is the moral lighthouse in our slightly less sophisticated world. When she announced she was getting married I cried tears of joy, Amber cried tears of sadness and Sean began sketching her wedding dress.

And finally to me, a girl who loves Mexican food and bowling and low-budget horror films, gently flying solo into the abyss: no brothers, no sisters, two parents who years ago deemed it better to carry on life apart, on separate continents in separate time zones with separate hearts. Perhaps I'm only now realising as I stand here, not quite young and not quite old, that their situation might not have been an easy one. That a family doesn't necessarily work better together.

I've learned that after a while, it can get pretty tricky to always make the right decisions, to do what everyone else expects of you and to make people happy. We discard the days, the weeks, the months, the years on the journey towards the destination as somewhat unimportant compared to the magical days of a future where we aim to one day be. But they will suddenly merge together and we will realise that *this* day, *this* week, *this* month, *this* year, these little, insignificant things culminate to form our lives, all joined together, like a map of the stars but instead right here on earth: a thousand lives crisscrossing, at times colliding. But the secret is not to avoid the collision. If the horizon blurs and the plans fade, just think of the places travelled, the things seen and the strangers now known as friends: it all happened because you once made what you had thought to have been a mistake.

Chapter Two – The Art of Intent

Cause…

Battle commenced one windy Friday morning last September. There was something in the air that day; I felt restless, almost as if suddenly, and without warning, my life wasn't enough any more, any sense of pride or ambition had vanished. My mind ached like a lead weight. *This wasn't me.* That was the only thing at this point that I actually knew to be true. The historical swirls of self-doubt that continually crept in weren't going to win this time. Not that morning. Not today.

I was at the beginning of a food shop at the supermarket across town and, as I walked briskly through the automatic doors, I stopped for a moment to look up at the final leaves on the trees, clinging on with the same sense of stubbornness. I had decided in a combined haze of high spirit and spirits to push aside the idea of law and pursue my dream of becoming a photographer. It had me taken two years at law school to arrive at that decision and the leap hadn't felt quite as wonderful as I had imagined. The disapproval of my father, moored somewhere off the South of France with his latest girlfriend, was evident. A short conversation resulted in us both hanging up the phone, which was surprising, as I thought he might relate given he felt the exact same sense of inadequacy about family life. Naturally, I had come to the conclusion that from that point on, I was on my own.

As I dragged the bags of shopping up the steps to our flat, I felt as if the air had been knocked out of me. The big supermarket was quite the commitment in terms of travel but a worthy respite from the express shop around the corner which, although convenient, was half the size and half the value. They even had a car park with trolley bays. I noticed this and despite not having a car was reasonably impressed. These days, I had time on my hands to appreciate such details. I pulled open the door and struggled inside, my fingers throbbing from the weight of the tinned goods. There was a note from Amber on the kitchen counter that read: 'Please buy milk.' I picked up the five-pound note and slid it into my jacket pocket.

After unpacking the contents of my bags into the fridge and cupboards I noticed the grey clouds heaving above me through the kitchen window. It couldn't rain now, I thought. My day hadn't been productive enough to be shut indoors. Quickly I pulled on my leggings and trainers and set off into the light downpour, determined to complete a run, determined to succeed at something that day. But in a few short minutes the light shower turned torrential. I stood at the very wet news-stand to shelter from the downpour under a sky of protective blue tarpaulin. I could feel the sting of a re-opened blister niggling the heel of my foot. I crouched down precariously to slide my foot out of my trainer, briefly easing the pain. A man in a large cream mac with a money belt attached to his waist began to pay me particular attention. He had caught me lingering. It was obvious I wasn't his usual customer. I picked up a magazine that looked fairly respectable and pretended to read it as water dripped through the plastic sheeting.

'It's not a library,' he said, restacking his stock. 'You want to read it, you buy it first.'

I nodded subserviently and retrieved the five-pound note from my jacket pocket.

As I walked home with my unwanted copy of *Business Life* magazine I flicked through it briefly. On the cover was a successful, dark-haired businessman named as one of the top five financiers who'd brought back the economy from the brink of disaster. He worked at Giles and Morgan. I rolled my eyes. They were the company to whom I'd submitted a series of photographs for consideration six months ago and heard nothing since. Amber's friend Nick, who worked there as an account manager, had advised me to corner the financial sector and supply lifestyle images in return for a serious amount of cash. His words. By now the rain had ceased to a faint drizzle and I had succumbed to using the magazine as a shield on the short run home.

'Come on,' Amber bellowed into her phone. 'Don't be such a boring bastard.'

She wanted to go out for drinks that night but the truth was I was in hiding. I couldn't face another bad date, another bad restaurant, I just wanted to focus all my energy on creating my future, not further blurring my present.

'Would it help if I told you that we're meeting Nick and it might be another chance to talk about your photographs?'

It was a predictable effort from her but it worked just the same.

'Okay,' I agreed. 'I'll meet you there at eight.'

I looked down at myself in the hallway, in my comfortable bra and pants. I pulled the elastic with my index finger and readjusted my pant line. Maybe she was right – maybe I was getting boring.

The bar was in the City, which was a strange choice for Amber, but I knew her well and could tell from the start that this place was far out enough to a) pick up new men and b) hide from the old ones. Despite the unfamiliar setting, the situation wasn't exactly new. The bar was heaving and full of the type of young professionals I'd spent two years at university trying to avoid. I'd already lost Amber. Anyone who has ever been out with Amber has lost her, but as with most beautiful friendships between young women, I knew she wouldn't leave the bar without me. I had one quick look around and by chance saw Nick talking to Brian, a man who I had desperately wanted to meet to quiz about photographing an ad campaign for Giles and Morgan. I walked over, briefly finishing my glass of white wine, before licking my teeth for remnants of lipstick. I had told myself that one act of self-doubt equates to at least one act of bravery.

'Hi, Nick,' I shouted, pretending to only sort of recognise him. After all, I wasn't sure if he remembered me. He did and waved me over to the small crowd of men in suits.

'Great to see you, Jess!' he said. 'Of course you know James…'

I did know James, he was the deputy head of marketing at Giles and Morgan and the second person on my wish list to meet. I followed my eyes around the group, giving a quick 'hello' to everyone, suddenly becoming incredibly aware of myself.

'Well, I don't want to gatecrash a party and I've lost Amber so…'

'Don't be silly,' James insisted. 'Stay. I'm sure she'll pass us at some point.'

'I'll go and find her,' Nick said, finishing his pint, 'she's probably giving some man a hard time on the terrace.'

I was frozen, my feet pinned to the floor, desperate to mention my photography and at the same time terrified of mentioning my photography. And that's when I noticed the tall figure standing next to me. As I tried to pinpoint why he looked familiar it dawned on me: he was the face on the front of *Business Life* magazine. The man deemed a 'saviour', a fact I'd later learned by actually reading the article. It had been a particularly slow afternoon and once on the comfort of the sofa I'd been entranced into reading it cover to cover. I examined his face, his green eyes and his dark hair. Just enough stubble to be attractive, but still groomed enough to know he cared. I quickly looked away. If I'd learned one thing from my mother it was not to commit to the man who should be a fling, to stop lust in its tracks and rise above the chemistry towards something more sensible. More concrete.

As everyone continued with their own conversations I had somehow found myself drawn into this god of finance and Brian's conversation about inflation and shareprices. I nodded intermittently with the rest of the group, playing piggy in the middle with people's opinions about the economy. I could sense Charlie (I had since clocked his name) and the proximity of our bodies getting slightly closer. I could feel that sense you sometimes get when someone is watching you and you daren't look at them in case they're looking. Well, I finally looked and he was too. I smiled a nervous smile, thinking he would do the normal thing and look away, but he didn't. Instead he leaned over and put his hand on my shoulder.

'You don't have a drink,' he whispered directly into my ear. 'We can't have that, can we?'

As he motioned to the bartender I noticed that he had his initials embossed on his cardholder, a surefire hint in my own judgement that he was a vain, slightly arrogant City boy, but no, he wasn't that easy to dismiss. He was nice, actually.

'Going to need some help getting through this,' he said with an awkward smile. He handed me a bottle of champagne and two glasses, an indulgence I had previously thought was usually reserved for special occasions and New Year's Eve but for him, apparently, just a regular Friday night.

I looked up at him and into his eyes as they stared across the room. His face, with 'bad idea' written all over it. I felt like the secondary school newcomer eye-flirting with the popular sixth-former. This wasn't me. I knew he probably used this line on every single girl he met but I also knew that at this point, I didn't care. As he stepped closer I stayed composed. I knew we shouldn't. I knew that girls who slept with guys on a first meeting rarely saw them again. But did I even want to? I felt his hand skim the small of my back. I could have protested but I didn't. I didn't.

I felt him bite down hard on my bottom lip in the back of the taxi as we came to an abrupt halt outside his building. A harsh handbrake manoeuvre made by the taxi driver so we'd get the hell out of his car and continue this elsewhere. We stumbled out onto the pavement and as we reached the bottom of the glass-fronted building I knew that beyond this point was no man's land. If I wanted to back out, now would be the time to speak up.

As he slammed me into the wall of the lift I momentarily forgot who we were. I could feel his heart beating – or was that mine? I was trying to be sensible. I was the girl trying to get back on her feet, the feet that were now wrapped around his waist as he lifted me into the air. I could smell the remnants of aftershave on his neck, his forehead balmy and sweaty as I kissed it. We didn't make it to his apartment. Instead we gave in to ourselves and fell together in an entwined heap on the carpeted floor of the corridor. And even if it was just for tonight, he was mine. As he pulled me to my feet and led me to his doorway I picked up my underwear and forgave myself. Start again tomorrow. Like sampling an indulgent chocolate cake in the midst of a diet plan, just start again tomorrow.

Six hours later, the sun had risen, and I lay in his bed wide-awake. Carefully and calmly, I made a slight gesture to move: beating him to the punch, avoiding the vacuous apologies from both of us, of a busy day ahead filled with lots of things to do.

'Don't go,' he said, smiling as he pulled me back into his warm body.

'I need to…'

'What?' He smiled. 'What do you need to do that's so important?'

'I need to phone someone,' I said.

'Who?' he quizzed with his eyes still closed, the curly tuffs of dark hair on his chest rising and falling as he spoke.

'My... dentist,' I said, beginning to smile.

He wrapped his arms around me, cocooning me in the smell of the night before. By now, the sun was streaming across the bed and we were drenched in it. It wasn't love. It was two people not wanting love, which somehow seemed even more perfect.

Effect...

Present day. Using clues from the past to plot a strategy for the future. It was a balmy afternoon and as I looked out onto the rainy London street, I could feel the dryness in my eyes from my tears that morning. A dull, fuzzy headache served as a mental reminder of the sharp pain I felt inside, deep within the concave cavity that had once carried my heart. I noticed people on the pavement below unaffectedly going about their day – doing their best to ignore the torrent of water around them. The British are quite fearless when it comes to rain; things just seem to carry on as normal. I looked at my watch. Still no sign of the van but I could now feel the vibration of my phone in my back pocket and assumed that it was the removal men offering an explanation.

It was Amber. I let it ring out. I waited for the ping. I could handle a message, but I wasn't yet prepared for a conversation. The text read:

Dinner with Sean and me?? We are DYING to see you

On this busy street, on this particular afternoon, I was waiting for a transit van to drop my things off at the flat I was moving back into with Amber after a brief spell of living in heaven with Charlie. They were supposed to be here at 4.30 p.m. and as there was still no sign at 6 p.m, I decided to put the phone back into my jeans pocket and hopped my way up the stairs to our flat. I looked around at my new yet familiar home. The home I had shared with Amber and had to move out of, in, shall we say, a rather immediate manner: full of smiles, giggles and promises. Instead of once being our girls' world that we used as a hideaway from the rest of the universe, it was now the flat I had once left to move in with him. The one I had left in the hope of building a life with someone I now felt I no longer knew.

I opened my phone, still at that stage of expecting to see a text from him, for which I hated myself, and instead texted Amber:

Yes, definitely! Can't wait – I'll meet you there.

My thoughts were basically that if I filled the text with enough hearts and dancing girl emojis I would perhaps deflect the scent of how devastated I was to be moving back here. I walked into my empty room that was once filled with all the objects of my life and sat down on the edge of the bed, the bare beige walls almost consuming me. The fact that nobody else had moved in yet showed just how quick the decision was made to leave – and how even more quickly it was made to return. It was all *too* quick. I had it coming to me.

After two cups of tea and a sort through my piles of mail

I plucked up the courage to start opening a few boxes that I had managed to squeeze into the back of the taxi: just work things, thank God, it seemed that all the sentimental stuff was still in the van. I pulled out a large, leather portfolio of black and white photographs, the ones I'd taken in the second year of my law degree and had been so excited to put together and hawk across the city. I laid out my portfolio and fingered the plastic covering. It was bubbly now and the dog-eared corners were ageing… nothing at all like I remembered. Along with forgetting who I was for a short time, it seemed I had also forgotten what I wanted to be.

This would be my priority now: my only option of survival. I reminded myself about the one golden nugget that I'd learned since all this had unravelled: something that nobody had told me at the start. There will be sacrifices. I call it spinning plates. It's a balancing act that usually consists of the metaphorical weighing scales whereby your love life succeeds and your career goes down the pan, or your career booms while your love life's shot to shit. Or in my case right now, both, crumbling in my hands at the exact same moment. I smiled at the irony.

And wasn't it funny that the moment when I knew I had to end it was the exact moment I'd never wanted to stay more.

As I poured a glass of water and pulled myself up to sit on the kitchen worktop – an annoying trait which Charlie didn't mind but Amber always hated – I could see one good thing about being on my own: I could finally do as I pleased. Prove to myself that I could. Prove to my parents that they were wrong. The continual back and forth motion with Charlie – the euphoric highs and desperate lows – were now over. It was time to create space for myself and for the new, to give myself the opportunity to get it all wrong. Fuck things up to the *nth* degree. Barefooted and barefaced amongst the boxes, I was willing to risk all that was certain in my life for the very possibility of wanting something more.

The restaurant was heaving. I'd strangely missed the noise, the crowded bar, the way you had to navigate through the masses just to meet your friends, to breathe. As soon as I caught sight of them I felt relieved.

'Sit yourself down, Jessica Rabbit,' Sean said with a warm smile. 'I mean, I knew it wouldn't last long but three months? Jesus, Jess, I've got cheese in my fridge that I've had longer.'

'Yes,' I said, nodding dutifully. 'Get it all off your chest now, will you? And we were actually together for nine months,' I declared proudly as I walked around the oblong table to kiss Amber. 'And what do you mean you didn't think it would last long?'

Amber pulled me in and looked me straight in the eye.

'You did the right thing, bubs,' she said boldly.

I knew she was right but the pain in my stomach was still fighting the concept – it made a deep, heavy lurch as I sat down at the table, causing me to wince.

'Seriously, though, are you okay?' Sean quizzed.

'I need to find a job. And quick,' I replied.

'Our rent's due on Thursday,' Amber remarked, before hesitating. Her voice shrinking to a gradual fade as she saw my expression.

'She only moved out three months ago, I think she can remember when your rent's due,' Sean said, rolling his eyes.

I reached out to sip my water, my hand paused on the glass, as a thought I had buried caught up with me.

'Is it really as bad as it looks?' Amber said, placing her hand on my wrist.

'Well, let me fill you in, shall I?' I pushed the water aside and exchanged it for wine. 'I've left my boyfriend's home…'

'Ex-boyfriend,' Sean muttered.

'Ex-boyfriend,' I quipped. 'Half my possessions are on my bedroom floor while the other half are under house arrest in a transit on the other side of Westminster that has the word "penis" written on the side in dirt. So in answer to your question, things have definitely been better.'

'He's such a dick,' Sean spat.

'He's not, though,' I said, sipping my wine again. 'Things just didn't work out.'

I reached for the bread basket, realising I hadn't eaten at all that day.

As I buttered a piece of fluffy white baguette I felt a hand on the back of my chair.

'Jess – fancy seeing you here, how is everything? How's Charlie?'

A bomb of silence dropped on the table.

It was Sasha, the PR hound who lived two floors beneath him. She obviously didn't have anything better to do than keep track of the comings and goings of the building.

'Oh, I'm fine, he's fine, I think. Well, I don't know actually because we're not together anymore – we split up about a week ago.'

'Oh, I see,' she said, giving me the same vacant look that I'd seen several times over the past seven days. 'Well, sometimes these things just don't work out. He's pretty handsome, though. That's got to be tough.'

I nodded in agreement, to both parts, with a small smile that indicated that it was her cue to leave. I wanted to vomit as the overpowering smell of her perfume lingered in the air. I remembered the sweet, distinct floral smell from the building's lift.

'She's definitely going to drop by his place tonight as a "shoulder to cry on",' Sean said, watching her leave. 'She couldn't get out of here quick enough! I could actually see her smirking – who does that?'

'Well, good luck to her,' I said, mustering a fake smile. 'Maybe she can handle him better than I could.'

'Maybe she's got that condition,' Amber said drily. 'I saw a documentary about it: when somebody delivers some bad news, they can't help smiling.'

'Or maybe she's just a cow,' I said, bluntly.

'So, just to clarify,' Sean said, 'are we allowed to say his name?'

'Yeah, why not?' I replied.

'Because she just did and you look like you'd been shot.'

'I'm okay, really!' I protested. 'It's all for the best. Please can we just talk about something else?'

'I won't even mention his name,' Sean said, running his forefinger across his lips.

'And don't remind me how attractive he is either,' I said, searching for the emergency cigarette I'd borrowed from the doorman on the way in. 'All anyone's been saying to me is how attractive he was. It's pathetic,' I muttered.

'He was,' Sean said as Amber shot him a look of outrage. 'I'm sorry. But he absolutely was.'

After we'd eaten, I could still feel the remnants of the food stinging the roof of my mouth.

'So what else have I missed?' I said, looking at Sean to change the conversation.

'Amber's in love. A bit,' he said coyly.

'Oh please,' she said, as cool as ever. 'Today's idea of love is closing your Tinder account.'

'And have you?' Sean said, raising an eyebrow.

'Course not,' she replied. 'But I definitely go on a lot less.'

I stared at her until she gave me more answers.

'His name is Patrick,' she said.

'Patrick,' Sean repeated drily. 'He's definitely over fifty.'

I laughed.

'He is, yes!' She downed the remainder of her martini defensively and tried to get a waiter's attention for the bill. Sean and I glanced at each other like two schoolgirls banished to the front of the bus. She was too cool to be drinking with us and as a result was forced to hang around with the fifty plus Patricks of the world.

'Is he retired?' Sean asked.

'No, you fucker!' Amber cried. 'And that's it! I'm done! No more questions!'

The next morning Amber shuffled into my room in her dressing gown balancing two cups of tea. As I blinked through last night's make-up, for a brief moment I had forgotten where I was. The room looked bigger without my stuff in it. She sat down on the end of my bed as I noticed a small damp patch right above the window frame.

'We have damp,' I said, gesturing to the wall.

'I know,' she nodded, lying down next to me. 'I've missed coming and getting into bed with you of a morning. I even had to buy my own shampoo, and razors…'

'I knew you used my shampoo.'

'I knew you knew,' she said, leaning her head against the rickety wooden headboard. 'I know it's hard, Jess, but it's for the best. You can't be with a man like that. You're too… nice.'

'I hate that word,' I said, reaching for my tea.

'He was part of a scene that's just not for you – believe me, I've been there.'

'It's knackering, you know, pretending to be someone you're not all the time.' I looked down into the rim of my mug and could see the faint brown mark from all the drinks that had gone before it. I ran my fingernail over it in a faint attempt to remove the stain.

'You'll be all right,' she said. 'You've got to think about your own life. And now you can do whatever it is that you want to do… like shag that gym instructor you always fancied.'

'But I don't want to,' I said, quietly.

'Yet,' she said. 'You don't want to yet.'

As she left the room I knew I had no choice but to trust her. Trust her optimism. Trust that she knew what she was talking about. I pulled a box towards me and began to pull the clothes out. I stopped at a dress I had bought for a job interview. It was creased. I carried on pulling out endless streams of coats, jackets, tops, shorts – any mundane action to stop me from thinking. I reached right to the bottom of the damp box and that's when I felt it. A black jumper that had accidently been packed up in the frenzy. It belonged to him. I ran my fingers down the leather elbow pads and across a loose thread in the sleeve. A small fault within a ream of beautiful fabric, just like our relationship. In our short time together, he had created the loose threads and I had begun to pull them and before we knew it all we had was a tangled ball of wool. Using the black hair tie from around my wrist I pulled my hair up and pushed it loosely away from my face.

'Don't think,' I said to myself out loud. 'Just fold your clothes.'

SUMMER

SUMMER

Chapter Three – How to Get Lost in Reality

It was hot – the kind of heat that London isn't prepared for – when train tracks melt and people begin bulk-buying ice at the supermarket. Grassy public parks become a carpet for Prosecco bottles, factor twenty-five and supermarket plastic-bag picnic hampers. During the light evenings, a sense of heady weightlessness fills the air. Problems disperse and are exchanged for gin and tonics, despite the fact that city girls become forced to unleash their pale legs, hidden for ten months of the year beneath 100-denier tights. These heated times are unusual in Britain and must be relished during every single hour. Summers are precious to us; they're unpredictable but always ever so fleeting.

By summer I had weathered the storm and woken up on the last day of the last week of the last month of the last year that I was *ever* going to feel so shitty about myself again. Up to that point the feeling of emptiness was indescribable but a weekend spent hiding under a duvet, my computer conveniently open on his social media, had led to an intervention from a higher power.

According to my friends I was spiralling and I needed to get back to the real world: a distraction from the dull ache that had resided in my chest every day since Charlie and I had split. I wanted to scream, open a window and shout loudly into the world, a vast release or a call to the gods to do something, something bigger than me; bigger than us. Instead I brushed my teeth and made my first steps back to reality; the joyous purgatory between a dream and a slap in the face.

Since my break-up from Charlie, I had tried a number of tactics when it came to trying to give myself a reboot. First, I'd sampled staying in; reverting to the familiar by putting myself under house arrest and refusing to leave unless the house literally caught fire around me. I had stocked up on food, wine, toilet paper and bin liners. I'd tried box sets, starting the novel I'd always wanted to write, and spring cleaning my entire wardrobe by first piling the contents of my wardrobe high onto my bed, followed shortly by a deep sense of regret midway through. In the end, I just threw away half my possessions. All in all, it had been good for feng shui, bad for home economics.

And, of course, I'd tried going out. What's more fun than dressing up and dancing to music playing so loud that it drowns out your own thoughts and engulfs you in a different sound – the sound of fun and guilt-free solitude, Amber had asked me. True, there's nothing quite like feeling the beat of your own heart, moving freely in a dimly lit room full of strangers, bodies in unison with the distant odour of sweet sweat lingering in the air. I'd tried more sedate nights, too – restaurants with old friends, not in one of our regular haunts, somewhere new, with no memories or sentimentality attached. Here, we indulged in two of the most delectable things human beings can do together: gossip and eat. And still, I missed him.

But it wasn't until I'd divulged in an evening of speed dating, a collective group of people given three minutes to sell themselves without appearing desperate, that I even considered the idea of a rebound. Not always the answer, I admit, but a strong case can be made for forcing myself to see how life could be a little different. Perhaps not with the person I thought I would be with, perhaps not even someone I would want anything to develop with beyond this one event, but nevertheless, a surefire way to thrust myself, quite literally, out there into a new beginning and leave the pain of the past behind me. And I'm not just talking about sex, I'm talking about something a little scarier: chemistry. An addictive feeling that can exist with or without being naked. A bond between two people that can unfortunately neither be forced or faked. But in order to see it, I had to test myself. Give someone else a chance. Everything starts from somewhere and how would I know if I didn't at least try. In this instance, however, I did run the risk of rebounding with the wrong person. A person who made me miss the person I was hiding from even more than before. It's a risk – a toss up between getting too attached to something that's meant only to be fleeting, or if things do permeate, commit to something different from where you thought you once would be. A new chance, but in my book a risk worth taking if the alternative lies within the safety of the past.

In order to move on, sometimes you need to get moving. Having lived in a busy city, it may be time to escape to a leafy suburb complete with riverside walks and the need for waterproof clothing. The main importance of this activity is getting away from what I've been used to, playing opposites enabling my mind to wander into another energy setting. There is nothing more reassuring to me than seeing the sun set above a skyline I'm not used to, knowing that when the sun rises, hopefully, new possibilities will arise too. Parks also offer enough escapism to imagine, just for a second, that I am in the countryside: another world where trees, fresh air and open space collide. Looking around, I can see the beneficiaries firsthand, couples strolling hand in hand, joggers, readers and dog walkers. There is no better feeling than when the warm sun beams down on your face as you walk down a rickety path through the giant trees.

But it's always a comfort to know that an immeasurable sea of people inhabit the earth at precisely the same time as me. The people of my zeitgeist, comrades and fellow friends at arms. I mentioned the need to move forward, but of course this is not truly possible without the honest reverberation of human connection: or my friends. Those rare friends who sacrifice their precious time to sit and listen to the repeat realisation over and over again as if it's their first time of hearing it; all seeking a common destination of happiness as we pass the ball of encouragement back and forth between us. Under such honest tuition, there is no need to self-monitor. Advice comes in waves, and we may listen. This familiar buffer against the self-harm we often do to ourselves is the only outside eye we have. I take pleasure in carefully observing the fellow wildlife of others, comparing myself to what we deem is the norm. And when I feel the void, I know that I can always rely on the guidance of others in the bourgeoisie of our social climate. They wouldn't dare let me date if I'm not ready to move on, or let me befriend a new person who isn't exactly a support. They love me. They care. I should listen.

And so on to the next day: if only I could see that day that I'm imagining. Something I can see beyond how many miles, across how many oceans, aboard how many planes. Revisiting that landmark of the day that tipped the balance. The day that forced all toleration to crumble, the day a choice for something new took hold and the rewards of change had come to fruition. No longer do you have to test the boundaries of what your heart can take but instead you can be happy. Emerging from the flood, a slightly better, more water-resistant version of a person, to have the ability to travel through life again this time, returning slightly less scathed. I listened to the beat, to the sound of my heart, a drum-like pounding saying: use this, use today.

Chapter Four – Virtual Insanity

Checklist for Modern Romance:

- An electronic device for downloading free text messaging services. Cultivating digital friendships often involves a lot of backwards and forwards so free messaging is somewhat vital.
- As important as the ability to download digital dating platforms is the step of deleting them when the time comes for monogamous romance.
- A squidgy heart for the optimism of a swipe right.
- A tin heart for the rejection of a swipe left.
- A nice photograph of yourself: nothing too fancy and nothing too casual. You need to look your best but not like you're trying.
- Healthy food you will pretend you are eating.
- Photographs of sunsets you will pretend you are watching.
- Covers of books you will pretend to be reading.

Sean was going on a date and I had turned up for moral support, barefaced apart from a facial nose strip, and ruining the ambience of his pristine bed linen with my dark green joggers. I watched as he casually laid a crisp, white shirt, navy blue leather watch and aftershave next to my feet which were adorned in a pair of woollen bed socks, and surrounded by enough junk food to feed a family with five teenagers.

'You're not seriously going to eat all that, are you?' he said, glancing over at my stockpile as I reached for the Oreos.

'Sure am,' I replied, biting the packet open with my teeth. As I watched him towel-dry his legs on the edge of the bed it was clear I had nowhere else to be on this first Friday night in June.

'Who is he anyway? I don't think I've heard you mention his name before.'

'I met him online. I've not really spoken to him that much or at all. But judging by his online profile he's got the body of a Greek god.'

'Sounds terrific,' I mused, licking the cream from the centre of my biscuit.

'And it's just a bit of fun, anyway,' he said, as he disappeared into a row of hanging trousers, rooting for his shoes in the bottom of the wardrobe. 'He's more popular than frickin' Helen of Troy by the looks of things.'

'What do you mean? He's a bit of a slag?'

'Not everyone who enjoys sex is a slag, Jess.'

I screwed up my face. 'I know. I'm sorry.' I'd offended him.

'And it wouldn't hurt you to get online and see what's out there. You've been staying in for weeks, it's a one-way road to…'

'Depression?' I said, finishing his sentence and reaching for another biscuit.

'I was going to say obesity.'

I returned the biscuit to the packet.

'So you don't mind that they're seeing other people?' I said, propping myself up against his pillows. It was something completely new to me and I needed to know more.

'No, why would I care?'

'My God, I'd care. I don't think I could date more than one man properly.'

'No offence, sweetie, but you couldn't date one man properly.'

I toasted my can of Diet Coke to his cocky remark as he took a step back to look at himself in the floor-length mirror, spraying five strong bursts of cologne. I closed my eyes as the smell fell over me like a blanket. I lay back down onto his pillow and could feel myself plummeting into a sugar low, the aftermath from all the snacks I had consumed. As I re-opened them I caught sight of Sean as he held up his phone and snapped a picture of his reflection.

'Who are you sending that to?' I asked, with one eye open.

'No one.'

I threw him a look mixed with curiosity and a touch of envy.

'Don't hate the player, hate the game, right?' he said, carefully choosing a filter for the picture before pressing send.

It was a philosophy I was still trying to understand. He turned to me as I played with the toggle on my joggers. I smiled, a deliberate film of chocolate covering my teeth.

'Oh, that's really pretty,' he remarked, climbing over to lie down on the bed next to me. I made room as he flopped on his side so that our faces were almost touching.

'If I can't be with him then why can't I just be with you?' I whispered, carefully moving an errant hair from his forehead.

'Because we're both pricks and you deserve better.'

I placed a hand on Sean's chest, fighting the urge to close my eyes again.

'So you think tonight's going to be fun?' he said, lying back to face the ceiling.

'Yes, I think it's going to be good,' I said, supportively.

He shot me a sarcastic glare.

'Great, then!' I continued. 'I think it's going to be amazing. But I wouldn't take my word for it – I haven't even showered today.'

We lay there next to each other as I felt his big arm wrap round me.

'Okay, Jess, I love you but you have to leave now, he'll be here in ten minutes…'

I dutifully packed away my biscuits and half-eaten bag of crisps, carefully dusting the crumbs off his bed as I moved. I put on my coat, tightly gripping the twisted top of the open packet of biscuits, and made my way home.

I threw my carrier bag of half-eaten food on the table in the hallway, turned on the lamp and shut the door behind me. Amber was out so I had the flat to myself. I walked into the bathroom and turned on the taps, the water thundering out in large gulps as it filled our small bathroom with steam. I sat down on the toilet seat and waited for the bath to fill.

Sean's honesty lingered in my mind but I knew I had to do things my own way. I felt the coldness of the floor tiles beneath my bare feet. I pulled out my phone and for some indescribable reason opened a string of text messages from Charlie. I'm not sure what I was hoping to achieve but the sight of our relationship history, laid out in vertical block texts, took my breath away: the war rooms. I scrolled through the old messages that marked the end of a ceasefire: anger, spelling mistakes, accusations. I began to type a white flag but stopped myself.

After all, how do you say in a text message: I'm just not over you yet.

After my bath, I created a profile using an almost bearable picture of myself taken two years ago at Amber's birthday party and kept all other personal information to a minimum. As I tapped my fingers on the edge of my desk, debating whether or not to use a fake name, I came to the conclusion that this would inevitably get me off on the wrong foot.

I scrolled down the selection of men's faces and skimmed over a couple of profiles. How could I go from a man like Charlie to someone who lists 'adventure' as a hobby? In an act akin to pulling off a plaster, I set my profile to active and took a big gulp of the gin and tonic I'd prepared as liquid courage. I leaned back in my chair to assess the damage to my soul. At that moment a 'ping' sounded, nearly knocking me off my chair as a private message popped up in the bottom right-hand side of my computer screen.

It was from a man called Harry. It just read, 'Hi.' I hesitated. I could feel the dryness in the back of my mouth as I took another well-earned sip of gin. I typed back 'Hi' and clicked on his profile. He was good-looking but not intimidatingly attractive. He owned a surfboard. He played rugby at the weekend. As I delved deeper into his collection of photographs, another ping ensued. I opened up the private message that read:

Just looking at your picture in Sydney Harbour. Great view. Always wanted to go there.

The picture was taken on a holiday with my dad. A summer break designed as a father–daughter bonding exercise but resulted in him being called back to work, leaving me alone in an unknown city with nothing but my passport, my rucksack and his credit card. I ran my fingers along the computer keys and swiftly began to type a reply.

Yes, it was beautiful. A really unique experience!

I didn't know whether the exclamation mark was a little too much to end with. That maybe I appeared a little too fresh – too excited about all of this. But then I saw him typing a reply. My blood ran cold as I wanted for the ping.

I know this seems forward but I was wondering if you'd like to get dinner or drinks tomorrow night? Nothing major. Just casual.

How long did I have until I had to reply? I thought. I wasn't ready for this. Not an actual date where I would have to physically see another human being. I clicked back on his picture and could feel the weight of the past restraining me from replying. An image of Charlie flashed into my mind as it suddenly dawned on me that I probably wouldn't see him again… or kiss him. I won't have him as a wingman when I wanted a drink after work or to see a bad movie with when no one else would.

And then I remembered that last night in his apartment: the very last night, the arguing, the shouting and then, tears. I pressed send. And how was I supposed to feel?

'Morning,' I said chirpily the next day. Marlowe had invited us round for one of her famous home-cooked brunches, a chance to pull open the glass doors and let in a bit of sunshine. I'd been let into the house by Amber, who didn't look at me but immediately returned to the kitchen wearing an oversized grey hoodie – a familiar indication that she had a hangover.

'Please don't talk so loud, I feel like shit,' Amber said, motioning me into the kitchen.

'Well, this is great,' Marlowe said, as she pulled the filter coffee from the stand. 'Everyone's hungover and I'm in the bad books with George because I didn't tape the sports channel last night.'

'I stayed in last night. I'm not hungover,' I said, wrapping my arms around her waist from behind.

'Tell him to tape his own shit,' Sean said, downing his coffee.

Amber pulled off her hood. It was clear it had been a late night.

'So how was the date?' I asked, unleashing the tiger that is Marlowe and her questions regarding other people's love lives.

'Who was it last night!?' she shouted.

'It wasn't a date,' Sean said, rolling his eyes. 'And seriously, Jess, if I have to watch you eat one more packet of Oreos on a Friday night I am going to fuck you myself.'

'How rude,' I whispered. 'But grateful for the offer all the same.'

'A whole packet?' Marlowe mouthed.

I nodded.

'So who is he, anyway?' Amber asked.

'I met him online.'

'Kinky?'

'Nah – straight up,' he said, pouring himself another coffee.

Amber looked at him and laughed.

Their sex jokes were always shared only with each other and both myself and Marlowe were more than happy to remain in the dark.

'Amber, I forgot to tell you,' Marlowe said, searching the kitchen worktop for some papers, 'George was working in Berlin last week and met a fashion buyer. I asked him for his business card for you. They're an e-commerce start-up, supposed to be pretty cool. Thought you might be interested?' She handed over the card. 'Take it, it's yours.'

'Cheers, Mars,' Amber said, studying the design. 'It looks great I just… begrudge taking it into the office.'

'Why?' I asked.

'Because it will get passed on and handed over for someone else to take all the credit.'

'Happens all the time at my work too,' Sean said with a mouthful of croissant.

'Amber, you're the first in and last out every day,' I said, outraged. 'I barely even see you these days. How can they not notice everything you're doing?'

'I don't know,' she said, sliding the card into her jeans pocket.

'Why don't you start your own company?' Marlowe said. 'Then you might actually benefit from all those extra hours.'

'I don't think that's really an option for me. Besides, it's not really the best economic climate to start a business.' She stood up to pour herself some orange juice. 'Fucking government.'

'Where is George, by the way?' I asked.

'Shanghai – 'til Tuesday. That reminds me, I've got to pick up his suits from the dry cleaners.'

'For God's sake, Mar...' Amber said.

'Leave it, Amber,' I whispered, under my breath.

'So, what are we going to do about Jess's lady parts?' Sean said, quickly changing the subject.

'My what?!' I shouted, half spitting out my cereal.

'We need to get it eaten before it passes its sell by date. Which for women these days is around what... thirty-five?'

I shook my head in despair. Seven years of friendship and he still rendered me speechless.

'I'm kidding, obviously,' he said. 'But seriously, think about it. Take the standards down a notch and open your mind to what's out there.'

'Lower the standards. Great advice,' I said sarcastically.

At that point Elsa called for Marlowe from upstairs. 'Coming,' Marlowe shouted, taking one last sip of coffee.

We all watched her leave the room.

'I'm sorry, but am I the only one who can't believe what I'm hearing?' Amber said, in a hushed voice. 'What a total prick. Pisses off to Shanghai for a week and kicks off about the sports match he's missed. Not interested in his wife – or child!!'

'Look, he's basically a Prince William lookalike who keeps her in designer furniture,' Sean said.

Amber raised her eyebrow at him.

'I'm just saying,' he continued, 'there's give and take.'

'You're right, the grass isn't always greener on the other side,' I said as Amber looked at me. 'And it isn't necessarily worse either. It's just… not our business.'

'You're right,' Sean said. 'It's their marriage. And it's not our business.'

The next night, after a two-hour debate with myself about whether or not to cancel, I put my hair in heated rollers and pulled myself together. It was drinks, maybe dinner and, as he said so himself, totally casual. I cast my eyes over my open wardrobe. If I wore my black designer dress on a first date, he would probably think I was high maintenance even though it was a sample sale purchase and cost no more than a bottle of supermarket wine. I slowly put it back on the rack and dabbed a tissue across the small hairline cuts on my legs (a regrettably bad idea to have shaved my legs standing up in the shower).

On my way out the door I stopped in front of the mirror in the hallway and planted dark red lipstick across my lips that provided a hint of class and would also act as a deterrent in case he tried to kiss me: a Hadrian's Wall of red, sealing off my mouth from Harry, in case he turned out to be a sexual predator or worse. I looked at my reflection in the mirror. Good luck, I said out loud, quietly knowing that should probably be whispered to Harry more than me.

Outside the tube station I walked over to the man I vaguely recognised from the picture. He was taller than I had imagined with dusty blond hair in a perfectly coiffed style.

'Harry?' I said, smiling.

'Jess.' He offered his hand for me to shake before quickly changing his mind and kissing my cheek. 'Firstly, may I say you look beautiful and secondly, thank you for showing up.'

I smiled at him. Still no words but at least the pounding in my chest had ceased.

He had booked the table for eight thirty and together we strolled to the restaurant nestled just around the corner. Harry looked back as we walked against the evening sun and as we approached the corner of the pavement I noticed him do it again.

'Are you okay?' I asked.

'Yeah, it's fine. I'm just looking for my ex-wife. I've got a restraining order but you can't be too careful.'

I looked behind us as we crossed the road.

'Jess, I'm kidding,' he said, as I hit his arm and began to smile. 'You looked so bloody nervous coming out of the tube, I thought I'd better do something to lighten the mood.'

It had worked. He was funny, and despite my nerves he had made me laugh all the way to the glass doorway of the restaurant where we were hit with low hung lights and the smell of incense. We were seated at a table next to the open window where he gazed at me with expectant eyes to start the conversation.

'Great to be here,' I said, with all I could muster.

'Great to be here too,' he said.

In the midst of a silence that would have made a funeral seem energetic, I did what every girl in my position would do: I escaped to the toilets.

I caught sight of myself as I stood reapplying my lipstick in the bathroom mirror. I was being difficult; perhaps it was even an act of sabotage so that things wouldn't work out. So that I wouldn't have to be brave and try something new. Harry was attractive, funny and from what I could tell, incredibly easy-going. But as I sat on the toilet, tallying up the laughs, I realised my newly surfaced pessimism was an altogether more difficult mountain to conquer. This wasn't about him at all. The problem was definitely me.

'You were ages,' Harry said as I returned to the table.

'Was I?'

'Thought you'd fallen in.' His eyes perused the wine list with a cheeky smile. 'So are you a big eater, because this menu's pretty pricey? I mean, I'm okay to just nibble on an edamame, if you are?'

'Well, I just saw on my way back from the bathroom that the couple opposite us left a hefty amount of rice behind so maybe…'

'What an excellent idea,' Harry said. 'I'll distract, you pilfer.'

I laughed as the waiter arrived to take our order.

'I was a bit nervous before tonight but, this is not so bad, is it?' Harry said, reaching for my hand over the table.

'Nope,' I said, shaking my head. 'It's not too bad at all.'

Give it a chance, Jess, I said to myself as Harry ordered his food from the waiter. Just give it a chance.

The car pulled up outside my door just short of eleven thirty. Although neither of us knew at this point if there would be a second date, he was brave and made the first move to kiss me. I turned away, a knee-jerk reaction that I later slightly regretted. In an awkward moment that felt like a strange end to an otherwise perfect evening, I gave him a small wave and closed the door behind me. It was a typical survival tactic. One I had to unlearn. Fast. As I opened the door of my flat, I slid out of my punishing shoes and immediately saw Amber on the sofa, seated with a box of tissues on her knee, surrounded by the used ones.

'A builder on the bus gave me his cold this morning,' she shouted. 'He was breathing all over me – first I could smell his morning breath and now I feel like I've trekked through the Himalayas.'

I picked up the tissues and carried them over to the kitchen.

'Well, let's not pass it to everyone, shall we?' I shouted, dumping them into our silver pedal bin before heading over to the sink to wash my hands. 'Fancy a cuppa?'

I poured us both some tea and sat next to her on the sofa.

'How did it go?' she asked.

I shrugged my shoulders, deflecting any questions about how the evening had ended, but as I watched her flick through the channels before deciding on a nature documentary, I smiled.

'It was actually really nice,' I said. 'I was a complete moron about the whole thing, though.'

'Of course you were,' Amber said, without looking away from the screen. 'He'll grow to love that though.'

I smiled and sipped my tea. Not there yet but definitely trying.

'You've got to see him again!' Sean bellowed at me down the phone the next morning. I was on my way to buy a new portfolio for my photographs and had decided to pass by the organic coffee shop for a morning boost. As I attempted to juggle my phone, my coffee and my handbag, I leaned against a post box to regain my grip on things.

'He wasn't as I expected, that's all. He was actually really funny,' I said.

'Look, this is not my first rodeo... as you know,' Sean said.

I nodded. 'Nope.'

'And it's not yours, either, so save me the innocent princess convo and tell me what you really thought. Would you sleep with him?'

'I don't know... probably?'

'And was he clean, well-mannered... wasn't a psycho?'

'Yes. All of those things.'

'Then just promise me you'll give it another go.'

'Okay, I will,' I said, biting my bottom lip nervously. I relented, 'I promise.'

'Jess, I'm being serious. You've got to move on now.'

'I know,' I said. 'I am.'

I rested my phone down on the post box considering the weight of what I'd just promised him, all the while knowing it was a promise I owed to myself too.

Chapter Five – Takotsubo Cardiomyopathy
(Or, in human speak – 'To die of a broken heart')

Dave the plumber was lying down on our kitchen floor as I hovered over him clutching his spanner. The tenants in the flat below had heard a loud dripping and after a rather tense phone call with our landlord we had agreed to get things checked out. To be honest, I knew that something was wrong when the water didn't drain in the sink, but like everything I'd ignored it and pretended things were fine. Things were *not* fine. As I leaned against the open fridge, tapping my flip flop against the floor, Dave looked at me.

'It's a hot one,' he said, wiping his brow with his work cloth. 'Apparently it's going to be the hottest summer on record – hasn't felt this hot in years.'

Dave was right. It was an uncomfortable, muggy heat that left you feeling drowsy and inexplicably tired. Despite my promises, I still hadn't phoned Harry. And to my shame I'd ignored two voicemails and several text messages from him.

'All done here,' Dave said, making an involuntary noise as he got to his feet. 'All fixed.'

If only everything were so simple, I thought, as I reached for the cash in my purse. As I watched Dave pack away his tools

I reached for my phone and unlocked the screen. To be honest, the stumbling block wasn't the memory of Charlie, let alone Harry. It was a feeling. I craved the euphoria of the past nine months: a strange addiction I'd garnered to feeling helpless. At the time my pain was special and now I was left in the numb void of normality. Takotsubo cardiomyopathy: the emotional equivalent of being smacked to the floor. And I am not talking about actual death, either; more of the kind of situation where you have loved somebody so deeply, in a world that is so perfect and happy, but then somehow, somewhere along the way things just, unravelled. For the lucky ones, this separation is mutual: you have both decided that things would be for the better if you went your separate ways. For the not-so-lucky ones the decision could have been made by only one of you. While one person is confidently beginning a life without you, the other is left in emotional limbo. But the real mystery lies within feelings: where do they all go once the battlefield has emptied? Just imagine sitting, on a Saturday night, across a table from someone you may find attractive but don't fancy, who is generally amusing but can't make you laugh out loud, someone who is not in any way a bad idea but in short, isn't *them*? Nature tells us that we have to keep evolving, keep edging forward and this act of survival is something we must repeatedly force ourselves to do.

Takotsubo cardiomyopathy, in medical terms, means to die of a broken heart. After heartache, you are free to remain in the empty space, reflecting on what went wrong or trying to pinpoint when the disintegration started and, most importantly, if there was anything you could've done differently to alter the outcome.

The truth is, there probably wasn't. If he wants to leave, he will leave. If she wants to leave, she will leave. And although you could wait for them to have a change of heart, the collateral damage you do to yourself in the meantime can prove instantly catastrophic. So instead of turning the magnifying glass on yourself, picking apart the very essence of your own being, try turning the focus to science and the biological reasoning behind the pain.

At such times it can feel as if the head and the heart are operating on different playing fields. Emotionally, we are swinging between moments of clarity and optimism. You even manage to convince yourself, even for a second, that this could actually be for the best.

The brain works on a much more pragmatic level. There are actual scientific names for the areas of your brain that are responsible for what you are feeling, be it memory, anger, arousal or unhappiness. The brain invests in feelings at a certain level both chemically and intellectually and it is this investment, a chemical reaction that attaches you to a person and their smell, their pheromones, their person. It is this attachment that makes detaching so very, very hard. Your brain has become chemically acclimatized to the other person being there, which is why we sometimes feel the pendulum effect swinging between one emotion and another. Your body is literally counter-balancing the way you are feeling in the hope that it can shift your levels back to normality. In human speak: trust your body and trust your instincts. It is only trying to heal.

When you first break up it usually precedes weeks if not months of arguments, snapping at one another, picking faults that aren't always there and generally creating space between you both. And out of nowhere there will come a day when the arguments cease, when the quiet creeps in and you have no plausible reason to contact each other: no messages, no texts, no phone calls. Whether you talk the ear off a friend or sit together in silence, sometimes we cannot take the burden alone. I talked about it to death, to the absolute maximum that my friends could handle. They were my touchstone, my rock in the waves. They were my only sunrise.

As I stood at the kitchen sink pretending to inspect Dave's repair job while not really knowing what I was checking, a small, lime green parakeet flew in and rested on the windowsill. 'Little bugger!' Dave muttered as he made his way out of the flat. I had never seen a bird that colour in this part of London before. They usually stick to the leafy suburbs of Richmond or Kew Gardens, places where people pay large sums of rent to see birds like that: a half mix between watery green and yellow. As I stared at the red tip of his dark green beak he looked right back at me. Almost through me.

Growing up I was in the top grade, highest in the class and proud recipient of the 'most likely to achieve great things' award. A tongue-in-cheek certificate was given to me on my last day of school that was now moist with damp at the bottom of my keepsake box. Looking around at the eggshell paint crumbling from the plastered walls of our kitchen, I couldn't help but smile at the irony.

The truth was I failed my second year of law school. A fact I had been unable to tell my classmates, let alone my parents. The bright, ambitious star pupil had failed at her first attempt to truly succeed. In fact the only person I had ever told was Charlie. It was a moment of honesty in one of those late-night conversations, caught between the sheets, somewhere between night-time and morning. He turned to me, in that nonchalant way he saved to placate serious moments, and explained that perhaps it was just a case of the wrong dream. After two years of feeling like an underachiever, lying to everybody in my life, he had pushed me forward and funnily enough, almost back into the person I thought I could be.

With him, days turned into weeks, weeks to months and that was that. Before we even knew ourselves, we became an 'us'. He owned a tall, glass-fronted apartment overlooking the Thames, a bachelor pad complete with hi-tech gadgets that I didn't dare touch. Men in finance tend to be bad for reputation but fantastic for consumerism. In those days the fancy life had swallowed me up and I was foolish enough to think that I deserved it all.

'Look,' he said, turning to me one night over dinner. 'You're here near enough all week anyway – why not just move in and then you never have to leave?'

I looked at him as I ate my jacket potato, slightly dubious about his proposal.

'I don't know,' I said, putting down my fork. 'What will Amber say? We just renewed the contract on our flat.'

'I'll pay it,' he said without flinching. 'Just be here for me.'

And in a move that would make Emily Pankhurst turn in her grave, amongst the grated cheddar cheese and baked beans, I agreed.

It's embarrassing to admit that you've been hurt. It's not a shame as such, like bankruptcy or the time Amber accidently sent me a naked selfie, but more of a signal to others that you're not that capable after all. That some things, when left in your hands, do *fail*.

I sat down at the kitchen table and closed my eyes, my pupils making spectacular light shows in the dark. I pictured that night, a few weeks ago, when everything had gotten too much. Charlie had been up all night at the office closing a deal that had netted the company a fair amount of money and had decided to celebrate by staying behind for a drink. But with Charlie this was only ever where it started. Months of jovial rumours about strippers, cocaine and office lock-ins combined with promises that, of course, none of it involved him, had built up to me standing alone in his kitchen with no clue as to where he was – the harsh sound of the buzzer stabbed me awake, I walked to open the front door and there he stood at the door swaying, for the third time that week.

'Where have you been?' I asked, noticing he was dripping wet. His shirt was unbuttoned and I could see the water shine off his stomach.

'I've just been out with the guys from work. Don't start,' he snapped defensively. From experience I knew that an argument in these conditions was pointless. I turned off the light and made my way back to bed, my sleep disturbed by the sounds of dry heaving coming from the bathroom.

The next morning I continued my day as usual. I began making myself some breakfast in the kitchen – some fruit, yoghurt and a very large cup of coffee – when I heard a bang coming from the bedroom. I had expected him to crawl in, unkempt, dry-mouthed but instead he was dressed for work, freshly showered and smelling of aftershave. A sight that was surprisingly more worrying than the night before.

'Just so you know,' I said as he sat down at the breakfast bar, 'I'm not one of those girls that will fill your role of nagging wife.'

'What do you mean?' he said, without looking at me.

'You clearly want someone to be at home waiting for you while you go out and do god knows what with god knows who. But that's not me…'

'Give it a rest, Jess,' he said, opening his newspaper.

I slammed my favourite coffee cup into the sink, making us both jump as the handle snapped off, shooting a shard of cream pottery into the air. I looked over at him as he stood up and left, the door slamming behind him. And knew that would be it until the early hours of the next morning. A repetitive dance we both did, until one of us grew brave enough to stop it. I started to pick up the broken ceramic from the sink, trying not to cut my fingers through the murky water.

I suppose the worse part was that I never knew for sure. I couldn't prove my instincts. Instead, I carried my fears like heavy weights. A weight that became unbearable in the end.

The parakeet was still sitting on the window frame. I slowly and carefully reached for my camera that was nestled beside the microwave. In two clicks I had managed to capture him: alone, far from his familiar surroundings and desperate to spread his wings and fly away.

I know how you feel, little one, I said out loud. I know exactly how you feel.

Chapter Six – Cheap as Chips

I stared at my bank statement in disbelief. I knew things would be dire but the digits in front of me sent shockwaves through my soul. The figure typed in bold at the bottom highlighted the grand total I was worth. And it wasn't much.

I grabbed my keys and bankcard and briskly walked across the road to the ATM inside the local newsagent's. I needed a second opinion. I'd even had the audacity to wear a Jean-Paul Gaultier black blazer for my excursion, one of the many gifts from Charlie, a perfect fit in terms of cut but less so in terms of reflecting my means.

I stood in the queue, fourth in line behind two builders, an old lady and a teenage boy, who was probably more flush with cash than I was. As my fate was delivered, my fears were confirmed: I was four pounds short of zero. I had proved it was actually possible to be worth less than nothing. As I put the magazine I was holding back onto the rack, I realised I needed a financial intervention. And I had an idea. I dragged myself home, lost in a sea of commuters: a sheep in wolf's clothing.

The sound of loud vibrations was coming from my phone on the kitchen table. I had six missed calls from Amber and a voicemail. I dialled to listen: 'Jess, I've just had a call from our landlord to say our rent payment has bounced. I said there must have been some mistake. Please can you sort it as I'm stuck at work?' I put the phone back down on the table and typed out a brief message:

Yep, I'll sort it, will pay it in cash by the end of the day

I looked again at my bank statement: I had no other choice but to sell my soul to the devil. I put the stereo on to block out my internal wailing and opened the doors to my wardrobe, pulling out two small boxes of handbags: two Fendi, one Chanel, and a couple of Marc Jacobs' bowlers. As I ran my hands over the high-quality leather I felt like a fraud. This was the wardrobe of someone successful, someone who had her life intact, and as I was neither of these people, something had to give.

I ran a quick search through Google for second-hand designer shops. Although it was painful, I wasn't naïve enough to ignore the fact that having a roof over my head would be far greater than any memories I was still holding onto. A small shop popped up in Islington with a purple catchphrase written in violet across the website: 'One man's trash is another man's treasure.' I shook my head in disbelief.

Twenty minutes later, I exited the tube, my hands clutching a plastic bin liner full of possessions like a prisoner on his last day serving time. A small bell rang out as I walked through the rickety shop door. The smallest woman I had ever seen, with a halo of orange hair, pulled a curtain back from behind the till.

'Hello, darling,' she said. She reminded me of my grandma.

'Hello,' I replied. By now the bag was weighing heavily in my arms and the decision to actually sell off our history was weighing heavily in my heart too.

She took several minute steps over to me. 'What's that you have there, sweetheart? Are you looking to sell?'

I nodded and placed the plastic bag on the counter. Without a minute to spare, she had ripped it open with frail fingers that were stronger than they looked and tipped the contents over the glass worktop, meticulously sorting through them with an experienced hand.

'Time to get rid?' she said, fingering the stitching.

'Something like that.'

'From a certain gentleman?'

I nodded again, exhaling.

'Well they're good stuff: real quality pieces.'

'So how much do you think?' I said, focusing on the reason I was here. The facts. The financials.

'Well, I can give you £500 for the Chanel, £350 apiece for the Fendis and £300 for the Marc Jacobs.'

I looked down at the bags and took a deep breath.

'How does that sound?' she said.

'Sounds great,' I replied, knowing it would cover one and a half month's rent and a few weeks' worth of food if I ate like a borrower.

As she counted out £1,500 in cash I began to peruse the shop.

'This place is really lovely,' I said, running my fingers through the silk scarves hanging down.

'We opened in 1981. Can you believe that? I bet you weren't

even born!' she said, stuffing the large wad of cash into an envelope.

'My name's Jess,' I said, not knowing why I felt the need to introduce myself.

'Rita,' she smiled.

'You know,' I continued, 'those bags, they were a gift from someone – I feel a bit guilty selling them. I just don't have a choice. I've gotten myself into a bit of a rut financially and these are all I own of any real value. Sad really, isn't it.'

I ran my fingers over the worn leather.

'This is literally all I was worth to him.'

She smiled. She could see my face turn red as I fought to hide my embarrassment.

'You just did what you have to do,' she said, simply. 'There'll be others…'

'Bags or men?' I asked, my lips creeping into a smile.

'Both,' she said handing me the envelope.

I pulled the rickety door behind me and gave her a short wave through the window. I looked down at the envelope poking through my bag. Unless I was willing to sell every possession I owned, it was the motivation to find a money-paying job.

I lay down on the living-room carpet, my legs stretched out behind me, surrounded by lists of all the magazines that I had sent my photography portfolio to. I decided to take matters into my own hands and try to speak to somebody about a possible placement. I could feel the butterflies of nerves in my stomach as the tone rang out. I sat there, crossed-legged, picturing the office I was calling. Picturing the person who may answer the phone. After four, possibly five rings, a stern-sounding lady picked up.

'You're through to *Redsky* magazine, how may I help you?'

'Hi, I was wondering if you could put me through to your creative director, Laura. I sent through a portfolio of photographs for her perusal and I was wondering if it had been received?'

'Is she expecting your call?'

'Not exactly.'

'Then I'm afraid I can't put that call through. Can I help you with anything else today?'

'No...'

'Thank you, have a lovely day. Goodbye.'

It was a ten-second phone call then the line went dead. I drew a red line through *Redsky* magazine. I moved on to the next one.

After several awkward exchanges with receptionists, operators and refusals to connect I had reached the last name on my list. A warm sensation rose in my stomach and I knew that it was time to take a different approach. I dialled the final number.

'Good afternoon, *Inside Style* magazine.'

'Hello, I was wondering if I could be put through to Matt, your creative director? I sent through a portfolio for his perusal and I was wondering if it had been received?'

'Is he expecting your call?'

'Yes,' I lied.

'One moment, please...'

I could hear the line connecting, as I waited with bated breath to see if my tactic had worked.

'Matt Baker.' His voice was low and serious.

'Hi, Matt, it's Jess here. I sent through a portfolio for you to have a look at. I'm interested in a photography position and just wanted to check if you'd received it?'

'Hi, Jess. You know it's not exactly ideal to ring someone up in the middle of the day, unannounced.'

I nodded silently. 'I know,' I said out loud. 'I'm sorry, it's just…'

'Listen, give me two seconds,' he said, cutting me off. 'I'm searching my emails, what was your full name?'

'Jessica,' I said, quickly, making sure as not to waste any more of his time. 'Wood.'

'Here we are. Okay, I'm looking at your CV… hmmmm… okay… to be honest, you have very little experience for a full-time position. I mean, you haven't even taken a degree course at this level.'

'I know,' I said. 'I studied law and then…'

'My advice would be to get some formal training behind you and if I'm honest,' he continued, 'perhaps even a job assisting first. But in this climate, that's pretty competitive too.'

The sound of silence at the end of the line signalled our conversation was over.

'Well, thank you for your time,' I said.

'And don't call people in the middle of the day, it's annoying.'

'I know,' I said. 'I had no other choice.'

'Listen Jess, I can tell you want this from the outrageous way you chose to get my attention. You've got balls. Maybe when you get a little further down the line, and take the steps I suggested, then send it back through. There are always projects coming up.'

'Thanks, Matt.'

I hung up the phone and sat amidst the numbers. I needed experience to get a job and a job to gain experience. My head hurt with the confusion. Using the fabric from the arm of the sofa I pulled myself up and tidied away my paperwork.

The first to arrive for dinner was Amber. Well, she didn't exactly *arrive* as just came home from work like any other evening. She made her way to the toilet while talking quietly on her phone, giving me a slight wave on the way through. Moments later Sean knocked on the door, bringing with him a full Chinese and two bottles of wine under his arm.

'I can give you some cash for that now,' I said, wrestling for the bottle opener that was somehow caught between a wooden spoon and a spatula at the back of the drawer.

'How?' he said.

'I sold some stuff.'

'Like what – a kidney?'

At that point Amber strolled in. 'Looks tasty,' she said, peeling off one of the plastic lids.

'Who was on the phone?' I asked.

'Oh, no one,' she said, pulling out four wine glasses from the cupboard.

The buzzer sounded from downstairs and I ran over to let Marlowe in.

'Sorry, I'm late,' she said, shaking out her umbrella and making her way up the communal stairs to our front door. 'George's flight got delayed so I had to stay with Elsa but he's back now so I'm free – that rain came out of nowhere!'

She poured herself a glass of wine and lit a cigarette while sitting next to the open window. I loved how she used our flat to indulge in all the guilty pleasures that she couldn't enjoy at home. She was perched on the windowsill like a girl guide round the back of a tree at camp.

'So what's happening with the job situation?' she said, taking a drag.

'Well, put it this way, if nothing's come up in the next month I might have to look into selling that kidney.'

'You could get a job in a café?' Sean said.

'Thanks but I'd rather kill myself.'

'It must be cold perched up on that pedestal…' he replied.

I looked at him blankly.

Marlowe winked at me in support from her window seat while Amber was leaning against the kitchen counter, once again glued to her phone.

'Amber, are you okay?' Sean said as she continued to type. 'Back away from the phone, you're not at work now,' he said, prising it out of her hands.

'Stop it!' she shouted. 'For fuck's sake!' She wrestled it free as the whole room fell silent. 'I'm sorry, all right – I've just had a bad day.'

I watched as she went into her bedroom, slamming the door behind her.

'Is she okay?' Sean said. 'What did I miss?'

'She'll be all right,' Marlowe said, looking like she knew something we didn't. 'So tell me more about this Harry bloke.'

'I don't know,' I said. 'There's not much to say. He's… nice.'

'Ah, nice…' Sean said. 'That'll get the girls queuing up.'

'No,' I said, 'not like that. He's really lovely. I like him. I think.'

At that point, Amber emerged wearing a pair of oversized pyjamas, giving off the overall feel that she was slightly calmer.

Marlowe smiled at her. 'You okay?'

'Yeah, I'm fine,' she whispered, although the look on her face contradicted her.

'Sit down,' Sean said. 'I'll dish out the egg fried rice.'

Amber sat down at the table, the sleeves of her dressing gown covering her hands as she held her phone tightly.

'It's been a couple of weeks and we've been back and forth and now I just don't know what to do,' she said, looking to us for answers.

That was always what happened with Amber. She would tell you eventually – it just had to be on her terms.

'About what?' I said, leaning forwards in my chair.

'Well, a couple of weeks ago, I was working on this new proposal for promotion. I've been developing a new business growth plan, completely in my own time, in the hope that one day my boss might look at it and see me in a more, I don't know, competent light. I'd shown it to Marlowe and it was good.'

'Really good,' Marlowe said, now seated with us at the table.

'Okay…' Sean said, knowing there had to be more to the story.

'Well, there is a woman at work, Linda. She's senior to me and literally questions everything I do. I can't win. But if I got the promotion I wouldn't need to answer to her. I would just be working directly under my boss.'

'Amber, just get the point, what happened?' I said.

'I mean, this promotion would be an extra £7,000 a year and it would mean that my voice actually gets heard rather than working every hour God sends on someone else's ideas.'

'Yeah, but what actually happened, Amber?' Sean said.

'I was called into my boss' office about two weeks ago and asked what progress I was making in this quarter. I discussed my development and what I hoped to achieve. He said I was ambitious and liked to see that in an employee. He made a joke or two. I laughed. And then he talked about how we should discuss my ideas further. He got up and put his hand on the back of my chair. The other hand went on my knee. I didn't move.'

We all sat staring at her phone, which was now in the middle of the table like a piece of evidence in a crime scene.

'I know I shouldn't have but I kept thinking about my position and how I didn't want to offend him. So instead I just nodded. I could feel his eyes follow me as I left the office.'

'But isn't that sexual harassment?' Sean said.

'Not exactly,' Marlowe said.

'Two days later he called me into his office again and told me he was giving me the job of project manager at the new e-commerce merger.'

'What, just like that?' I said, in cautious belief.

'Yeah. Just like that,' she continued, 'but when I got to work on Wednesday he said that the position would mean that we should spend more time together and he invited me to lunch.'

'Just the two of you?' Sean asked.

'Yes,' she said.

'Is he married?'

Amber sat in silence.

'Just be careful…' Marlowe said, answering for her.

'It's a work thing,' Amber replied, dismissively.

'Is he married?' I repeated.

'Yes.' Amber looked at me with wide eyes. 'So we went to lunch and to be honest it felt great: I was being heard, he was flirting and so what if I flirted back, it was totally harmless. But late this afternoon he called me into his office again.'

'Smooth.' Sean laughed.

'Go on…' I said.

'He told me how much he valued and appreciated me, now that he'd got to know me better and how he had come to rely on my opinion. And then he tried to kiss me.'

'What did you do?' I asked.

'I didn't pull away.'

'Amber, he's married!' I cried.

'I know! But I was scared, he's my boss and now I'm stuck in it. And I don't know what to do.'

At that point her phone pinged.

'You've got to keep him sweet,' Sean advised. 'Don't piss him off. You don't know what he might do…'

'But don't have sex with him either!' I shouted.

'It's a tricky one,' Sean said as he leaned over to look at the phone. 'He's typing…'

'What about my business proposal? I've worked for weeks on it and it's really good. I don't want to lose the opportunity.'

'Babes, I don't think he cares about your business proposal,' Sean said, drily. 'He's still typing.'

'Can we just change the subject?' she said, pulling her phone off the table.

After dinner, I stood in the kitchen by myself, clearing away the forks that we'd used to eat from the cartons.

'The upside of eating takeaway...' Amber said as she walked back into the kitchen. 'No washing up!'

Marlowe had left early to relieve the babysitter and Sean needed to be up early for a gym session. We were alone: just the two of us.

'You can't have an affair with your boss, Amber. He's married. What about his wife? Did you even think about her?'

'Hold your horses,' she said, defensively. 'I don't know that I am.'

'What if you piss him off? If he rewards you with a promotion, how does he punish you? It's your job. Seriously, take it from me, life without an actual career, at our age, well, it's not ideal...'

'I think you're overreacting.'

'I'm not,' I said. 'I know how hard you've worked to get here.'

I switched off the lights throughout the flat and went to bed, leaving Amber still texting at the kitchen table.

'Amber,' I said quietly. 'Trust me, it's not worth the heartache.'

I'd passed the piece of paper that was sellotaped in the window numerous times and wondered what loser would want to work in an off-road Italian restaurant. As it turned out, that loser was now me. After the equivalent of a car boot sale for the heart, I felt unshakeable and remembered the advert in the window, sandwiched between a children's clothes shop and a pharmacist.

I found myself in front of a small stone building that had been transported from the Italian coast. Terracotta pots hung from the windows and a small layer of condensation gave the windows a slightly blurred feel. I made my way through the door and could immediately smell homemade soup and strong coffee. Through the customers that were gathered around the counter, I saw a large man with a tidy, jet-black beard and, assuming he was the manager, made my way over.

'I saw the advert in the window and was wondering if I could apply for the position?'

'Which position? Chef or waitress?' he replied.

'Waitress,' I said quickly, slightly thrown at the prospect of being hired as a chef.

'Maria, can you bring in the large case of tiramisu?' he called towards the back of the room.

I noticed his dismissive attitude and tried to hold his attention. 'I can bring in a CV if you'd like,' I continued. 'I live just around the corner...'

'Not necessary,' he cut me off. 'Can you come back at midday to help with the lunchtime rush?'

'Of course,' I said.

'Ask for Guido.'

'Who's Guido?'

'Me,' he said.

I left hastily before he had time to reconsider and returned two hours later, after a quick sandwich and dressed in a white blouse and black trousers. I'd tied my hair into a high ponytail and put on some lipstick so that I felt a little perkier.

'Hi, Jess,' Maria, the woman I'd heard on my earlier visit, shouted from the back of the restaurant. 'I'm Guido's wife.' She led me through the door reserved for staff. 'Next time,' she said, 'you must enter from the side door on the left. The main door is for customers only. I don't mind but Guido doesn't like it.' She held out her small delicate hand for me to hold. 'Follow me, the steps are steep.'

'I'm sorry, I didn't know,' I said, as I looked back at the daylight disappearing as we descended the stairs.

'Toilets are through there and you have your own locker in the side room in the basement. I'll give you two minutes to freshen up and then see you out on the floor, okay?' Her accent was thick and Italian.

I dutifully hung my beige trench coat in my locker, changed into my black leather loafers and washed my hands in the basin. A yellow neon light bulb shone down giving my skin a jaundiced tone. It would be a steady income. And for that I was grateful.

The following morning, my trial shift had proved successful and I was now a fully-fledged member of the team. I stood on the pavement on the dawn of my first full shift at Guido's and pulled out my phone from my bag. There was another missed call from Harry. Another call unanswered, but this time I decided to handle things differently. I pressed redial and listened for the ringing tone. After what seemed like an eternity of doubts that perhaps he'd seen sense and found somebody new, he answered.

'Harry,' I said. 'It's Jess. How are you?'

'Jess, I'm fine thanks. Nice to hear from you.' His voice sounded surprised, as expected.

'I saw that I had a missed call from you and so, I just thought I'd call to say… well, hello… and things…'

'It's good to hear from you, Jess. Yeah, I did ring. Quite a few times, actually.'

'I know,' I said. 'I'm sorry…'

After a brief pause, he continued. 'So, why ring now?'

'Well, I was thinking we could meet up again,' I said, wincing.

'Sure. I mean, I've never met a girl who cost me a week's salary just to eat noodles. Maybe we could go to the Ritz for tea this time?'

I laughed out loud. 'Thanks for making a joke,' I said, smiling. 'Is that a yes then?'

'Yes,' he replied. 'That's a yes.'

'Listen, I'm just at work but I'll give you a ring later to choose a good restaurant. Second thoughts…' I hesitated, coming to the realisation that a night out with the remains of my bag money might not be the most logical idea, '. . . why don't you come round to mine tonight after work and I'll cook us a pizza or something?'

'Sounds great,' he said. 'I'll see you then.'

Nine hours later I sat in my kitchen opposite a man I'd only met once but felt as if he belonged there. And I was still in my work clothes, which I couldn't decipher as meaning that I didn't care, or I cared too much not to notice.

'Okay,' I said, 'I told you about my failures at cookery, now tell me your most embarrassing story.'

'Fine,' he said. 'As you know, I've played rugby since I was young...'

I nodded as he took a sip from his bottle of beer, slowly beginning the anecdote but starting to laugh already. His chuckle was contagious.

'I was at school and playing rugby for the team. Now, this was a big game, the final of the county championships so basically the FA cup final of rugby for students. For some reason, I'd had an Indian the night before with the lads...'

I closed my eyes in anticipation. A small burst of laughter escaped my lips.

'Eh... don't look at me like that,' he said, 'go with it...'

He smiled widely at me but I couldn't help it. I wiped my eyes, which had now filled with tears of laughter.

'Wow, you're a good audience,' he said, chuckling. 'So, anyway, it was half time and I made a quick dash to the changing rooms, as you can imagine, quite quickly.'

I put my hand over my mouth.

'To cut a long story short, it was too late to check if there was any toilet paper: far too late. And there wasn't.'

I screwed up my face. 'What did you do?'

'I took my socks off and used them,' he laughed.

'So what happened?'

'I played sockless.'

Both of us burst out laughing: two loud and heavy laughs from the opposite sides of the table.

'It was all well and good until I remembered that I still had to play the second half.'

I reached over to pull a piece of kitchen roll from the side, my face aching from the strain.

'So, do you have any more stories for me?' he said, pulling his chair closer. 'Not necessarily in that… genre, of course.'

As I started to think I felt him lean into me. He kissed me.

'*Fucking wanking bastard taxi driver couldn't find Hungerford Bridge.*'

At that point I heard Amber slam the front door behind her and make her way through the hallway, shattering our rosy evening by turning the air blue.

'Sorry, I'm late, Jess. It's bloody pissing it down out there. Goodbye, summer.'

Christ, this is it, I thought to myself. The amount of men who could handle an angry, dripping wet Amber were few and far between.

'Hi,' she whispered, suddenly realizing that we weren't alone.

'I'm Harry, nice to meet you.' He went over and shook her dripping wet hand, sliding the soaking umbrella off it and putting it down by the door.

'I don't want to interrupt, I'll just go to my room,' she said, quietly making an exit.

'You don't have to…' I said.

'No way!' Harry continued. 'Plenty of room for three. Why don't you two go and put your PJs on and we can all get another beer and watch a film or something?'

Amber questioned me with her eyes as to whom this man was and why he was telling her what to do.

'Come on,' he shouted. 'I'll nip into the lounge and find a film.'

Before sauntering off to her bedroom Amber shot me another glance from behind the door, unable to hide her wry smile.

'I like him,' she mouthed.

'Me too,' I whispered.

AUTUMN

Chapter Seven – Oh, Starry, Starry Night

I suppose the thought of autumn always appears more attractive to me than the reality of it. I'd fantasize about sheltering in shop doorways, shaking out umbrellas amidst ankle-drenching puddles and drinking freeze-dried soup stirred from a packet into a cup.

As the first nips of the season could be felt, I was still working as a waitress at Guido's and had saved enough money to buy a new camera and tripod. My relationship with Harry had gone from semi-permanent to full time and to give an idea of where we were headed, he was staying over at our flat most weekends; the relationship wasn't open but the bathroom door still remained closed.

Looking back, it seemed as if time had suspended itself over summer, a period of just a few weeks when nothing and everything had happened. Some memories stood out, others had faded. I didn't know at the time that it would all catch up with me. Like a jolt or a shudder, a reckoning for the anticipation of a moment, one in particular, that changed everything…

Believers of astrology have long interpreted astronomical happenings and the position of stellar constellations as influencers of the earth's condition, affecting the key substances of human form. In other words: our lives. Only in the last few centuries have scientists learned to grasp the importance of the stars and their impact on the human race. Even now, the galaxy's vast stretch of darkness remains mysterious. Nothing is clear.

It may run a little deeper than whether or not a Sagittarian is compatible with a Virgo, but it could govern the very direction of our trajectories: our happiness, our loves, our sadness, our mistakes, they could all be cosmically linked. For the sceptics perhaps it's just a matter of gaining perspective of our size in comparison to the universe but it still begs the question as to whether we are actually in control of any of it *or* if the constellations are merely a guilt-free director of everything that happens day to day: the rising sun, the moon, the stars… and me.

I lay awake as the wind whistled through a small crack in the windowpane. I looked over at Harry sleeping next to me – thinking how a collection of little steps forward could culminate in such a colossal change. I slid out of bed trying not to disturb the covers and perched on the edge, wrapping my large towelling dressing gown around me. I could feel him stir.

'Are you getting up?' he asked, from a sleepy haze.

'Yeah, I need to. Early start.' I could feel his head gently lift before flopping back down on the pillow and back to sleep. I left our bed a little too easily that morning and ran myself a hot shower.

I was getting ready to meet Cathy Abbott. A few weeks previously, I had posted a blog on an online photography forum looking for anyone who may need an extra pair of hands assisting with their work: unpaid, of course. I had since received an email from Cathy who had a studio at her home in West London.

After two bus rides across the city and a wrong turn at Sloane Square, I wove my way through the shoppers clutching a small piece of paper on which I'd scribbled her address. I arrived five minutes early. The exterior was painted white with a probably once-thriving flower basket now left hanging empty above the door. I gave three sharp knocks of the rusty gold handle and waited.

'Jess,' she beamed as she opened it. 'How lovely to meet you.'

Cathy was late sixties, perhaps seventy, who had a mass of long blonde hair clipped up in a shaggy bun on top of her head. Her face was free from make-up except for a trace of burgundy lipstick that had been slightly washed away by a cup of tea or coffee.

'Would you like a drink?' she said, leading me through her hallway.

As I took off my shoes I looked around at the museum of Cathy Abbott which hung on the walls: family photos, an old clock and three framed black and white landscape pictures hanging in unison across the staircase.

'Did you take those?' I asked.

'I did. It's actually the Lake District, *beautiful* part of the country.' She stressed the word beautiful so that it was at least three syllables longer than usual. 'Have you been?'

I shook my head. 'I would like to though.' She guided me into the studio; an extension on the back of the townhouse that smelled of rolled-up cigarettes and oil paints. She moved a pile of books from a stool to let me sit down.

'I paint too,' she said, 'but you just want to help out with the photography stuff, right?'

'Yes, that would be great. What I really need to do is gain some experience. That's what everybody keeps telling me, anyway.' I looked at the painting of a half-finished nude standing on an easel. 'I just want to learn a bit more about art and your work.'

'I'll be honest,' she continued, pulling out a brown leather portfolio case. 'I only saw your post by chance as I don't really look at those online forums. I usually go on recommendations but I was having a flick through and for some reason, you caught my eye.' She handed me her folder as I sat down. 'These were taken in 1986, would you believe.'

I looked at the images of five young women sitting on the floor of a studio against a white background.

'I read that your pictures were in American *Vogue*,' I said, waiting for an animated reaction. But instead, she just smiled and nodded.

'So you can start by coming Tuesday and Thursday mornings. I'll leave some of the editorial stuff for you to examine on the computer. Nothing too airbrushed as that's not my style but you'll get the hang of it. Sound good to you?'

'Absolutely,' I said, smiling.

'You should really get going on your own shoots too,' she said in a matter-of-fact way. 'In order to last in this game, you have to create your own style.'

I nodded, a tingle of inspiration that had long been forgotten rose within me as I flicked through her work in the folder.

'And do me a favour?' she said. 'Pick a style that won't be

replaced by a machine in ten years' time.' I smiled at her as she stood, hands on her hips. 'Better to make yourself irreplaceable in this digital world,' she said.

'Would you mind if I stayed for a bit today?' I said, almost without thinking. 'I could tidy up or help you with packing?'

'Well, let me see. I was making a start at archiving my work,' she said. 'I could always use an extra pair of hands with that – but it's not too exciting, I'm afraid. I tell you what, I'll put the kettle on, shall I?'

'No, I will,' I said jumping to my feet. 'I want to make myself useful.'

As I stood holding the dry tea bags, waiting for the water to boil, I could hear she had put the radio on and was beginning to pull open boxes. I had the urge to get back inside and help an indication that this might be more than a stepping stone. I was exactly where I needed to be.

I left her house that evening at 6.30 p.m. In just under nine hours I had archived thirty years of style and attitudes right through from the Seventies to the Nineties. I walked back along to the bus stop, this time in darkness, evidence that the cold nights were getting longer by the season. I phoned Harry to tell him I would be later than planned but as I pulled out my phone that's when I remembered: we had arranged to go out with Sean that night to celebrate some big news, something that had proven too important to tell me over the phone. And I had completely forgotten. It was the reason I had swapped shifts at the restaurant and why Harry had been invited as a chance for them to get to know each other a little better. I moved along to the back of the bus and sat by the window. As

I wiped away the condensation on the glass with the edge of my forefinger, I noticed that it was a full moon. Bright, bold and hazy in its glow. A shining beacon in an otherwise pitch-black sky. I followed it with my eyes for three bus stops.

'So what exactly is this news?' Harry asked as I marched him down the stairs outside our flat.

'I don't know, he wouldn't tell me,' I replied. Having sat around in leggings all day at the studio, I had changed into a dress and even managed to paint my nails emerald green before being hustled out the door by Harry. He hated to be late. I hated being rushed. Things were tense.

As the taxi pulled up outside the restaurant I caught sight of the moonlit sky again.

'Jess,' Harry bellowed from the taxi.

'Yeah, I'm coming,' I said, following him outside.

Sean was alone at the table and with what looked to be his second cocktail.

'Finally!' he shouted.

'Sorry we're late, mate,' Harry said, shaking his hand. 'Nice to see you again. This one wouldn't get out of the bathroom.' He signalled to me as if I were an unruly teenager. What I really wanted to say was that he didn't need to apologise on my behalf to my own best friend but I held it in reluctantly.

'Where is everyone?' I asked. 'I thought we were late?'

'You are.' Sean rolled his eyes. 'Marlowe's not coming because George forgot to tell her that he was away – so she's looking after the bambino. And Amber will be here when she gets here.

When that will be is anyone's guess. Tell me, are your friends as reliable as mine, Harry?'

I looked over at them both, chatting animatedly about the journey over here as I sat in my chair in relief: relief for central heating, relief for not having to talk anymore – relief that I'd made it. I didn't know what was wrong with me. In the back of the taxi I could hear myself being difficult, tutting at every question, snapping at Harry for no reason at all. In all honesty, I had been trying to distance myself from the thoughts that I'd been having for weeks but that somehow made them stronger. Something wasn't right. I'd felt it the night before when we were making dinner and last weekend at his house making pancakes. For weeks, I'd sat on my feelings in the hope they'd go away but this feeling of claustrophobia and the fact that he was still being nice to me only seemed to be making things worse.

'Sorry I'm late,' Amber cried, 'the tube stopped mid-tunnel and I had no idea how long it was going to take.'

'Yeah, I hate when that happens,' Harry said, buttering a piece of brown bread.

'So what's this news?' Amber asked, jumping straight in.

Sean leaned forward and straightened his cutlery. 'Well, you know how I hate my job?'

'Yes,' both Amber and I said in unison.

'Well, I was headhunted for a design position at a menswear label, Jack Saunders, about a month ago and I went for the interview yesterday.'

Amber leaned forward from across the table. 'Jack Saunders is pretty special. I have clients who want to stock their stuff.'

'Well, they called me up today and I got it. They've given me the job!'

'Oh my goodness, that's amazing,' I cried, reaching for his hand across the table.

'So this means that I get to see my own designs being made into actual clothing. I won't have to cut and stitch someone else's pattern pieces anymore, I'll just be working on design.'

'Well, I think a celebration is in order,' Harry said, trying to get the waiter's attention. I watched as he ordered a bottle of champagne for someone I loved but he barely knew. A twinge of guilt panged inside me.

'Why don't we go out tonight?' Amber said. 'Like properly out, we haven't done that in for ever.'

'Oh I'm in!' I said, for once not having to apologise for the lack of money.

'Great,' said Sean. 'A dry martini followed by a dance followed by who knows what?' he said, winking.

'I'll just join you for the martini,' Amber said, drily.

As we got up to leave I caught sight of a couple standing by the bar: a tall man wearing a suit, talking energetically to a woman with a bouncy blonde blow-dry, hanging on his every word. Sharp suit? Yep. Good shoes? Yep. Attractive woman? Absolutely. It was the perfect look to keep a woman on her toes. They don't get a chance to feel permanent and so they never stop trying and so develops, in my experience, a cosmic connection based on flirtation and fear. You don't feel safe enough to let the mundane creep in. Or, dare I say it, be any type of ordinary.

We arrived at a club in the centre of Soho: the home of punks, gays, rebels and queens. As usual, Amber knew the guy on the door, so we bypassed the queue and made our way down the spiral staircase. The music was loud. I couldn't hear myself think. It was exactly what I needed. As Sean and Harry went off to find the bar, I led Amber onto the dance floor.

'Are you okay?' she shouted, being pulled into the frenzy.

'I'm fine,' I said, almost forgetting that I was speaking to someone who could see right through me. It was a strange phenomenon that often occurred between us whereby I didn't have to tell Amber anything. She already knew.

'I get it, Jess,' she said. 'But stick with it because he likes you – a lot.'

'I'm just not ready to go down that road yet, Amber. I'm not ready to… settle down.'

'Settle down or just settle?' she said, wincing.

I could see Harry stood at the edge of the dance floor looking out of place and a little lost.

'I'd better go,' I shouted, nodding in his direction.

Amber kissed me on the cheek. 'I'm going to find Sean…'

We parted ways and I made my way back through the tight crowd.

'Sean dumped me for a bartender – here you go…' Harry said, handing me a vodka soda.

'Thank you,' I said. I watched as his face changed colour with the lights. Just one kiss, maybe that was all I needed, just one kiss to prove it was still there.

'What the fuck are they playing! Is it supposed to be retro-cool?' At that point a tall, slim woman pushed past me.

'Charlie,' she shouted. 'Over here!'

I loosened my grip on Harry and turned around. My eyes

darted around the room, the rotating lights now blinding me. And that's when I saw him, slowly making his way through the crowds. Charlie Rainer.

It was as if a fireball had ripped through the sky, knocking me fifty paces. I knew the rule of fate but didn't listen. When you've reached a point when you wake up and no longer think of him, when you don't notice men who look like him in the street, when you think it's safe to mention his name, something in the outer universe strikes back: fate will take over and right there, he'll appear. Both together, in the exact same moment, we were written in the stars. He strode over, giving me a maximum of ten seconds to prepare myself but instead I remained glued to the spot unable to speak.

'What are the chances?' he said, almost nervously.

'Hello,' I replied, the music drowning out my heart, now beating in the back of my throat.

'You look amazing,' he said. It was at this point that he would usually put his hand on the back of my thigh and kiss me – but that wouldn't be happening any more.

'All right, mate?' Harry said from behind me. I could feel Harry's hand resting on my back in an act of ownership. It took everything in my power not to shrug it off, violently.

'Charlie, this is Harry,' I said. I couldn't bear to make the introductions, never mind small talk.

'Hi, Harry,' Charlie said, looking at me.

'We're out with Sean,' I said, 'He's got a new job so we're celebrating.'

'Pass on my congratulations to him. So, how are you?' Charlie said, pulling me to one side.

'I'm fine. Nothing new.'

Harry looked at me, halfway between stunned and confused.

'Sorry, I can't hear you for the music…' Charlie said reaching for my arm, pulling me in closer.

'I said, I'm here with Harry.'

'Oh,' he replied. 'Well, like I said, you look amazing.'

I leaned in. I thought he was going to politely kiss my cheek but instead he just lingered, halfway between my neck and my ear. I could smell him. The earth shifted.

'Charlie, what are you doing!?' the ten-foot blonde shouted, bringing us both back into the room.

'We should go,' said Charlie, motioning her on. 'Enjoy the rest of your evening.'

He looked back at the two of us; our reunion shot to stardust.

'Come on, let's go,' I said to Harry, walking back onto the dance floor. And that's where I danced. I danced to any song that was played for however long they played it. I danced until my feet burned, until my thighs ached, until I didn't think of him anymore.

The streets outside were littered with flyers and polystyrene boxes as I paced the edge of the pavement, trying to keep warm waiting for Amber to find her coat. Soho in the early hours was a beautiful mess, filled with people buying guilt-free kebabs, drunkenly texting exes, staggering sideways to find their friends.

'I don't get why she checks it in,' Sean said.

'She always does,' I replied. 'She's scared it'll get nicked.'

'Well, if I'm honest I'd rather it did than go through this faff.'

This is ridiculous. I'm going to find her,' he shouted, adamantly. 'I've got a bartender waiting with a hot tub in Shoreditch.'

I reached my arms around Harry who was warm in the cold wind as my phone vibrated in my pocket.

'Is that you or me?' he asked, checking his pockets.

'Me,' I replied. 'It's probably Amber…'

I opened my phone to see the name 'Charlie' light up on the home screen. I hadn't seen that name in months and it ripped through my stomach like a firework.

'Back in a minute,' I said to Harry, walking towards the edge of the pavement.

I reached the side of the road and turned the phone over, my hand trembling in anticipation. I opened a message which read:

I'm sorry.

'About bloody time!' Harry shouted to the others climbing up the stairs of the club.

'This is vintage,' Amber shouted to him. 'If someone steals it, I'll absolutely die.'

'I've never known anybody to absolutely die before,' Harry said, smiling. 'The man fell thirteen storeys and absolutely died. She was run over by a lorry and absolutely died…'

Amber came trotting over to me, wrapping the large camel coat around her.

'Cab time,' she said. 'Who's with who?'

'I'm with Jess,' Harry said, still feeling he had to state the obvious. But this time I stopped him.

'Actually, I've got a splitting headache,' I lied. 'Could we just see each other tomorrow instead?'

'Yeah of course,' he said, his nonchalant charm making the situation less volatile. I wondered if he knew. If he could smell the regret on me like a stale perfume. I kissed him lightly on the cheek and left.

The back of the taxi felt comforting. I looked over at Amber who was staring out of the window as I sat there deep in my own pool of thought. I didn't know what I was doing or why I was doing it, but in spite of all of this, I'd still chosen to drive away.

I sat at the kitchen table and opened my phone: two words. How can two words possibly mean so much? How can two words emotionally pin you against the wall? I turned my phone over as Amber walked into the kitchen.

'How's your head?' she asked.

'Fine,' I paused. 'It wasn't about my head.'

'I know,' she said as I sat and watched her put the kettle on. 'Fancy some toast?'

I nodded.

'Well, if it makes you feel any better, me and Sean were dancing erotically and I caught sight of someone I know from work… soooo, that should be round the office by Monday.'

I laughed limply. 'I bumped into Charlie when I was with Harry in the club. He was with his new girlfriend.'

'Wowsers… girlfriend?' She looked over as she slid the bread into the toaster.

'Well, whatever she was, looking at me like I should be jealous.'

93

'And were you?'

'I don't know…'

'I bet that put the wind up him. How did he look?'

'He looked different. Sad. Sort of.'

'It's not your problem, Jess.'

'I know, but as soon as I saw him I… I don't know…'

There was a pained look written on her face. 'Do you want to be with Harry?'

'Yes,' I said, confidently.

'Do you want to be with Charlie?'

'No,' I hesitated. 'I don't think so.' I rested my forehead on the kitchen table. 'You know, I lied to Harry tonight. I actually lied to him.'

Inside I felt ashamed – but not sorry.

'I think I know what the problem is,' Amber said, bluntly. 'For the first time in years you feel safe. And he doesn't make you work for it like Charlie did. Does he text back?'

'Always.'

'Does he text you goodnight?'

'Most nights.'

'Well, there's the issue. It's not that there's anything wrong, you're just bored, that's all.' She began taking her make-up off with a face wipe, offering one for me to do the same.

'So why did I leave him tonight?' I said, wiping my eyes, ignoring the sting.

'Because there's no drama kicking off so you have to compensate for it. Just do something to shake things up a bit.'

'With Harry?'

'Yeah.'

'Like what?'

'I don't know, relationships aren't my forte, Jess. Can't you both go away for a few days?'

'I'm not sure it'll help.'

'Just don't throw it all away for nothing. Because that's all you get from men like Charlie. Literally: *nothing*.'

Later that night, I climbed into bed and lay there in the cold sheets, staring up at the dark, blank ceiling, my exhausted body fighting desperately to sleep. The full moon was still out in force and the events of the night were flashing through my mind. Fate may have brought us back together again, but our destiny is determined by our own actions. And this time, I was going to do nothing at all.

Half an hour later my phone pinged in the darkness. I pulled it towards me as my eyes adjusted to the light. It was Charlie:

Are you awake?

I typed out 'yes' but deleted it as soon as it had been written. After all, I was clueless, I wasn't some sort of sadomasochist and I wasn't going to willingly put myself through that again either.

A second ping:

I miss you.

I looked down at the phone and hesitated for a moment. This would be the crucial moment, the point where I would have to fight or flight. I put it on silent mode and rolled back over in bed. Perhaps it was the alcohol or the dancing, but in that moment, I just didn't have the strength to go through it all again. Suddenly, a loud, harsh buzzing blasted from my phone, sending a piercingly loud vibration out into the quiet night. I quickly answered it so as not to wake Amber.

'Charlie, it's 4 a.m.,' I whispered. 'What do you want?'

'You,' he said, calmly.

The sound I heard coming from his mouth, I'd heard a million times before. There was a longing for me, and despite my denials, it was mutual.

'Where's your girlfriend?' I snapped, hoping a rebuttal, spat out, might knock me to my senses.

'She's not my girlfriend, Jess.' I could hear him breathing. Guttural.

'Don't, Charlie,' I said. I wanted to hang up the phone but I felt pinned to the bed. I could hear him, right in my ear. I could picture his face. I wanted him.

'Remember when I would get home from work and you'd be there. Christ, I couldn't keep my hands off you…'

'What am I doing now?' I said, unable to stop myself.

'You're sitting on top of me,' he replied, breathing heavily.

As I heard his moans I reached down and touched myself. I wanted him. I needed him – only him.

'I love you,' he cried as he came. 'I fucking love you, Jess.'

I lay there motionless, I couldn't breathe. I walked over to the window and pulled up the heavy sash, letting the cold night air hit my face. Everything was silent… halfway between despair and ecstasy. In just one night, a force had taken over the shattered pieces of my life that I had somehow re-aligned. Whatever it was – fate, the stars, coincidence – it rendered me powerless. It had a cosmic hold over everything. And I just couldn't let him go.

Chapter Eight – There Once Was a Girl Who Swallowed a Lie, Perhaps She'll Die

'Forgiveness': a conscious, deliberate decision to release feelings of resentment toward a person who has harmed you.

There was once a girl whom I sat next to during art hour in school, the one time of day when we could pack away our work and paint, draw or build whatever we wanted to as long as it was our own, as long as it was unique to us. On this particular afternoon I had decided to build a kite. I tied purple and turquoise ribbon to its tail and drew a bright yellow sun with orange rays in the corner. At the end of the hour the teacher would ask us to place them all on the mat in front of us. As the teacher held my kite high in the air, said girl threw up her arm and claimed it as her own. There was a loud sound of applause followed by a sticker from the teacher. I didn't say anything but just sat there, silent in my rage. I did confront her, once the crowds had dispersed but by then it was too late. I forgave her, but I was invariably unsure of whose fault it actually was, hers for claiming my work as her own or mine for not highlighting the injustice. And here we still were, decades later: Charlie had lied to me, but I had let him. That's the funny thing about forgiveness, it's a concept I still struggled to distinguish from my own admission. Was it his fault for lying, or my fault for staying silent?

I walked into the kitchen and poured myself a glass of orange juice as Amber emerged on her way to a yoga class.

'Can I come?' I said, handing her a glass.

'To yoga?'

'Yeah.' I was trying to pass it off as nonchalance but really it was a faded attempt to cleanse myself from the night before.

'Sure,' she said, putting on her Lycra hoodie.

I smiled at her without speaking.

'You're being weird,' she said, filling her water bottle at the tap. 'Look, you've got ten minutes until we have to leave. I'm not waiting.'

Half an hour later I lay on a mat borrowed from Amber, my eyes closed, focusing on my breathing. I couldn't understand why I hadn't started this sooner: a moment suspended in relaxation away from the world and most importantly away from the thoughts inside my head.

'I can hear you breathing,' Amber muttered from the mat next to me.

'Sorry,' I said. I tried to lie back down again but by this time I was all fidgety. 'Amber?' I continued.

'Shhh, you're not supposed to be talking,' she replied without even opening her eyes.

'Amber, what do you think about forgiveness?'

'Has all the deep breathing gone to your head or something?'

'No.'

'Well, if you're talking about Charlie then no, it's not a good idea.'

I lay there with my eyes closed too; trying to get back into the yoga zone and the positive energy, but all I could think about was the night before and the sound of his heavy breathing down a very much consensual, two-way phone call. I tried to focus on the rising and sinking of my chest, the feeling of weightlessness, the prickly feeling of the yoga mat against my sweaty back – and the sheer speed at which I was unremittingly being dragged back into the past.

'So I'll see you later tonight,' I said, on our way out of the gym.

'Actually, I'm going for dinner with someone,' Amber said.

'Well, I'll see you later on then…' I shouted after her as she buried her head into her phone. She looked back briefly, giving me a slight wave as she crossed the busy street. I wasn't the only one being weird that morning.

As I got home that dreary Sunday morning, I made my way into my bedroom and pulled open the curtains. A pile of dirty laundry lay strewn on the white wicker chair in the corner of the room as I scooped up what I could and carried it to the kitchen, wrestling it into the washing machine. I closed the door and briefly rested my head against the cold glass. I had come to the conclusion after the pre-dawn phone call with Charlie that getting involved with yet another man was not at all what I needed. What I wanted was pretty clear to everyone but me. I needed to be on my own. But first, I needed to talk to Harry. Unlike Charlie, he had emotionally put himself on the line and the least I could do was be honest with him. He was owed a conversation.

*

If there's one thing to make you feel proud of your friends in London, then it's their first step onto the property ladder. A homeowner is somewhat of a rarity in the city, akin to the snow leopard or white rhino. We know they exist, but we rarely meet them. In a sea of renters they emerge after years of saving and demonstrate to the rest of us how life could be… if only we didn't shop, or use electricity, or eat on a regular basis.

I had arranged to meet Sean to view a flat he was considering buying, having been told by the current owners that if he arrived that day they would show him exclusively before start of business Monday morning. His new job would provide him with an income that would allow him to evolve from a house-share and for the first time, branch out to a place of his own. It was a monumental moment and one that I was dying to witness.

'Wow,' I said looking out through the bare bedroom window. 'You're going to have to put some curtains up. Half of London can see you!'

Sean arched an eyebrow, a look I'd seen a few times.

'Or not…' I said, my voice fading. I walked across the uncovered floors to the concrete fireplace and ran my hand across the smooth surface. 'I'm ending it with Harry,' I said.

'What? Why?' Sean said, surprised. 'I was only with you last night. When did you decide all of this?'

'It's just not right,' I said. 'Amber thinks I'm an idiot…'

'Amber thinks everyone's an idiot. You know yourself what you want, Jess. Life's too short: me of all people should know.'

'Do you think Paul would've liked it?' he asked, looking out of the window.

His name still hit me like a sucker punch.

'I think Paul would be very proud of you,' I said, standing at his side.

'I just don't know how we managed to fuck everything up,' he said.

I laughed. 'Me neither. But we're getting better.' I squeezed his hand as we stood together in the vast, empty room. 'So, do you think I'm doing the right thing?'

'I don't know, Jess,' he said, through gritted teeth. 'I think you should do what makes you happiest. You can't choose who comes into your life and you can't choose when they leave, either, so stop taking so much of the responsibility. Because this is it, this life, there won't be another. There isn't some magical place beyond here that we're rehearsing for. Well, I don't believe there is anyway. It's funny, when I used to think of what life would be like in the future, perhaps this very day was the one I was dreaming of. Would I have done things a little differently, loved a little less harder, if I knew that it was destined to end? No. Because I was introduced to feelings that I didn't know I had, that for the first time had nothing to do with my own wellbeing. And now I know that it's possible.'

I wondered if he knew of his importance. That he wasn't just a by-product of a terrible accident. I reached out and flicked the back of his ear.

'Ouch!' he said, pulling his head away.

I looked over at him as we both crept into giggles.

'Do you think it's too big?' he said, pressing his hand against the glass.

'Yes, definitely,' I said. 'Miles too big.'

'Isn't it a bit indulgent to be looking at a flat this size with it just being me here and no one else?'

'Life's too short,' I said, relaying his own advice. 'You've earned this one, Seany. You've earned every brick.'

'Oh fuck it,' he said. 'Why not, eh? If the mortgage repayments bounce I can wait tables with you in my spare time.'

I smacked him on the arm as we made our way back to the estate agent who was waiting patiently outside in the corridor. I took one last look at the view before I left. Being responsible for all of this: now that was certainly something to aspire to.

I had arrived fifteen minutes early and had brought with me the maroon jumper he had lent me one chilly night, just in case he mentioned it and wanted to take it back. I was sat in the bar around the corner from Harry's house: a neutral ground that didn't harbour any memories. It was almost last orders, and ten minutes later he walked through the door and approached my small, round table by the window. I was already on my second diet coke and had been running through my head exactly what I wanted to say. I had thought about just telling him that it just wasn't working, but then he was going to think that part of this was his fault. And it wasn't. I waved as he made his way over to the table. He leaned over as he usually would and kissed me on the lips as he usually did.

'Fancy another drink?' he said.

I shook my head.

'I'll be back in a minute then…'

I watched him as he stood at the bar and then came back

with a pint of lager. I knew I was bordering on insane for ending things, but I also knew that you can't live, all the while pretending.

'Are you okay?' he said, sitting down.

'Yeah, I'm fine,' I said, lying.

'How's your head?'

'My what?'

'I'm talking about your head, you said you had a headache last night when we left the club.'

'Oh, yeah, it's fine now,' I said, lying again.

'So what's this all about then? Only I've got to be in the office early tomorrow and it's not like you to want to meet on a school night.'

'It's not working,' I said, my mouth running away with itself before I could stop it. It was insensitive and too easy to say.

He took a deep breath and looked at me for about three seconds too long. 'So that's what this is about?'

'I don't want you to think this is about you. It absolutely isn't – it's all me.'

'I know,' he said.

'What do you mean you know?' Perhaps it wasn't the reaction I was expecting.

'Jess, I've never treated anyone the way I treated you. I was there for you. I got involved with your friends, usually I'm not that keen but with you… I just dived right in.'

'I know,' I said. 'I just don't know what happened.'

He reached out to hold my hand across the table: his were warm and mine were freezing.

'I'm sorry I've been awful to you,' I said.

'Jess, please. Just give it some more time.'

'Harry, I really like you, I do,' I said, moving my hand away, 'but time isn't going to help anything.'

'Is there someone else?' he said, looking me directly in the eye for the first time since he arrived.

'No,' I lied.

And maybe that was the problem: with Harry, lies came spilling out effortlessly. I didn't even have to think. I hadn't lied to Charlie once. I couldn't.

'Well, if that's it,' he said, 'I'm not going to say I'm not disappointed because I am but if that's how you feel…'

'It's how I feel,' I said, defiantly. I reached down and searched through the carrier bag wedged between my legs. 'I brought back your jumper. It's in here somewhere.' I rooted through the bag trying to free it from under a large plastic bottle of water.

'Keep it, Jess. I don't need the jumper, for Christ's sake.'

I called off the search and raised my head above the table.

'Look, I'd better go. Like I said, I need to be up early.'

'But you didn't even finish your beer?' I said, suddenly wanting him to stay.

'Take care, Jess,' he said, standing up. And with that he walked out of the bar.

I'd gotten what I deserved. I sat and watched the bubbles rise to the top of his beer. I felt terrible, cruel even. But it was the most honest thing I had done in months.

An hour later, I opened the door to my flat to the sound of cheering and clapping from the room next door.

'How did it go?' Amber shouted from her bedroom.

I threw my keys on the side and walked through the hallway to find her cross-legged, painting her toenails on the bed. I took off my coat and glanced at the loud chat show blaring from her TV screen in the corner of the room.

'What are you watching?' I said, yawning.

'Just some American trash reality thing.'

'How was dinner?' I asked.

'Good,' she said. 'It was a quiet one actually.'

I sat down on the bed next to her and wriggled my shoes off. 'How was your day?'

'Sean is buying a flat and I've ended things with Harry.'

'I gathered,' she said, picking up her wet pieces of cotton wool. She leaned over to turn the lamp off as the room stayed lit by the glow of the television.

'Move over,' I said, wriggling under the covers. 'You're hogging my side.'

We slept together that night, our legs entwined beneath the duvet, safe, secure, listening only to our dreams and the sound of the television.

It was a Tuesday night and for the third time that week I scooped my hair up into a ponytail and tied my black work apron around my waist. I was running ten minutes late for my shift at Guido's, having lost track of time at Cathy's studio. As I desperately searched the locker room for a pen I could hear my phone vibrating in the side pocket. Give it two minutes, I thought to myself, and it will go to voicemail. I stared at my reflection, stark under the harsh lights above the mirror, and ran my finger over a pimple on my chin that hadn't been there that morning. After a brief pause it started buzzing again. Flashing in big white letters was the name 'Charlie'. I looked up the stairs to the restaurant. It sounded loud and bustling. I could hear a waiter shout for bread in the kitchen as I slid out of the staff exit and under the doorway of the smoking area.

'What do you want?' I answered, abruptly.

'It's Charlie, are you okay?'

'I'm fine. Look, I can't talk, I'm at work.'

'You're at work? Where do you work?'

'I work at Guido's, the Italian place opposite the tube.' I don't know why I told him; the words had spilled before my brain had time to stop them.

'I need to talk to you,' he said, 'it's important.'

I could hear the lunch staff finishing their shift in the changing room and knew it was my turn to take over.

'Okay,' I said, desperately needing to leave. 'I'll ring you at 11 p.m., that's when I finish.' I paused. 'I have to go.'

As soon as I'd put the phone down I felt a rush of either regret or excitement. As usual with him, it was impossible to tell.

I walked into the restaurant and was greeted by Maria and two of the locals.

'Sorry I'm late,' I said, hiding the state of panic I was in.

'Slow down,' Maria said, 'the boss is away and I won't tell him.' She gave me a small smile and straightened the knot at the back of my apron.

For the next few hours I tried to focus on the table numbers, the food, the wine, the specials, but I couldn't shake the thought of Charlie from my mind. Every face of every man that came in seemed to look like him. I was angry, angry towards him for taking over my life again and angry towards myself for letting him.

The restaurant was busy and the central heating had made the lower part of the restaurant feel like a furnace. I could feel the sweat trickle down the back of my neck. It was five consecutive hours of constant running, the type of distraction that my mind so desperately needed but that had sent my body into spasm. By the end of the night, after placing the last chair upside down on top of the table, I sat down gently on the cold, floor tiles.

'Jess,' Maria said, in her thick Italian accent. 'Is everything all right?'

'Fine,' I said.

She turned to me and handed me a small loaf of bread wrapped in cling film. 'For breakfast tomorrow,' she said.

I smiled. 'Thanks, Maria.' I took off my small black apron and made my way down the stairs, glancing back briefly to give her a wave. A look passed briefly between us. Perhaps she knew.

I sat down on a rickety chair in the locker room and tried to assess the situation. I had two choices: I could block him out and forget the past year had even happened, or I could face him and ultimately get the answers I needed. I took my coat and my handbag from my locker and left. The cold metal steps dug into my shins as the ring started. A tingling sensation ran through my hands as he answered.

'Charlie, it's Jess,' I said.

'Thanks for calling back. How was work?'

'Fine. Quite busy, but fine.'

'I didn't even know you had a job. How long have you been working there?'

'Three months. But then, you don't really know much about me these days do you?'

'No. I suppose not,' he said, softly.

After months of rehearsing this conversation in my head, I was struggling to find the words that I wanted to say.

'So what's this about then?' I said. 'Because I'm outside and it's cold and I just want to go home.'

'I miss you,' he said.

We sat in the pause where neither of us spoke.

'How was your night out last week?' I said, diverting the subject. 'It was strange bumping into you.' I tried to keep things factual, beating off the emotions with my imaginary iron fist. All the while a secondary voice ran through my head telling me to keep it light. Don't get drawn in. Just. Keep. Things. Light.

'I really miss you, Jess.'

There was another pause from both of us.

'I don't believe you,' I said. 'I just don't believe you anymore.' I said it in the way a newsreader might deliver bad news, almost professionally.

'I know I made a mistake, but if you could just understand that I didn't mean to hurt you, Jess.'

'But you did.' I hesitated. I could feel myself welling up inside but tried to disguise it by clearing my throat. 'Look, I'm not sure what you're trying to prove, Charlie, to me or to yourself, but please don't. Don't use me as some form of entertainment because you're bored with your girlfriend... or whatever it is you call her.'

'She's not my girlfriend, Jess.'

'Charlie, I don't care…'

'I just want you,' he said.

I could feel my hands start to tremble.

'There's something I think you should know,' I said. 'I'm sorry too.' The lightness in my voice had all but gone as I succumbed to the weight of what I wanted to say. And the words just flooded. 'I'm sorry things didn't work out between us but now it's time to start again, with this job, with everything. These past few months, everything has just become a bit of a mess. It's my own fault, I know. But I just need to focus on turning things around now.'

'I see…' he said.

'And by doing this, by turning up out of the blue, well, you're not helping me to do that.'

I could hear him breathing at the end of the phone. 'Well, I wouldn't want to be the one to stop you,' he said.

I sat there, on the stone-cold steps of the fire escape. 'I love you, Charlie, and I hope that you find what will make you happy.'

And with that I hung up the phone.

They say that it is far easier to forgive someone you hate than someone you love, and it was true that even after all he had done, I did still love him. But like that kite I had worked so tirelessly to create, he had cried ownership, but I had been given the skills to make it.

I went to bed that night without a single feeling of regret. And woke up the next day as someone who had been hurt, but was still striving forwards, carrying that feeling with me instead of hoping it would go away. I had finally forgiven him and at the same time, and more importantly, maybe I had forgiven myself. And did I regret the heartache? No, because if there was one thing I had learnt, it was that forgiveness is possible.

Chapter Nine – Goodnight, Head/
Good Morning, Heart

There was red wine, two glasses and single white rose left on the glass coffee table. This time he had really made an effort, Amber thought, as she took off her coat and waited for her boss to arrive. She looked around at the hotel room and took in the surroundings. It was an affair. There was no getting away from it. In fact, they were bordering on a cliché. She looked down at the pamphlet resting on the pillow, the prices of room service listed. Although she knew it would be charged as a business deal, she couldn't help but feel pleased with herself about her worth. And that's just what it was. A deal. She got the setting where the price of scrambled egg reached double digits. And he got, well, her.

As she walked into the bathroom her sense of pride for handling him in such a way was monumental. By all account he was falling for her. A rapid development that she could feel was on her side. She was running the show and, as always, the ball was most definitely in her court. She could hear his key turning in the door and smiled. She knew it wasn't real. He was the equivalent of an invisible friend, someone who existed between the two of them, but not in the real world.

'Amber,' he shouted through the door.

She always waited a few minutes before she replied. It felt nice to be wanted. She slid off her dress in front of the bathroom mirror and stood confidently assessing the new black underwear she had bought. It had taken her longer than usual to pick it. With him she needed something classic and elegant. He wasn't into the cheap nylon twin sets that seemed to appeal to her own generation. He was older, and to Amber's delight, much harder to please. She sprayed three squirts of perfume and rearranged the thin, black stockings around her thighs. She was ready. She wanted more. And he didn't stand a chance.

'Listen,' he said, cautiously. Just two hours later and she lay in his arms as he stroked the top of her arm gently. 'There's something I really need to talk to you about.'

'What is it?' she replied, sitting up so she could see him.

'This whole thing is really very lovely but we still need to remember to be careful. I noticed that you said "see you later" when you left the office today. Now, that may have just been a slip of the tongue, I know, but we really need to be doing a better job of hiding things.'

Amber looked at him, her neck flushed. She snapped herself out of the feelings creeping in. 'Yes, yes of course. I'm sorry.'

He saw the look on her face and ran his hands through his grey hair nervously. 'Because this is fun, Amber, but I'm married. And that's very important to me.'

She could feel a burning heat rise towards the top of her back. Maybe she didn't have this worked out after all. But maybe it was too late. 'You could've at least waited and had this conversation whilst I was wearing clothes,' she said, pulling the bed sheet around her. 'Might've made me feel like less of a prostitute.'

'Don't be like that, Amber. I just don't want you thinking this could be anything more than it can be. Don't make me the bad guy here, there's two of us in this bed.'

As she felt his hand on the small of her back she wondered, quietly, how she had got here. His words, spoken in shame, had hurt her. It was only supposed to be a bit of fun. But her heart had caught fire and she had gone up in flames.

Although my social media might tell a different story, I have very few friends. When I was four years old I made my first friend. Her name was Lucy and she was my best friend: a nursery school partner in crime disguised in a denim blue dress and pigtails. She moved to Canada before we'd reached the age of ten, before real life had got in the way of seeing who could do the best handstand or who had been the first to spell their own name, before the teenage years of boys, periods and fallouts over borrowed clothes. After several failed attempts to search for her on social media, I don't think I'll ever know what happened to Lucy, where she is now or the person she became: just a tiny friendship in a large passage of time. And, of course, it would be totally inappropriate to invite her round to play – though I wish I could. Now I spend my days gossiping with Cathy or Maria, both of whom are over the age of sixty, trying to explain to them that yes, I *do* have 643 friends on Facebook, but no, I *don't* have anyone to go to the cinema with on a Friday night.

They look at me confused, and to be honest, so am I.

The rain splattered against the window as I sat dry, perched on a stool in Cathy's studio listening to an old record player that she had dug out of the loft following a conversation we'd had about the influence of music.

'Who's this?' I said as a raucous, croaky voice tore through the speaker.

'Janis Joplin,' she said. 'One of the best.'

I was an hour into retouching a portrait of an author that Cathy had taken earlier that week. I could see her feet tapping and moving to the music, her hips rocking back and forth on the stool beneath the easel she was working on.

'Can I ask you a question?' I said, as she smiled. She put down her paintbrush next to a bottle of white spirit and leaned over to turn the volume down.

'Sure,' she said, now that she could hear me.

'How long have you been married to your husband?'

'Forty-eight years,' she replied, followed by an outburst of laughter. 'I bet you can't imagine being with a person for that long. He works for Radio 2. You'll meet him one day I'm sure.'

'Wow, that's... impressive!' I said, as I turned back to my work and adjusted a few more levels on the picture. 'Don't you ever get... bored?' I said, feeling as if I were testing the waters of what she would be happy to talk about. I quickly looked for her response, hoping I hadn't offended.

She started laughing again. 'Jess, it's not a question of being bored. Yes, he can be a real arsehole sometimes, but you just have to stick together, like glue.'

'How did you meet?'

'We met at Woodstock in 1969. He was the sound engineer

of a travelling rock group and I was a backstage photographer. I'd just turned twenty-one.'

'You were at Woodstock?!' I cried.

'I was, hence the unlimited number of Janis Joplin vinyls back there. I'm a bit of an addict.'

'What was it like?'

'It was… messy. Exactly as you would imagine, really. I've still got an album of my shots somewhere. I'll dig it out for you. There was this one picture of the crowd – I remember standing there, and this woman was dancing with her eyes closed, she had two big daisies drawn on her cheeks and a bikini top on – my God, she was gorgeous! That picture made it into *Rolling Stone* magazine!'

I could feel myself gazing at her, transfixed.

'It was all about freedom and experience,' she said, getting up and drawing her legs underneath her on the green velvet couch. 'Love who you want, take what you want…' She gave me a look. 'A certain psychedelic drug…'

'You took LSD at Woodstock?!' I shouted.

'We all did! The drinks were spiked with it backstage. Just don't tell my kids…'

I slowly turned back to my desk, smirking uncontrollably at the thought of Cathy Abbott on LSD.

'Oh, it was a fabulous time, Jess, all about energies, auras and spiritual stuff. I still think about it sometimes, usually when I'm on my own, doing the gardening. I'm a lot older now so it's evolved more into creating flow within plants and interior design. You've just got to sense it… to *feel* rather than think all the time.'

'You can sense auras?'

'I think I can, yes.'

'Well, what about me, then?'

'You sure?'

I felt ready to accept what came my way.

'Well, what do you think?' she asked, sipping her coffee.

'I'm okay,' I replied.

'I didn't ask if you were okay; I asked what you're thinking?'

'I don't know,' I said, suddenly feeling slightly embarrassed. 'I'm… transient. I'm just leaving myself open to the possibilities, I suppose.'

'Well, how did you end up here, in this studio in my backyard?' Cathy asked, diligently.

I ceased avoiding the question. 'Well, I originally went to university to study law…' I was ready to give the pre-prepared speech I had rehearsed in my head and relayed 101 times before, detailing how it hadn't been for me and how I had wanted to follow my dream instead, but this time, for some unknown reason, I stopped myself.

'And…?' she said.

'I failed my second year. Turns out I wasn't clever enough to be at such a good university. My dad had paid the fees and it was a private institution, so I didn't want to, I don't know… let him down by re-sitting and then probably failing the third year too. So I told him I just… didn't want to do it anymore.'

I looked over at Cathy to see if she was still listening. And she was, intently.

'But I did meet my best friend Marlowe there so it wasn't all bad… and Amber too, in a vain attempt to rescue the whole situation.'

'It must be hard running in such successful circles when you feel that way,' Cathy said, rubbing her bare feet beneath her on the sofa.

'I guess it just wasn't the place where I needed to be.' I looked out of the small panelled window framing Cathy's back garden. It wasn't something I was going to dwell on. 'Anyway, weren't you were going to tell me about my aura?' I said, feeling myself growing intrigued.

'If I'm honest you seem to have a lot of confusion surrounding you. It's the main reason I gave you the job. And that's not surprising as you're obviously going through your Saturn returns.'

'My what?' I said, trying not to sound alarmed.

'Saturn returns, darling; we experience it at different stages in our lifetime. Anyway, I've got a doctor's appointment before lunch so I'd better be making a move.'

'But what is it exactly?' I said. 'You can't just say that and leave!'

She stopped as she reached the door.

'I can see you're interested so I'll digress. Technically it's when Saturn returns to the exact place where it was at your birth – emotionally. It's why girls your age usually feel confused and a bit lost. Can't you Google it or something? It's what you kids seem to do with everything these days.'

'And my aura?'

'I've got to go!' she said, putting on her coat, laughing.

'Just tell me about my aura, Cathy, please…'

'It's a personal glowing field. When it's at peace, so are you. Think of the effort it takes to cling onto something compared with the ease of letting it go. Trust me, I've been around long enough to know it works. You just need to focus on your energies, your personal space, make it less… *chaotic*. Why don't you look at feng shui? It's the year of the yin fire rooster, awakening and triumph, so now would be the perfect time.'

I sat there in the harsh realisation of my aura.

'Oh Christ, I have really got to go,' she said, checking her watch. 'Just finish the retouches from Monday's shoot and then you can let yourself out. I've got to get my knee checked. Trust me, Jess, be young for ever: it's no fun getting old. See you on Tuesday. Bye, darling.'

'Bye, Cathy.' I watched her leave in a fluster of wellington boots, prescriptions and umbrellas.

It wasn't the most relaxing place, my home, on the fourth floor of a red brick building on a busy road in London. I could hear the neighbours and their conversations late at night, their television sets and their arguments.

I arrived back there that night and immediately pulled my laptop onto my bed, typing 'feng shui' into the search bar. As soon as I pressed 'enter', hundreds of online tutorials popped up, cascading down my screen like a waterfall. 'How to choose crystals', 'Architecture and you' and 'It's in there, find it!' It seemed people all over the world were exploring ways to calm down. Of course, my intention was to just watch a couple and then vacuum the living room but once I'd started I couldn't stop clicking. Continuously, the sidebar was recommending one after the other and my mind got lost in all the ways to look after the inner you in what can only be described as a beauty tutorial for the soul.

By midnight I had learned that the lucky colours of this particular Chinese year were red, pink, purple and burgundy. I glanced at the eggshell walls of my bedroom: far too small for burgundy and I was never really a fan of purple. It was at that point a dusty pink shirt caught my eye from inside the wardrobe. I held it up against the wall and instantly knew: it would be the colour of my new-found sanctuary.

I awoke bright and early the next day to transform my personal space into a haven of positive energy, and after a quick trip to the local hardware shop to buy paint and a mirror ball, designed to 'eliminate all negative chi', I looked at the contents strewn on my bedroom floor, then walked over to my computer to turn on the sound of Jimi Hendrix, a guitar-riddled, heart-inducing rendition of 'Red House'. It was played as part of his set at Woodstock and I was hooked. Above the shrill of the guitar I could still hear Amber in the kitchen, making a sandwich for lunch, an unusual activity in the middle of the day when normally she should have been at work and the flat would be empty.

Before I began, I covered all surfaces with some old bedding and flicked the lid of paint open using a screwdriver. Once open, the pale pink paint didn't look too daunting. I delicately drew a single, gunky brushstroke on the wall and stood back to take it all in. After pausing to assess the damage I gained speed, lacquering the thick paint onto a roller, the creamy liquid smoothing every crack and damp patch.

'Jess,' Amber said, knocking lightly from outside my door.

'Coming!' I shouted as I turned down the sound of the psychedelic Sixties.

'What are you doing in there?' she said, confused. 'And what's that on your face?'

'Oh nothing, I'm just painting,' I said, wiping a smear of pink paint from my cheek using the corner of the old T-shirt I was wearing.

'Well, just to let you know, I'll meet you at Marlowe's tonight,' she said. 'I've got to do something after work.'

'Oh damn! Yeah, I forgot…' I said, before realising I didn't have any plans anyway. 'No problem, I'll see you there, about eight then?'

'What's with the bin liners?' she said, noticing them scattered across the floor.

'I'm de-cluttering.'

'De-cluttering what?'

'My life.'

There was a brief pause as she searched for words. 'Okay. I'll just see you later then,' she said, putting on her coat.

'Why are you here anyway, in the middle of the day?'

'I'm working late so I'm starting late.'

'Wait,' I said as she went to leave. 'Is that my black wrap dress?'

She turned and gave me a wave as I attempted to tell her to wash it this time before returning it, and that I didn't want the sleeves stretched like before, but it was too late. She was gone. Looking around at my half-finished job, I turned the volume of the music back up and carried on with the painting.

*

I arrived at Marlowe's house at the agreed time. By now the paint fumes were stinging the back of my nostrils so I thought it best to get some fresh air by walking the three kilometres to her house by the river.

As usual, it was immaculate and I was just admiring the cream carpet through the window when I could see her walking down the stairs, bouncing Elsa on her hip. She led me through to the kitchen as I put down the bags of food shopping I'd bought on my way over.

'Thanks for coming round,' she said. 'I could kill George sometimes. He's away in Manchester and thought it best to stay over rather than get back late. So now I'm stuck here for a couple of days. I did have some paperwork I wanted to finish but never mind... Daddy can't exactly help it, can he?' she said, talking to me through Elsa.

He absolutely can, I thought as I watched Marlowe sit down on the sofa, exhausted.

'I'll pop the garlic bread in the oven and open a bottle, shall I?' I looked over at her, thrown together topped with a messy ponytail and wearing odd socks. Normal for me. Normal for anyone. But not for her.

She rubbed her hands through her hair and sat down at the breakfast bar.

'No offence, Mars, but you look knackered,' I said.

'Thanks very much,' she laughed.

I handed her a glass of wine. 'Merlot for Marlowe?' She humoured me by smiling at my terrible joke.

'Fancy talking about it? I'm a good ear,' I said, sitting down across from her at the kitchen table.

'I wouldn't even know where to start,' she said, rolling her eyes.

'Mars, stop being the responsible one for a minute. It's me you're talking to.'

'I don't want to moan, Jess, but I'm just sick of these walls. I'm literally tearing my hair out.'

'It's okay...' I said, weakly.

'I'm sick of my only conversation being in a high-pitched voice or shouting over the top of Peppa Pig. It's not me. Correction, it's not who I *was*...'

'It's not for ever,' I said. 'You're still you.'

'That's all anyone keeps telling me. But George is never here, he's always away, and when I ask him to spend more time at home he just flies off the handle, going on at me about the mortgage.'

'You can't look after everyone all the time,' I said, softly.

At that point the doorbell buzzed and I could hear Sean and Amber chatting loudly outside. Marlowe wiped what I thought was a small tear from her eye and smiled through the glass door as she let them in. Amber waved at Elsa, who was in the living room watching television through the open door.

'Apparently you're supposed to limit TV to just two hours per day...' Marlowe said, as she walked them both through.

'Oh let her crack on, that's what I say,' Sean said. 'As long as she's not smoking a joint in there – let her get on with it.'

'What a sweet thing to say about her daughter,' Amber said, following him into the kitchen.

Sean had brought around playing cards, which he dealt out

between us as I put three large pizzas onto plates and made a token gesture of health with a bowlfull of washed salad.

'So what happened to Harry?' Marlowe said. 'I never even got to meet him.'

'He was nice…' I said.

'That was the problem,' Sean piped up. 'If you're nice in this dating climate you may as well have a rare strain of herpes.'

Amber nodded as she tugged at her dress.

'Amber, you need to tighten that wrap dress, honey,' he continued, barely looking up from his cards. 'I can see everything.'

'Sorry, I probably should have worn a bra with this,' she said, adjusting it.

'Are you not wearing a bra?' I said, trying to look.

'No, I'm not. Is that all right?'

'You had a bra on earlier today?' I said.

'Who are you, the bra police? I had one on today and I don't have one on now. Is that a good enough answer for you?'

'I didn't say anything,' Sean said. 'I've seen it all: from all of you. Remember when Marlowe was breastfeeding? I saw her full boob on most occasions.'

'It wasn't full boob,' Marlowe said, 'just the nipple…'

My eyes stayed transfixed on Amber as we continued playing cards. She was definitely hiding something.

'Are you sure about Harry?' Marlowe said quietly.

I nodded. 'Yes. I'm sure.'

'And there's no one else?'

'Nope.' I didn't want to explain to the table that I'd indulged in phone sex with my ex that was so intense it had contributed to the end of my relationship.

'Okay, Amber, any more news on the old, married guy front?' Sean asked, deliberately changing the conversation.

'Nope… not much,' she said, looking down at her hand. 'What about you? How's the new job?'

'It's a bit of a shit show with the new team to be honest, but we're getting there.'

'Would you mind if I popped by?' Marlowe said. 'I'd like to see where you work.'

'Any time,' Sean said. 'Come by one morning and we can go for lunch.'

'You know, I was walking down Oxford Street the other day with Elsa and I caught sight of myself in a shop window and I didn't even know it was me, seriously – I didn't even recognise my own reflection. How tragic is that?'

The three of us listened to Marlowe as she spoke.

'I've got clothes in my wardrobe that belong to a fifty-year-old because they're comfy and easy to move in… I'm pathetic.'

'You're not pathetic,' I said, softly.

'And it's not for ever,' Amber reassured her.

Marlowe looked at me. 'See…?'

'Mars, why don't we go upstairs and have a sort through your wardrobe? Let's set fire to some of those clothes you're talking about.'

I watched as she followed Sean through the hallway, stopping for a brief moment to pick up a toy left lying on the stairs.

'I hope she's all right,' Amber said, reaching for another slice of pizza.

'You're sleeping with him, aren't you?' I whispered across the table.

'With who?' Amber asked innocently.

'Your boss!'

'No, I'm not! Not really...'

'Amber,' I protested. 'He's married.'

'I'm not sleeping with him, okay?'

'But what about the bra?'

'Jess, I mean this in the nicest possible way, but you think you know everything that's going on... with everybody, but you don't. And once you get into the real world you'll realise that some of the men out there can be pretty shit – not just Harry and his crime of caring about you too much, but properly shit. Then perhaps "nice" won't seem like too much of a problem.'

I sat at the table, unable to find the words to defend myself.

She took her wine and followed the others upstairs as I remained at the table alone and by her accounts left outside of the real world.

It's a world quite literally at our fingertips, strapped to devices that give us everything we could ever dream of, using bandwidth and search engines to take us further beyond our capabilities as humans, but it seems that even with the thrust of such technological masterminds, we're still not as close to each other as we might want to be. It occurred to me that evening that such advances are changing the ebb and flow of a long-term friendship. Through screen time we somehow become acclimatised to how things change and get quite nifty at being able to disguise text messages of concern and congratulatory posts, without actually *being* there. As well as online friends we need real-time friends, people to call us out on our flaws, sitting across from us, in the same space, at the same table, unflinching. Social media was designed to bring us closer together but as that evening had suggested, maybe it had driven us all further apart.

Chapter Ten – Doing the Wrong Things to the Right People

A gust of wind took flight, knocking a series of leaves, dust and crisp packets into the air. It was a late September morning and as I walked briskly through the park, the sunshine tearing through the almost bare branches, I wrapped my scarf tightly around my face to protect it from the grit. I needed to get to the printing shop at the foot of the Southbank to pick up some photographs that I had taken using Cathy's camera. I hated the thought of riding the rush hour tube and avoided it at every opportunity. Hundreds of people pressed up against each other in packed trains, struggling to move, aligned like sardines. On that particular morning I wanted to breathe, take in the autumnal air – not stand with my face pressed up against a stranger's armpit.

I wove in and out of the tourists walking slowly along the river, momentarily blindsided by dogs and the occasional push-chair, and rushed through the door of the printer's, handing them the small ticket and twenty pounds in cash. I opened the packet and placed them down on the glass counter. There they lay: the first fruits of my labour. Cathy had helped me with the composition in the local park and although they were just trees, I actually felt quite excited. I folded them back into the packaging and made my way to the restaurant.

The faint glimpse of progress had made work quite enjoyable. Guido was out of town again so it was just Maria and me for the entire afternoon. The place was completely empty, apart from an older lady called Brenda who wore fur and plastic coloured beads. She was a regular and so didn't mind us cleaning around her as she sat at the counter sipping a bowl of soup.

By now I was on my third coffee of the night, leaning against the counter discussing the difference between freshly ground coffee and instant. Four months at Guido's had me hooked on the various blends and now I barely made it through a shift without a sample of at least one, freshly ground from the machine.

'Don't you just love autumn?' I said to Brenda as Maria looked on, carving a joint of salty prosciutto.

'Absolutely not,' she said. 'It's too cold and plays with my arthritis.'

I had actually grown fond of coming here most nights. I liked the smell of the food, the familiarity, and the small talk. Even the uniform didn't seem so bad after a while. As with most things, I'd adapted. In four short weeks, four pink walls and a cleansing crystal from Cathy, I had managed to de-clutter and de-stress my life. I was now alone. And it was perfect.

As I got up to rinse the residue of coffee from my cup, a clatter of hail suddenly hit the window like grit. I rushed over as the door blew open in the wind, bashing heavily against the concrete wall. I wrestled with it, tethering it closed as the heavens tore open. Hail the size of ping-pong balls began hitting the glass and Maria quickly signalled to me to help her carry in the outdoor furniture.

'Let me do it!' I cried in the wind, not wanting her to get wet. But she wouldn't listen. My face was splattered with rainwater as I lifted the seat covers from the metal frames. We both sprinted through the downpour and gathered all that our arms could carry. As I ran back inside and peered up, I noticed a tall figure stood on the pavement across the street.

'Bravo,' Brenda said, as she straightened out the cushion covers. 'It looks apocalyptic out there.'

As I dried my ponytail with a tea towel, I walked up to the glass to get a closer look. I knew in my heart it was him, but needed further confirmation. And I was right. Dressed in a navy blue trench coat, no umbrella, Charlie crossed over and made his way inside.

'What are you doing here?' I asked, dripping water from my clothes all over the terracotta floor tiles.

'I need to talk to you,' he said, gently.

'Well, you can't, I'm working. Jesus, you're soaking.' I pulled his arm and led him to the door, hoping no one had seen us. But Maria had and was making her way over with a selection of embroidered tea towels.

'Here,' she said to him, 'dry yourself on these.'

'Thanks,' he said, towering over her, dutifully drying his hair and face on the delicate, cream tea towel.

I made my way behind the counter and returned with a carrier bag. 'Just put them in here,' I said, taking the damp towels from him. 'I'll sort them.'

'What time do you finish?' he said.

'Eleven,' Maria said from behind the counter before looking at me, exasperated.

'Eleven. All right, I'll come back then.'

I walked back over to Maria who was pretending to tidy the worktop.

'He's very attractive,' she said as he left.

'Nice bum too,' Brenda said, watching him leave.

I left by the staff exit at about ten past eleven. I could see Charlie across the street waiting for me.

'You know, normal people send a text or email. They don't just show up at people's work, Charlie. I'm walking home – whatever you've got to say, you can say it on the way.'

By now the rain had stopped but the wet air still had traces of moist, glittery dampness.

'Wait – slow down,' he said, catching me up. 'I know I've ruined everything, Jess, but can we at least try to talk?'

'What about?'

'Us.'

I avoided looking directly at him.

'There isn't an *us* any more, Charlie,' I said. 'There hasn't been for a while now.'

For a brief second he appeared hurt. 'I just need to know if there's a chance?'

I took a breath. I could feel my heart pounding as I tried to remember everything I had previously rehearsed: at the bus stop, in the shower, make-believe arguments in my own head where I would be so articulate once the day finally came where

I could finally confront him. But standing there, amidst the vacant words, I just let it all go.

'I'm not part of that scene, Charlie, or will ever be part of that scene.'

'I know you won't. That's why I want you, Jess. You're exactly what's right for me.'

'I was sick of everyone looking at me like I'd won the jackpot just to be with you. Well, it's a bit of a shit deal if I'm honest, Charlie, being with you. Maybe they should try it for themselves. Maybe now they have.'

I continued to walk home as he reached down to touch my hand. I snatched it away without turning back.

'Please, Jess, don't do this…'

'And besides, I'd be risking a whole lot more now, now that I'm actually happy.'

'Jess, look at me,' he said, standing over me.

But I couldn't. I wanted to walk through the door to my flat and close it firmly behind me: on him, on us, on all of it.

'Come here, will you…' He wrapped his arms around me. I squeezed his wrist as I somehow managed to break free from his grip, relatively unscathed.

As I reached the corner I felt a pull on my arm. Before I knew it I was pulled in as he kissed me hard on the mouth: no apologies, no excuses. With all the will I had in the world, I pushed on his chest to leave me. I could hear a voice screaming inside of me to run away. But it wasn't heard. Instead we stood on the pavement, like two fighters post match. We had given it all. And now given in.

I stood in the kitchen waiting for the coffee to brew, still thinking about the events that had unfolded the night before. As the toast popped up I heard Amber stir.

'Morning,' she said, packing up her handbag on the kitchen table. 'Listen, I'm probably going to be working late again tonight,' she said, pinching half a piece of toast from my plate.

'Okay,' I said.

'Are you all right?'

'Yeah,' I replied.

'Oh and Jess...' she said, noticing the two cups of coffee I'd poured, but choosing not to say anything about it, 'could you get the plumber to come round and look at the sink again? It's still not draining.'

I nodded, wondering if she knew what I was doing. I doubt she did; after all, I certainly didn't.

I walked back into the bedroom where Charlie was sitting up in bed, flicking through my copy of *A Sacred Space and How to Create It* that he'd found slotted down the back of my bedside table.

'I like what you've done to the place,' he said, reading the back cover.

'Do you like pink?' I said sarcastically as I pushed the bedroom door behind me with my foot. I put the coffee down next to him as he grabbed me and pulled me into the bed.

'So what does the mirror ball do?' he said, looking up at it turning slightly.

'It eliminates my bad chi.'

'Your bad what?' he said with a snort.

'Stop it, Charlie. I'm being serious.'

'I know you are,' he said, putting his arm around me. 'But I'm not sure I understand.'

'It just prevents bad things from entering your life, that's all. It's a safeguard.' I felt a wave of stupidity run through me as I said the words out loud.

'Well, you've got me for that now. I'm not going to let anything bad happen to you.'

I rested my head back down on the pillow and stared up at the ceiling. 'I'm going to buy my camera today,' I said, excitedly. 'I've been saving up for months. You'd be surprised how much money you can save by cutting out coffees and eating in all the time. Fancy coming with me?'

'Ah, would love to, Jess, but the office is manic. So proud of you though,' he said as he kissed the tip of my nose.

'I'm really excited about it. Cathy has helped me so much these past few weeks. The only help, actually.'

Charlie rolled over and pulled me closer as I stared up at the mirror ball hanging above us. 'You know, there are a lot of people who would like this to fail, Charlie.'

'Then let them. I don't care, Jess. I really don't care what they think.'

'I'm just sick of explaining things to people...'

'Then don't,' he said.

We lay there for the next twenty-five minutes before finally getting up to face the world and like that mirror ball that hung above our heads, I knew that I was going to have to work out a way to deflect all the negativity around us.

A few weeks later, Sean texted me to arrange a lunch and also, I presumed, an opportunity to sit me down and ask me what the hell was going on.

'How's the man cave?' he asked. 'I thought he'd taken you hostage.'

'I know it's been a while. I know it's a surprise. I guess he's my weak spot. One that always seems to find me.'

'Yes, life has a way of doing that. But listen, I'm not complaining.' he said. 'I've not seen you this happy in months.'

'So you heard about me and Charlie, obviously.'

He nodded. 'Amber told me...'

I rolled my eyes.

'Don't do that, she's just looking out for you.'

I began to read the menu, using the wine list as a distraction from having to face his gaze.

'Are you happy?' he said.

'Yes.'

'Then why do you care what anyone else thinks?'

I put down the menu. 'I don't know, it's just, Amber's got quite an opinion and when it's hammered into you constantly, it becomes very hard not to listen.'

I unfolded my napkin and laid it across my knee.

'Anyway,' I continued, 'let's talk about you, how's the new flat?'

'Big,' he said. 'What on earth possessed me to think that three bedrooms would be a good idea?'

'I'm sure it's spacious enough for entertaining the troops,' I said, with a smile.

He let out a short, sharp laugh, before subtly clearing his throat. 'So what about Amber, have you heard from her?'

'I saw her the other week before work but that's about it…'

'Hmmm. I saw her the other day for a quick drink. She's sleeping with him you know, her boss.'

I rolled my eyes again.

'You didn't hear it from me! But I really think you should talk to her, Jess…'

'Does she like him?' I asked. 'Like, seriously like him?'

He nodded. 'But you know what Amber's like who knows really?'

'I do,' I said, bluntly. 'And I think she does.'

Sean fell silent and looked over his shoulder discreetly.

'What?' I said.

'He's fifty-eight,' he whispered.

'Oh God!' The shock had caused my hand to leap over my mouth. 'But we knew he would be, didn't we? I mean, that's Amber all over.'

'I bet he's a cool fifty-eight though,' Sean said, 'like a clubbing, bar-hopping fifty-eight.'

'He'll have to be to keep up with her,' I laughed. I topped up my water and took a long, broad swallow.

'You know it's Paul's anniversary today,' Sean said, catching me completely off-guard.

'I knew it was this time of year. God, I miss him.'

'Me too,' he said, smiling.

It seemed that by getting caught up in my own world for a short time, I'd lost sight of the things that actually mattered.

'Can you believe it was four years ago today?' he said, soberly.

I shook my head. 'Nope.'

'You know, I spoke to Ryan the other day, remember him? He was the small, bald guy who used to pay for all our drinks?'

I laughed. 'Yes, I do remember Ryan. He tried to kiss me once outside a kebab shop in Clapham.'

'Well...' he laughed. 'I bumped into him at the gym and he said a lot of things changed for him after. He doesn't even go out that much anymore.'

'You just forget sometimes, don't you,' I said, 'that none of this is actually important, dating and part-time jobs. I mean, don't you ever get fed up of us all whining on about ourselves all the time?'

'Don't say that about yourself, Jess. I think having an unbelievably hot banker wanting to be with you is a really big problem. Huge, in fact.'

'He's not a banker!' I laughed, throwing my napkin at him. 'But you know what I mean,' I said, taking hold of his hand, 'everything must seem pretty trivial now. But you've handled it all brilliantly.'

'Not today,' he said, shrugging, 'but like the weather it will pass.' He closed his knife and fork together and pushed aside the plate.

'Can I ask you something?' I said.

'Fire away...'

'Do you think things are meant to be?'

'What do you mean?' he replied.

'Do you believe in fate?'

He looked at me, even more confused.

'Take us here, right now, do you think it's been, in some way, predetermined?'

He thought for a second as I watched him. 'I think things work out the way they're meant to, if that's what you mean and, believe me, it's taken a long time for me to be able to say that. But, yes, I think they do.'

'So you think we have a destiny?'

'Not really,' he said, 'but I think there're a few signs along the way.'

'But how do you know what the signs look like?'

'I'd say that smile you've been carrying around on your face is one of them.'

I held his hand and kissed his fingers gently. 'If only everybody else was just like you,' I said, smiling.

'Don't listen to them, Jess. After all, what do they know?'

I arrived home that afternoon and could hear Amber excessively scrubbing the bathtub. I knocked gently on the bathroom door and pushed it open gently.

'What are you doing?' I asked, seeing the bottle of bleach, the yellow rubber gloves and a large plastic bowl of water.

'I'm cleaning.'

'Okay,' I replied. 'For any particular reason?'

'Because I wanted a bath last night and I couldn't, given the ring of gunge that had formed around the top.'

'I'm sorry, I didn't know,' I said, pulling back the shower curtain in an attempt to look at what she was describing, and help.

'You wouldn't know, you haven't been here,' she said, sharply.

'No, I know. I've been at Charlie's.'

'Pfft – should've guessed,' she said, wiping the hair away from her face with her wrist.

'What's that supposed to mean?'

'That's where you are, that's where you always are and I'm here, the only one giving a shit about anything!'

'Is this about the mould in the bathroom?' I said, confused.

'No, it's not about the fucking mould in the bathroom,' she said, throwing the gloves into the tub one at a time. 'It's about you not taking responsibility for anything, ever. Leaving me to have to clear this whole mess up.'

'What do you mean I don't take responsibility for things? Amber, what have I done?'

'You haven't done anything Jess. That's the whole point. You're off, you're gone and that will be it until the next time.'

'Next time?'

'The next time he decides that you're not the one he wants, then you'll be back expecting me to drink tea with you on the sofa again, just like old times.'

'That was way harsh, Amber,' I said, taken aback.

She looked at me, unflinching. 'He'll fuck you over, Jess. You just wait and see.'

She left the bathroom and I reached down to retrieve the sponge discarded on the floor. I couldn't understand what I was being vilified for. Sean was his own boss now, Marlowe had a baby and I was being blasted for being with a man who made me happy. A man who had a job and a car, who wasn't swiping right behind my back or whose monthly bills weren't paid for by his parents. Things were, quite rightly, changing. After all, who wants to remain stuck in a series of late nights that consisted of bar-hopping, bed-hopping, leaving the club at 2 a.m., throwing up in the toilet, throwing up in the sink. Yes, those times were exciting, but they are over.

It was time to grow up.

Sean stood in the hallway of his flat and placed his keys down on the small ceramic dish by the door. He took a deep breath and slowly made his way through to the kitchen, opening a loaf of bread, placing two slices in the toaster. He closed his eyes and remembered carefully what it was like to live there with Paul. He could still see him stood by the fridge, his charismatic smile that took Sean's breath away, still swept across his face. Although it wasn't easy, it was time to move on and his new home would be the perfect setting in which to start again. He poured himself a glass of water and drank it down, feeling the cold liquid line the side of his throat. It felt comforting.

It may have seemed like he was coping. Like he had coped. But inside was still the realisation that nothing would be the same again. He walked over to the dark, wooden desk at the side of the room, turning on a small table lamp and sitting down at the table. With ease he pulled out a series of sketchbooks and began reading the notes written haphazardly down the side. Work had proved a valuable distraction these past few years and this particular night wasn't any different. As he sketched out the outline for his spring/summer collection, from nowhere, the pain hit him. There, away from the eyes of anybody he knew, he cried for the fact of losing him, for the life that he used to live and the distant memory of the man he used to be.

That night I arrived at Charlie's flat and could hear the distinct sound of music coming from the other side of the door. I turned my key in the lock, slowly, and let myself in.

'I finished work early,' he said, standing there with a bottle of beer in one hand and a tea towel in the other. 'Don't worry, the beer's organic.'

'Are you cooking?' I asked, both surprised and slightly scared.

'Well, I wanted you to relax. Focus on your Zen.'

'How long have you been waiting to work that one in?' I said, glancing at the white polystyrene containers on the table.

'They're from this health food store near work that someone had told me about. I bought us a vegetarian lasagne and some dairy-free, sugar-free, fun-free brownies that, to be honest, looking at them, could probably be used to re-grout the bathroom.'

As he continued with his attempts at dinner, I decided to vacate the emergency area and instead walked over to the window. The people below looked like ants, all going about their business. I continued to watch as some waited for buses, others carried food shopping across the bridge, many walking quickly to catch the last train home.

'You okay in there?' I shouted to Charlie. He turned up the music that was playing from the kitchen. An album we always listened to. He remembered.

'I don't recall ever seeing you cook,' I said as I passed the kitchen and watched him, unsuccessfully, try to cut free the lasagna from its container.

'This is why,' he said, almost slicing a finger. 'So what did you do today?'

'I saw Sean for lunch. It was Paul's anniversary today,' I said, opening a bottle of beer for myself.

'Jesus,' he said. 'How many years is that, three?'

'Four,' I said.

'That's got to be tough.'

I watched as he struggled once more to cut the plastic using a butter knife, his hair strewn across his face. 'For Christ's sake!' he shouted as it flew off the table onto the floor. I casually sipped my beer, trying my best to hold the laughter in.

'Well, looks like the bad karma got us after all,' I said.

He glanced at the mix of tomato sauce and pasta sheets, trying in vain to scoop it loosely back into the container.

'It'll be all right,' I said, as I handed him a bottle of beer. 'We'll just have to eat it down there, like cats.'

And just like that, Sean was right. In the midst of everyday normality, somewhere between dinner and the washing up, the signs do come. You just need to pay extra special attention to them and open your heart to what's meant for you.

Chapter Eleven – You, Me… Oui

Voulez-vous fuir avec moi… ?
Would you like to run away with me… ?

'Tomorrow.'

It was the first thing I'd heard that morning. As if we could just pack up and go on a whim. And we could. I looked at the shape of Charlie's nose, the smooth contour of the bridge leading towards the tip and then the mouth. It had already been booked. We were going to Paris.

It was going to be late-night walks, long baths and cocktails before dinner, rich cheese in butter croissants and strong coffee in foreign streets: celebrating familiarity within a certain new-ness. But in the midst of this new kind of relationship, I knew that it was important to still retain an element of mystery; a sense of magic to keep the excitement going in what can often be an overload of time, intrusion of personal space and an awareness of the realities of human function. Which is why, when I arrived at the station the next morning, the idea was mixed with excitement, and just a hint of trepidation.

A fear set in that, from this point on, he would know things, things he probably shouldn't. Like the fact my hair was naturally a dry frizz, that I shaved my legs using a man's disposable razor or the fact that I didn't dispose of it at all as the packet suggested but rather used it repeatedly for several shaves. Up to this point the ample space in his flat had allowed me the precious luxury of being able to hide behind a wall of mirrors and hair straighteners, an effortlessly put together show pony without a single errant hair or facial blemish. There was only one thing I knew as I packed my case: this would be an insight into what was real.

Construction cranes dotted the London skyline as I began my sprint towards St Pancras International train station. I hadn't been up this early since Christmas day, 1995, and although I had promised to be on time – early, even – I had spent most of my short morning fawning over a suitcase full of clothes that I had been forced to quickly pack the night before.

By now, I was running over twenty minutes late. It had been my intention to buy the both of us a croissant and wait for him on the platform like a scene from a Nouvelle Vague film, but here I was sprinting through the light rain, trying to balance a beige trench coat, which I had deemed to be very Parisian, a handbag and a suitcase that appeared to have two left wheels. I checked off the items mentally as I ran: comfy underwear, good underwear, straighteners and a Continental plug already attached to the hairdryer. I skipped through the small row of taxis occupying the front pavement, and skidded across the squeaky marble floor, my unruly suitcase travelling in the opposite direction. And that's when I saw him, clutching two coffees and a newspaper: relaxed and well put together.

'I'm sorry,' I shouted, weaving through the last of the crowds.

'I knew you'd be late,' he said as he kissed me.

One of the things that I admired most about him was his ability to keep his cool in a crisis. We were now late: extremely late, but without so much as a mention, he carefully lifted my bag onto the security scanner and pulled two train tickets from his back pocket.

'Take your pick,' he said. 'Window or aisle?'

Inside I was feeling slightly more excited than I probably should've been. We had spent many a weekend at his place together so what was so different about Paris? Suddenly, and at the height of our new romance, we would be thrown together like cellmates. I looked over to see him reading the back page of a newspaper, gently resting one hand on my knee, thankfully oblivious to the stream of insanity running through my head.

I held up my phone to capture the image of the orange sunlight whizzing across the rooftops, and saw I'd received a text from Amber:

Bon voyage! Hope you remembered to pack some good pants xxx.

I smiled to myself and slid my phone back into my pocket. I knew her well enough to know that it was meant as a peace-maker, and that meant a lot. After a few minutes of reading the newspaper over his shoulder, I reached for the packet of photographs still sitting in my bag, smoothing out the glossy surface with the palm of my hand.

'You should really get started on that,' Charlie said as he reached for a bottle of water from my bag.

'I know,' I replied. 'What do you think?'

He folded over his newspaper to get a closer look.

'Can I see?'

'Of course,' I said, handing him the envelope.

'Where were you?'

'Regent's Park. Cathy helped me with the composition.'

'Jess, they're really good,' he said. 'What are they for?'

'Just for me, I guess. I took them with my new camera.' I took the packet back from him and slid them back into the side pocket of my handbag.

'You know, if you really want to do this, I know a few people who might be able to help?'

'That's okay,' I said, dodging his remark by taking a sip of my water.

He smiled before going back to reading his newspaper. 'I literally had no idea you were that good. What else don't I know about you, eh?'

I wanted to tell him that this trip would be a tasting platter of life for us, that maybe at the end of it we would know, but as we entered the tunnel, somewhere between England and France, I decided to just sit back and enjoy the excitement.

We arrived in Paris mid-morning to the scent of rich perfume and cigarette smoke. At our hotel, Charlie had stayed behind in reception to sort out passports and paperwork and I stood alone in the lift as it ascended the five floors to the top suite. I watched as the different floors went trickling by before coming to a halt at the top as the doors clicked open.

The concierge had arrived beforehand with the bags, meaning

that all I was left to do was unlock my case and begin unpacking. The room was simple yet elegant. Thin white curtains billowed from the open window and laid on the bed were a pile of laundered towels. Two sets. I walked over to a fruit bowl left on a table by the window and picked two green grapes, popping one immediately into my mouth. In the bathroom I leaned in towards my reflection in the mirror, the harsh fluorescent white light above the sink beaming down on my face: every blemish and stray hair was on display, perfectly lit like a poor man's Mona Lisa. Great, I thought to myself, unpacking my make-up bag. Good job I packed the tweezers. I walked back into the room to retrieve them and saw that Charlie had since caught me up. He, too, had started unpacking. His was the type of suitcase with actual compartments and pressed trouser and shirt sets. A brown box sat in the middle, designed specially to contain his watch.

I opened my suitcase to reveal several dresses, one still damp from the dryer, cramped, hidden under a pile of underwear and a pair of cream silk pyjamas bought specially for the occasion. He laid out his bottles meticulously: aftershave, deodorant, followed by a pale pink bar of soap. I smiled to myself. He had his quirks too, probably things he'd been hiding from me, things like OCD by the look it. And so it begins, I thought to myself, the getting to know one another. I lay down gently on the fluffy white duvet and, as I predicted, he followed me. As history had taught me, I decided to embrace the want, after all, one day, I might miss this second, miss this moment. Miss the days we spent together, in Paris.

I clipped my hair up on top of my head and lay down on the pillow next to him. It was 3 p.m. and he was asleep. I could feel his arm around me as I lay, quietly, looking out of the window. I thought about London, which although just a two-hour train journey away, still felt incredibly distant. To add to this, and for the first time since I'd known her, I was missing Marlowe's birthday party. 'Go and have fun,' she'd said when I told her about our last-minute Paris trip. 'Just don't blame me if you come back pregnant.' Despite their difficulties since having Elsa and although she got annoyed with his working away all the time, Marlowe and George had withstood more than a romantic weekend away. George once told me that he knew Marlowe was different to the other girls he'd dated. There was something so serious about her. She was an adult before any of us. I will always remember her turning to me over a coffee one late afternoon in South Kensington. 'They can only treat you like shit if you let them,' she said. I sometimes missed a Saturday morning coffee with her, which usually turned into lunch that turned into dinner that turned into drinks and before we knew it, we were dragging each other home at 2 a.m., swearing that this time really would be the last time. But months had passed and with them, other responsibilities had quite rightly taken precedence. She looked after Elsa, and George, and all of us, really. Her maternal nature was often taken for granted against the louder, more extreme behaviour from the rest of us. And this phase, this unhappy outlook she'd recently slipped into, would inevitably fade and in time, she would be her old self again. She just needed to see it too.

'Are you asleep?' Charlie asked, nudging me.

'No,' I said. 'Just lying here, waiting for you to wake up, sleepy head…' I kissed the corner of his cheekbone gently.

'Well, what do you say we take a shower and go for a walk by the river? The table's booked in the restaurant at eight.'

'I'm not sure I want to leave anymore,' I said, pressing my cold feet into the back of his warm legs. 'This bed is just so comfy…'

'Eight forty-five,' he said, wiggling himself back down under the covers. 'We can push it back to eight forty-five.'

I stood over a vase of flowers in the lobby of our hotel. By this time, daylight had surrendered to darkness and I was waiting for Charlie to hand in our room key. I could smell the lilies, mixed with faint perfume from all the people who had left before us. The sound of the piano in the hotel bar drifted gently through the foyer, drowning out the sound of shoes squeaking on the marble floor.

'Jess,' Charlie shouted from the desk, 'you all right walking?'

I looked down at my gold sandals that were holding up surprisingly well for five-inch heels, scrunched my nose up and nodded. I walked over to him as he took my hand and led me through the revolving doors and out into the Parisian night.

'I wish we could do this more often,' I said, looking out over the Seine.

'We can,' Charlie said, squeezing my hand. 'Thames is a bit nippy, though.'

I laughed. 'You know what I mean. It's nice just to be on our own for a bit.'

'I'm yours and you're mine, in London, Paris...' he said, putting his arm around me, 'wherever we happen to be in the world.'

We crossed the street and came to a small restaurant on the corner of Avenue Montaigne. I stepped delicately through the rows of white roses carefully laid out around the outdoor terrace. The maître d', a striking woman with light brown hair and fluorescent pink nails, led us to a table in the corner of the terrace. It was central enough to be part of the crowds, quiet enough to be intimate. A row of orange heaters blazed out around us. I could feel their welcome warmth on my back.

I reached for a menu and began my mission to choose a starter. I could feel Charlie's gaze landing on me before quickly looking away as I caught him. On his third attempt it was time to confront him.

'What?' I said, laughing.

'Nothing,' he said, grinning. 'I just wanted to say that I meant what I said on the train, Jess. I would love to help with your work if I can.'

Although the gesture was sweet and his intentions were completely genuine, I couldn't help but resent the fact that he saw me as a girl who needed to be helped. I wanted him to see me as an equal, not a helpless damsel who needed rescuing.

'Thanks,' I said, looking back down at the menu. 'I'll bear that in mind.'

'Why don't you want to talk about it?' he said, leaning back in his chair. 'You know, Jess, I find you fascinating. You shove your photographs in front of my face and then back away when I try to talk to you about them.'

'I didn't shove anything,' I said.

'I just would like us talk about it, that's all.'

'But I don't need to talk about it,' I said, feeling flustered. 'And I don't need helping.'

'Sorry!' he said, raising both his hands in protest. 'Just trying to...'

'Help,' I said, 'you're trying to help. Which is good for you because you look like a hero but if I refuse, then I'm the bad guy.' He waited for me to finish. 'I'm sorry. I appreciate it, I really do, but this is just something I need to do for myself.'

'I have this friend, Steve, he's the head of...'

'Charlie,' I said, cutting him off mid flow.

He held his hands up again. 'Sorry! Jeez, sorry I mentioned it.'

Despite all the signs that this conversation was over, I should've left it there. But I couldn't.

'What's with the Mother Teresa act all of a sudden, anyway? You couldn't care less about my career before, why now?'

'Because I've realised what it means to you,' he said. 'And it's my job to help.'

'Why is it your job?' I said, digging deeper. 'Because I've suddenly become your responsibility?'

'No – because I love you,' he said.

'Are you ready to order?' the waiter stood at the foot of the table and began listing the specials in a thick Parisian accent. 'Madame, may I recommend the scallops, perfectly in season with a hint of chilli oil.'

'Sounds perfect, I'll have them,' I said, as he scribbled my order down and turned to Charlie.

'I'll have the same,' he said.

'You know, you can't do everything on your own, Jess,' Charlie said as he straightened his knife and fork. 'Like it or not, we're together now.'

After a three-course dinner, talking about anything but my career, he had left to go to the toilet and in my experience, probably to take care of the bill, which he usually did when he didn't want me to put up a fake argument. The definition of a fake argument being when you at least offer to pay your share of the bill, knowing only too well your card will more than likely be declined but in some way have saved face by making the initial gesture.

As I waited at the table for him, I glanced over again at the girl working behind the desk. From the way she wore her hair to the work shoes, freshly polished, I knew exactly how she felt to be working on a Saturday night. Another couple approached her and as I watched her smile the same smile that I did it became apparent how much I identified with her. Perhaps she wasn't as lost in her career as people expected, stuck in a filler job, just biding her time until something better came along. Perhaps she was taking her time to choose the right path. A path that would make her happy.

'Can I help you?' she asked, noticing me staring and assuming I wanted to order something more. Her rosy face was even more beautiful under a natural light.

'No, I'm fine, thank you,' I said. 'I was just thinking about what a nice place this must be to work. I work as a waitress too, in London.' For the first time I said this without having to justify it, or offer an apology or a throwaway comment. I was just a waitress called Jess. That's who I was.

'Oh really,' she replied. 'You know I have always wanted to live in London. It is actually my dream.'

'Well, take my number,' I said, scribbling it down on a napkin. There was something about her that I instantly liked. 'If you ever do come to London, let me know, it's nice to have a friendly face there.' As soon as I said it out loud, I realised how ridiculous I had been in rejecting Charlie's offer to help me. When you are in a position to help, you offer it, that's just what you do.

'You ready to go?' he asked, arriving back at the table.

'It was nice to meet you,' I said, handing the girl my number.

'I thought you said you didn't give your number out in bars?' Charlie said drily. 'I can see I'm going to have to keep an eye on you...'

As we left the restaurant I looked back and smiled at her standing in the doorway: my kindred spirit in Paris.

We followed the Seine down to the Notre Dame and turned right at a rooftop bar called Paradis. The music was loud and dense. Bodies piled haphazardly together amidst a large spiral staircase littered with half-filled wine glasses, couples, entwined, using the dim lights to their advantage.

'I got us both a surprise,' Charlie said, passing back two short drinks from the bar. 'It's strong. A mix of brandy, orange and whiskey that I know from previous experience will get you legless, which I can take full advantage of later.'

'Is that so?' I said, sipping it through a thin plastic straw. I pulled my hair over my shoulder in a vain attempt to cool myself down.

'Seriously, you look amazing, Jess,' Charlie said, sitting on a bar stool as I stood between his legs. 'I sometimes can't believe you're mine…'

'Charlie…' I said, trying to speak.

'Sexy…'

'Charlie…' I repeated, wriggling free from his grip.

'What's the matter?' he said, resting his forehead on mine.

'I love you too. I wanted to tell you because I know I might not show it like other girls do. But I love you – very much.'

It might not have been the first time I'd thought it, but it was definitely the first time I'd said it out loud. Amidst the scene of kissing mouths, low lights and partygoers I'd finally come clean about what was going on, on the inside. I put my arms around him and kissed him. Perhaps just for tonight, we were by ourselves and there was nobody there to answer to: we were in heaven.

It was our last day in Paris. As I stood in the vast open space of the Musée d'Orsay I was instantly transported back to London where I'd spent so many days wandering the large rooms of the National Portrait Gallery. Charlie was occupied with his Blackberry so I walked on ahead, gazing up at the gigantic oil paintings hanging either side of me. It was always the sense of history that stunned me. Hundreds of years documented in time by the swipe of a brushstroke: people, landscapes and objects all created from someone else's perspective. People we would never meet.

I journeyed on alone into the next room and looked at the huge frames hanging against the whitewashed walls before stopping beneath a painting of a woman sitting on a bench in the park. Most of the subjects in the paintings were women, their clothes identifying the period, their faces expressing their time. Although we lived in such different worlds, I couldn't help but see the striking similarities between the woman working in the restaurant last night, the girl in the picture, and me. As with all women, together we were watched, observed and commented upon, all with comparable feelings: same sense of happiness, same sense of sadness. It was a collection of not only art, but of souls too.

'Can we get out of here now?' Charlie whispered from behind me. 'If I hear one more comment about the "romance of Monet" I'm going hang myself with the cord from my audio guide.'

I tried to stifle my laugher against the frequent sounds of shushing. As we walked back through the gallery, navigating our way through the overcrowded rooms, we had reached the end of our first break together in Paris. And how ridiculous I had been in my attempt to hide myself, to cover up my flaws and blemishes.

While it is important to retain a sense of mystery, perhaps in a bid to preserve the magic, there is also something to be said for honesty: the unbrushed hair, snorting-when-you-laugh-kind of joy. Feeling lucky that you're the one person who gets to witness it.

As we approached the exit of the gallery and walked out into the daylight of the city, I was beginning to see that the real magic, the very thing that I was striving for, is seeing someone for who they really are, and loving them regardless; a private showing, just for you.

Chapter Twelve – So Human

A dream

Marlowe stood in the luxury of her walk-in wardrobe wearing a light grey T-shirt and tracksuit bottoms. She sat down on the cream cushioned stool in front of her dressing table and peered into the mirror at her face free from make-up, her hair tied loosely in ponytail around her ears. She looked at the person staring back at her: a perfect version of happiness, content in the knowledge that things for her were always going to be okay. Taken care of. A four-bedroom castle of designer interiors, the subtle hue of scented candles, housing what her life had actually become.

To the outside world, there were many reasons why Marlowe could be seen as the object of jealousy. To others, she had won the invisible race. It seemed that life was judged on the basis of four categories: self, partner, genetics and wealth, and she was striking out for first place on all four playing fields. But something, a feeling buried deep inside, told her that maybe she had become what she had feared most: merely an illusion. She had done what she had sworn she would never do: she had created a distraction from reality and lied to someone she loved – herself. Her days were spent carefully curating social media accounts filled with hot beaches, interior design ideas and carefully angled selfies. It did what it was designed to do: it showcased the ideal, the way that life *could* be. She had become a gold medal participant in hiding from the truth.

The reality

A sharp, loud buzzing came from the computer resting on the kitchen table, against the backdrop of an otherwise, silent house. The second time felt louder. For the past half an hour Marlowe had ignored it, trying in vain to organise her bank statements, but by now the intensity had grown unbearable. She put down her paper and walked over to it. Her intention had been just to silence it or turn it off so she could get back to her work. She stared at a message from a woman called Samantha. She couldn't quite read the words in front of her:

When can I see you? Stop ignoring my calls… xx

After what felt like a decade suspended in time, staring blankly into the glow of the screen, her suspicions had been confirmed. She placed the computer back down on the table and poured herself a large measure of vodka. For a brief moment she got lost in the dramatics, imagining Elsa, the separation and the heartbreak.

It pinged again: another message. It clearly had only been meant for George's phone but had been accidently synched up to the family computer. Against her better judgement and surprisingly unafraid of what she might find, she pressed her forefinger gently on the screen and watched calmly as a waterfall of messages began trickling down.

Having laid there for two hours, wide awake next to Charlie's snores, I decided I'd reached my limit and got out of bed. I was no stranger to occasional bouts of insomnia and knew by now that the best thing to do was trick my mind into believing it should be awake. There was no use fighting it, tossing and turning, praying for the sun not to rise; instead, I walked barefoot across the hard wood floor into Charlie's office to try and find a DVD from his bookcase.

As I browsed the selection of action films and box sets for anything that didn't feature a cameo from an American wrestler, I caught sight of a Post-it note that he had stuck to his computer monitor. I had written it when we first met: our initials in a love heart with a kiss. It was designed to be cheesy and silly, a throwaway joke, but he'd kept it. Despite everything that had happened between us, that little piece of paper had somehow stuck.

I sat down in his recliner chair and pulled my feet up underneath me. It seemed that together we had silenced a world of doubts but I was now left to perform the juggling act of splitting myself between two corners of the ring: having dinner with Charlie one night, while seeing my friends for a drink on the side. I decided that perhaps it would be a good time for everyone to sit down for dinner so that maybe, just maybe, they could finally leave their reservations at the door.

I turned off the lamp and walked back into the living room armed with a DVD and a dinner party to arrange. I was asleep before the end of the opening credits.

'How would you feel about having dinner with my friends one night?' I said over breakfast the next morning.

'Your friends who hate me?' Charlie said, filling his coffee from the machine.

'They don't hate you, Charlie, they don't know you – which is why I thought it might be nice to get together?'

'Sure.'

'Was that a yes?' I said, feigning surprise.

'Yes. Fine. I'm in your life and they're in your life, the least we can all do is make the effort to get along.'

I waited for a hint of sarcasm that never came. Instead, he was actually bordering on enthusiastic.

'Come round here!' Marlowe shouted down the phone. 'George is away and I don't mind cooking.' She sounded surprisingly excited. Maybe it was the thought of hosting a dinner for adults where the plates weren't plastic and neither was the food.

'Are you sure, Mars?' I said as I crossed the junction at Euston. 'I just need somewhere…'

'Neutral,' she said, finishing my sentence.

'Exactly. Not that there will be a problem. It's just well, Amber…'

'Have you talked to her?'

'No. Not since before Paris. I've been avoiding it, if I'm honest.'

'Jess,' she said, her voice loudened against the sound of

cartoons in the background and a police siren passing me. 'We are on your side, you know.'

'I know,' I said. 'Thank you.'

'Look, I've got to go, Elsa's shouting. I'll see you tomorrow at eight.'

'Are you sure this is a good idea?' Sean said on his way to work that morning.

'Yeah, I'm sure. I'd just like you all to get to know him a little better. Do you think you can?'

'But what if we hit it off and become best friends and then you guys break up again. Have you really thought about the consequences for me?'

'Sean…'

'I'm kidding,' he said, straightly. 'Of course, I'll come.'

'And can you sit on the jokes until after we've left, at least?'

'I can't promise…'

I stayed silent, hesitating. Perhaps this wasn't such a good idea after all.

'Don't worry, sweetie,' Sean said, 'nothing's going to go down on my watch. I'll see you there.'

'Hello,' she said, in a rush, as always.

There was a pause. I pressed the phone to my ear.

'Look, Amber, I just wanted to say I'm sorry. I've been a bit absent these past two weeks and…'

'I'm sorry too,' she said. For a moment she sounded deflated but she shrugged the moment off almost as quickly as it arrived. 'Anyway, what's the news?'

'Well, we're having a dinner over at Marlowe's tomorrow night and I would love it if you could be there.'

'I know,' she said. 'I already spoke to her. Of course I'll be there.'

'Thank you,' I said, 'that means a lot.'

'Let's see what he's got to say for himself, shall we?'

'He's a good guy, you know. You just need to get know him. That's all.'

'And I'll be happy to, tomorrow tonight,' she said.

'Absolutely no way!' Charlie said, laughing down the phone. 'If you think I'm walking into that lion's den you're mistaken…'

'You were fine when it was a restaurant.'

'Yeah, a restaurant with people: witnesses. Not a house where there's nowhere to escape to.'

'Escape to?'

'What if I want to order a scotch?'

'Are you serious, Charlie?' I said. 'Don't be such a child.'

I could hear him in the background loosening his tie.

'Can I at least bring someone to fight my corner?' he said, reluctantly.

'What, like a date?'

'No, just someone who can be on my side once the accusations set in.'

'Charlie, I don't understand…'

'James. Can I at least bring James?'

'Yes, you can bring James. Actually that's a great idea. Maybe he can hold your hand over dessert?'

'I'm putting the phone down,' he said. 'This conversation's gone on long enough…'

'Promise you'll come?' I said.

'Yes. I'll meet you there, tomorrow night, seven thirty.'

'Well, I did say eight but if you want to get there early then by all means…'

'I'm doing this for you, you know!' he said, this time being serious.

'I know and I love you for it. I'll text you the address!'

'Yeah, yeah…'

And with that he hung up the phone.

I arrived at Marlowe's house at quarter past eight and immediately saw Charlie's car parked on the driveway. I could only guess what they were talking about inside. I walked across the pebbledashed driveway and reached out to ring the bell, but Sean answered the door before I had chance to.

'Get in here,' he said abruptly, 'it's like being shut in the locker room at Canary Wharf.'

In all honesty, I was a little apprehensive about seeing Amber again. I didn't want to go through the small talk and pleasantries, not with her. But as she walked over to me in the hallway and gave me a kiss on the cheek, it was hard to remember why we were fighting. In fact, I don't remember when she last kissed me on the cheek but suffice to say it hadn't been a regular occurrence.

I walked into the living room and was greeted by Marlowe who handed me a glass of wine. I placed it down on the coffee table fearing that at this point, alcohol might only add fuel to the fire. I was here as the referee. I needed to keep my wits about me. I made a deliberate decision to sit next to Amber on the sofa and once everyone had started talking, felt this would be my perfect chance to offer an apology.

'I'm sorry I haven't been a very attentive friend,' I said, quietly to her. 'So much has happened with me and work and… everything else.'

'I've been a bit preoccupied with things too at the moment. Plus I know you've got Charlie to, you know, spend your time with.'

'Yeah but he's not you, Amber.'

'It's not what you think between us, Jess, with my boss. You probably think you know what's going on but it's not like that. I'd never deliberately hurt anybody.'

'I know you wouldn't. You don't need to explain anything to me. I shouldn't have been so judgmental. All I care about is that you're happy.'

'I am happy. See?' she said, showing me her teeth sarcastically.

'How did you like Paris, Charlie?' Marlowe said, finally joining us for a drink.

'It was great,' he said, clutching his beer. 'I've actually been before, for work, but obviously this time it was a lot more fun.'

'Well, it sounded fantastic and the food! I know when I went the food was just fantastic. I just said fantastic twice there, didn't I?'

'Three times…' Amber said, drily.

It was true that Marlowe didn't sound at all like herself, but at this point, in a room where we could otherwise hear a pin drop, I was just happy for somebody to be speaking.

'How's work?' I said to James.

'Pretty good. I don't know if Charlie's told you but we're working with Dianne Cagney at the moment.'

'Dianne Cagney?' Marlowe said. 'I've got two prints of hers in our bathroom.'

'Well, she's designing a set of billboards for us,' James replied. 'I think she's pretty great too…'

'I did my dissertation on that period,' Marlowe said, smiling.

'You did? I'd love to read it. I've actually taken a bit of an interest in her work since meeting her.'

'I'll get it from the study, remind me before you leave. Want another drink?'

'I'd love one,' James said.

Marlowe left the room with James, taking the conversation with them. I looked over at Amber who was running her index finger around her wine glass and Sean, who at that point met my eyes across the room.

'Great party,' he mouthed, before sarcastically giving me the thumbs up.

'Did you ever think when we first met that our lives would take us here?' Amber said.

We were sat at the table, part way through the main course with Marlowe and James laughing continuously at one end, while the four of us were at the other on the double date from hell.

'I was studying to be a lawyer then, so no,' I said, twirling my half-full glass on the table.

By this time, Amber had made the fluid transition from wine to gin that I knew from past experience was never a good sign and would inevitably result in a trip down memory lane.

'I wanted to be a model,' she continued. 'Can you remember? I used to get paid a fortune to sit there and have crap painted on my face.'

'And then you'd pay for the drinks all night!' I said. 'Fun times at The Edge...'

Amber laughed, trying her best to speak. 'That's where Sean took first prize for best solo dance act on Valentine's night.'

I laughed sharply, spitting out some of my wine.

'Charlie, he came off stage followed by a small Brazilian man covered in baby oil, carrying his pants! I've still got the photo somewhere.'

'You probably had to be there,' Sean said, slightly embarrassed as Charlie looked at him from across the table.

'My face hurts,' Amber said, wiping her eyes. 'Is there any more gin, Mars?' She floated her empty glass high up in the air.

'In the cupboard,' Marlowe said.

'I thought this was supposed to be a dinner party,' Sean told her as she topped herself up, 'not a free for all at Marlowe's liquor cabinet.'

'She won't mind,' she said, looking down the table grinning, 'she seems far too distracted.'

'I'm sorry about this,' I whispered to Charlie. 'I don't know what's gotten into her.'

'Just as long as I don't become the target,' he said, leaning back in his chair. 'After all, she's quite entertaining.'

'Ladies and gentlemen,' Amber began, clicking her glass with a teaspoon. 'I'd like to perform a little speech I had prepared for this evening. Mars, I can see you don't give a shit about what I have to say but if you could pull yourself away from your boyfriend for two seconds, I'd appreciate it...'

'Stop it, Amber,' Sean said, tugging at her arm.

'I'd like to thank you all for being here tonight. Charlie, thank you for gracing us with your presence, we are truly honoured, and Jess, thank you for accepting my apology, despite the fact that you were in the wrong.'

'I'm just going to the toilet,' I said to Charlie.

'Okay then, bye!' Amber said. 'Rude.'

As I reached the top of the staircase I stopped briefly to look at the photographs that adorned the walls of the hallway. I'd seen them a million times before but hadn't quite taken them all in until now. Arranged in lines along the beige wallpaper, there was one of Marlowe on her graduation day sporting a rather dubious fringe and lip liner, one of Marlowe and George on their wedding day in Tuscany and finally, right at the top, a gold-framed photograph of Elsa in the bath. I smiled and tiptoed across the hallway, avoiding her bedroom that was lit dimly by a nightlight.

I washed my hands at the basin and as always when I visited, borrowed two squirts of Marlowe's expensive hand cream. I had delayed things for as long as I could before having to go back downstairs. With Amber things were always impulsive but I still didn't know what had got into her. I could hear her muffled voice from beneath me.

'I've got it, Amber,' Sean said, calmly, 'just lift your sleeve out.'

'I think it's time we went home,' Charlie said, greeting me at the bottom of the stairs, chewing on the remains of an after-dinner mint.

I rolled my eyes and lifted Amber's coat from the bottom of the banister.

'Want to stay at mine?' I said as I led him back through. 'We can't let her go home like that on her own. Look at her.'

Charlie walked over to Amber, slowly holding out his arm. 'Here you go, you can hold onto me. Watch the step, my car's just outside.'

We watched at the doorway as Charlie laid Amber down on the backseat of his car.

'I really like him,' Sean whispered, linking my arm.

'See,' I said. 'You should trust me…'

'And might I just say, that is one nice ride he's got himself.' He glanced at the black sports car sitting at the bottom of Marlowe's driveway.

'Yeah, it's not bad. Cars aren't really my thing.' I said, smiling.

'I wasn't talking about the car,' he said, patting my bum as I climbed inside.

We drove home in silence. After dropping Sean off at his home, we continued on through the city towards my flat.

'Don't worry,' I said, reaching for my coat. 'I'll deal with her.'

I made my way to the front of our building, propping open the doors in preparation for her entrance. As they turned the corner I saw that Charlie had picked Amber up and was carrying her in his arms.

'You owe me for this,' he said, kissing me on the lips on the way past. 'Big time.'

'You okay, Amber?' I shouted, as they both passed by.

'Yeah, I'm fine,' she muffled, from under a pile of black hair.

As I stood in Amber's room, convincing her to drink some water, I texted Marlowe to say thank you for dinner that evening:

I'm sorry we left early. Hope you had a good night. xx

I stood at the foot of Amber's bed and watched as she contorted her legs to fight the sleep. She was holding her hands just below her stomach, massaging it softly in what I can only assume was a way of stopping the vomiting. I could hear Charlie turn on the television in the living room and desperately wanted to be with him. I wanted to bury my head in the sand and pretend I lived in a world where the two sides of my life could join amicably for at least one night. I was wrong. But I couldn't help but feel that I was in some way responsible – that I should have somehow foreseen this happening. After wrestling her into her pyjamas and watching her spectacularly pass out on top of the covers, I left her bedroom door ajar and made my way into the living room.

'Well, that went well' I said as he pulled my legs onto his lap on the sofa.

'I just don't understand why you have to fix things all the time. It is okay to just let things be.' He ran his hands over my feet, slowly making his way along my thighs.

'Charlie, we can't,' I said, pulling away. 'I left her bedroom door open.'

'I don't care,' he whispered into my hair. I could feel his hands moving down my jeans as my phone pinged from inside the pocket. It was a message from Marlowe. He gently threw it onto the table and continued his journey across my chest. I wondered about Amber. I cared if she could hear. What if she got up to go to the toilet? What if she walked in? By this time his hands had reached inside me: I let out a cry, struggling to stay unheard. Please stay in your bedroom, I repeated over and over in my head, please stay in your bedroom. There was no time to think. It was messy and awkward and immediate. As he pulled my legs around him, I felt the heat of his body and I was gone. Consumed. In that moment, he was everything.

Chapter Thirteen – It's a Girl Thing

London was my drug of choice and I had all the hallmarks of an addict. Apart from being a cosmopolitan metropolis where quite literally, anything goes, I find it gives you a similar feeling to when you go on a date with someone slightly out of your reach: almost impulsive, temporary, but above all, slippery. As with most unequal relationships you never quite manage to reach the comfortable phase where you're given the liberty of putting on ten pounds by eating pizza in bed socks, or when you are lulled into a false sense of security, descending into complacency. London calls for effort, a sense of direction and to top it all off a foray into the world of congestion charge and competitive rent prices. You are a permanent newcomer; not even at ease enough to chance a backstreet, safe in the comfort that you know where you're going. Without realizing, you end up lost, out of your depth, begrudgingly seeking help from a stranger.

In a desperate attempt to get back in the saddle, work-wise, I'd spent the previous week scouring the Internet for positions that would allow me to stretch my photography skills and also, in a rare dose of optimism, potentially get paid for what I wanted to do. As a result of my labours I was on my way to interview for a photography position at a local magazine, an alternative travel guide for visitors to the capital. The brief, from what I could determine from a hundred-word blog post, was for somebody who could navigate the city, documenting it in imagery in a 'unique and exciting way'.

I'd just passed the sign for Battersea Bridge, a result of getting off the bus too hastily, believing that I knew the way, only to find myself walking along the riverfront, lost and annoyed. The yellow sun cast a shimmer across the Thames and joggers sprinted past me, breathing heavily in the foggy atmosphere. It seemed that I'd taken a wrong turning somewhere off Sloane Square and was currently following a blue dot (me) along the backstreets of a warehouse forecourt towards a red arrow (them). I glanced up from my phone to see a small cabin with a man in a high-visibility jacket reading the newspaper, clutching a polystyrene cup of tea.

'Excuse me?' I said through the chequered glass window. 'Could you tell me where this office is?' I held out my phone so he could see my trajectory on the map.

'Let's have a look,' he said, taking it from me. 'You need to go along the green bay and out through the other side. There's a small grey building at the dead end – that's it.'

I walked off speedily in the direction he suggested.

'I can show you if you want?' he called out as I left.

'That's okay!' I shouted back. 'I'll be fine – thanks!'

I checked my watch and broke into a small jog. Here I was in the familiarity of Battersea, totally lost and navigating my way through a lorry car park. Luckily I'd worn my trainers and was carrying work shoes in my canvas tote.

'Jessica Wood,' I said as I finally reached the reception desk. 'I have an interview for the photography position.'

'Take a seat,' the man said from behind the desk. 'They'll be with you shortly. Would you like a tea or coffee?'

'No, thank you, I'm fine,' I said, straightening out my jacket.

I sat down on the squashy grey chair, changed my shoes and pulled out my portfolio from my bag. Through the window, the grey sky cast a thick weight across the river. I could see the sun trying so desperately to break through.

'Jessica?' A middle-aged man in a grey cashmere jumper signalled me to come over. 'Follow me…' Together we walked through to an office on the second floor.

'Thank you for coming in to see us,' he said, taking a seat at his desk. 'I've been looking at the sample shots you sent through in advance of our meeting today.'

I moved in my seat slightly, trying to gauge a reaction. I didn't realise how much I wanted the job until I could feel my hands trembling in my lap.

'And you want to work full time?' he said, without looking up from my CV.

'Whatever is available,' I replied. 'Preferably full time but I'm willing to work just a couple of days, if that's all you need.'

The back of my throat felt dry and scratchy. I tried to clear it quietly but couldn't take my eyes from the light blue water cooler in the corner of the room.

'And you took all of these yourself?' I could smell cigarette smoke and could see his yellowing fingernails rub the desk next to my folder. 'Clever girl,' he said, fingering the plastic covering.

'I started off with landscapes and then moved on to

portraiture. Your advertisement said that you might need both so…'

'I have to say, Jessica, I was impressed with your work here and the selection you sent over, but I'm going to be honest: your style is a little too delicate for our taste. We want someone who will blend in more with the overall feel of the magazine.'

I was crushed. I could feel a sinking feeling hitting my stomach as I faced the reality that I had let myself down, and Cathy, and anybody else who had taken the time to help me. 'In what way?' I asked, hoping that a little more clarification might help me to understand where I'd gone wrong. I could feel the dryness in the back of my mouth as I spoke. My voice didn't sound like my own as I heard it out loud.

'We're looking for someone who's a bit more robust in their approach. You know, fits in as part of the team with the lads. But that's not to say that your work wasn't impressive. I could just picture you running around town with your little camera,' he laughed.

I chose to give him the benefit of the doubt. Perhaps he couldn't see how patronising he was being. Despite this, and to my shame, I found myself almost desperate to make myself fit his criteria.

'So you want me to be more… manly?' I said, hoping that saying it out loud would help him to see the lunacy of it all.

'Your work is exciting, don't get me wrong, I'm not taking that away from you but I think you need just a few more years to toughen up a bit. I'm just a little concerned that it's a bit too feminine for what we're looking for on those big shoots.'

'But I thought the whole idea was to create a magazine that was accessible and appealed to young people?' I said.

'Yes, but the male demographic are the people who actually *buy* the magazine so it's really them we have to cater for...'

I smiled my way through frustration. 'I'm not sure I know how to make my work more masculine?' I said, calmly.

'And you don't need to. You're an exciting young girl. I'm sure there's a million magazines you could go and work for – and look at it this way: at least you won't have to carry our heavy photographic equipment across London.'

I gave him a small smile. Just what he needed, a reassuring response to an unfunny joke.

'I bet you've got a strapping man somewhere who can help you with that though, am I right?'

I readjusted myself in my seat. 'No, I carry my own equipment. It's usually fine.'

'Clever girl,' he said, for the second time. 'I tell you what: here's what I'm willing to consider. Why don't you go away and put together some pieces. A few generic shots: nothing too... bold. And then we can get together and see if it will work?'

'I don't wish to be rude, Richard...' I'd read his name from the plaque on the door but hadn't expected to be using it so casually. 'This isn't a joke, it's my career. I don't think you're taking me seriously as a suitable candidate. I'm sorry you don't think my work is in keeping with your magazine, but if I stay here in this office a moment longer, while you crush my dreams against your own agenda, then I'm afraid I might not pick up a camera again. I've taken two buses and walked for twenty-five minutes in drizzle to sit and be told that my work is too feminine and the very idea of me running around town with a "little" camera actually made you laugh out loud. In future, maybe you should have some consideration for the people on my side of the desk.'

I didn't know where it had been hiding, but for the first time, a runaway train of words had managed to trip off the tongue in a coherent and measured way and Richard had become the pin board upon which they had landed. The feeling was unique and satisfying, to say the least.

'Thank you very much for your time,' I said. 'But I think it's best that we end things here.'

I stood up on jellied legs and made my way out of his office. As I crossed the forecourt, time slowed down, the mist had cleared, and a faint rainbow had now broken through. I reached in my pocket and noticed that I had forgotten my gloves in reception – far too humiliating to go back for them, I thought. Instead I took a sharp turn back along the green bay and saw the man in high visibility still in his cabin.

'Did it go all right?' he shouted through the glass door.

'Fine,' I said, giving him a genuine smile.

I continued along the river and towards Battersea Power Station. I may not have got the job but I had done something equally as courageous: I had stood up for myself and for my future as I saw it. Not bad for a clever girl.

'You did what?' Sean said over the phone in a mixture of horror and amusement.

'Yeah, I walked out of the interview. I just couldn't do it, Sean. He was a soul-destroyer. He kept talking to me like the little girl who wanted to take photos in the big boys' club.'

'But you're happy to work as a waitress?'

'Yes.' As soon as I said it out loud, I knew it was actually true. 'Are you free for a coffee?'

''Fraid not, I'm in the studio – looks like I'll be here late. I'm already on my second packet of Doritos. Lord have mercy on my five chins…'

'Well, I think I'll ring Marlowe, see if she's free for the afternoon.'

'Good idea, Gloria Steinem – you two can go burn your bras or something.'

'It's not funny,' I said, shaking my head. 'It was humiliating.'

'So how long do you have?' I said to Marlowe, speaking to her as if she were a woman on parole.

'Three days…'

'What?' I said, pulling out my chair.

'He's back for three days and after a short cry and a long bath he agreed to give me a break for a while. I took a taxi through Bayswater so I'm now on my second coffee and quite a bit shaky to boot.'

'Oh Marlowe…' I said, taking off my coat.

'It's amazing what crying can do, isn't it? Anyway, no more talk about husbands, babies or adults. How are you?'

'I like how you don't class me as an adult,' I said, half smiling.

'You know what I mean, Jess. Any news?'

'Not really. I had the worst interview this morning. To be honest, I wish I could just work for Cathy forever. God, Mars, you'd love her. She was actually backstage at Woodstock, can you believe that?'

'So what exactly are you doing for her?'

'Just retouching and archiving. I'm sorting her work from the Seventies at the moment. She travelled the coast from San Francisco to Los Angeles. Can you imagine being a woman at that time? I bet it was incredible…'

I looked over at Marlowe but she was lost in another world.

'Great choice of café,' I said.

We were in a courtyard in Marylebone – outside, so that Marlowe could smoke underneath an orange canopy, the colour of a tangerine, which fooled us into thinking it was sunny. It was not. Instead, Marlowe was staring into space, playing with her lighter.

'What is it, Mars… come on, you can tell me?'

'Do you think I'm a bad mum?' she said, matter-of-fact and without hesitation.

'Not at all, why would I think that?'

'Because I want a life outside of Elsa…'

'Marlowe, no one thinks that. Where did this come from?'

'My parents do. They think I should just be happy to be married and paid for…'

'But you're not though, are you?'

'Not what?'

'Happy.'

She took a breath as if to speak. 'Never mind,' she said. 'I'm here now, may as well enjoy it. What else have you done this week?'

'Oh, I know what I need to tell you!' I said, suddenly remembering my run-in with Carla Walker. 'Remember Carla from the student union, the one who used to date the lanky guy Greg who…'

'Shaved his armpits.'

'I was going to say now lives in Leeds, but yeah, that one. Well, I bumped into her at Borough Market and she's having twins.'

'Bully for her,' Marlowe said. 'Sorry, that was *awful* of me. Good news. No, it's great news. Is Greg the father?'

'No, Mars,' I said, smiling. 'She has actually dated other people in the past ten years…'

'Ha!' she laughed. 'I don't know, I guess those people from university are all frozen in that time in my head. It's weird to think of her with someone else, though.'

'You weren't even friends!'

'I know,' she said, protesting. 'But it would be nice if they were still together. It may have been young love but it was real. I can tell!'

I watched Marlowe bite her fingernails, which always meant she wanted another cigarette.

'Have you eaten?' she said, grabbing her keys and purse.

'Nope, you?'

'To tell you the truth I haven't had much of an appetite lately. All of a sudden I'm starving. Fancy a spot of lunch somewhere in town? My treat.'

I nodded, downing the rest of my coffee.

'But it has to be a quick one, Jess, George is watching me like a hawk at the minute – thinks I'm going to defect or something.'

'It's lunch, Mars, what does he think is going to happen?'

Two hours into lunch and a bottle of white wine later, Marlowe was conserving juices like a cactus.

'I'm fine, really,' she said, only slightly slurring.

'Well, you don't look fine. You're all fidgety and haven't sat still since I met you earlier today.' I was being the kind of honest you are with someone after three glasses of Chablis.

She paused and pretended to read the dessert menu before discarding it back onto the table.

'Can I tell you something?' she said, leaning forward. 'And you'll keep it to yourself?'

'Of course.'

'I wish…'

'What?!' I said. 'Say it…'

'I wish I could be more like you.'

'Me! Have you completely lost your mind?'

'I mean it,' she said, adamant now.

'Mars, I'm a waitress who is also working for free as a photographer's assistant. Did you not hear me? I'm actually working for free.'

'No. You're following your heart.' She placed her forefinger down on the table adamantly, and left it there.

'Stop being so cheesy,' I said, 'especially when it's the wine talking.' I threw a serviette across the table, narrowly missing the end of her nose.

'No. I'm proud of you.' She looked at me for longer than was normally acceptable. For a brief second I saw something in her that I'd never seen before. Defeat. 'I don't want it to be like this for ever,' she said, holding my hand.

'I don't want it to be like this for ever, either!' I said, squeezing it. 'So cheers to that!'

She clinked my wine glass and a look of relief washed over her.

'Fancy going on to somewhere with music for a quick cocktail?' I said. 'Just a quick one to blow the cobwebs off.'

'Yeah,' she said, standing up. 'Just a quick one though, Jess. I don't want to be back late.'

We both left the restaurant insulting each other with the belief that this would be a quick drink; reassuring each other separately that we absolutely needed to get home.

'I'll have a gin and tonic,' I said, sitting down in the type of bar that Marlowe and George frequented. 'Order me one while I nip to the loo, would you?'

I walked up the white, shiny staircase that was all a haze and felt like a dream, hovering cautiously over the toilet pan. 'Just one drink,' I uttered to myself as I washed my hands at the basin. I considered my reflection and could see a smudge of red lipstick on the side of my face. I licked my finger and rubbed it gently to remove the stain. I thought very briefly about my interview earlier that day. And how far away it actually seemed. 'What a total bastard,' I whispered to myself as I rubbed my hand through my hair to ruffle out the layers.

Back at the table my drink sat waiting for me: a bitter tonic to a tiring day, a precursor to hours of stories, secrets and familiar jokes. In the gap between gin and tonic and tequila, we had caught the eye of a group of businessmen: four suits out for a good time. In their defence, our ability to laugh heartily without the usual amount of effort may have been a turn on. The fact that we danced to and from the bar may have appeared to them in some way attractive. But with what would be a thunderstorm of rain on their parade, we were actually not looking beyond ourselves for a good time.

'Marlowe,' I shouted above the sound of German tronic music. 'Do you fancy going somewhere else?'

'I can't!' she shouted, before turning on her heel. 'Actually, yes, let's go dancing!'

And then, somewhere between a good nightmare and a bad dream, the taxi took us across London to the nearest club that would accept us – six drinks in. It was a small, squalid nightclub in an unknown part of London. My head was already swaying – my feet sticking to the floor.

'Perfect,' I said as I pulled out my purse and paid for both our entry. 'Just get me a drink later,' I said to Marlowe who had already made her way inside. I positioned my heel at the foot of the stairs, which I believed at the time to be swaying, as I slowly attempted to let go of the handrail. I placed my foot down with trepidation as if stepping onto a roundabout that was already spinning.

'Do you need a hand there, love?' a blond man shouted, towering over me, trying to assist with my descent.

'I'm fine,' I said. 'I really don't need any help from a man, right now.'

Once inside, I set off to find Marlowe. I could vaguely make her out in the blurred crowds. But I knew that she was walking towards me and carrying two drinks.

'What took you so long?' she said. 'Here, drink this…'

I stood up straight and sipped my drink down. It was vodka. It burned. After the slow shudder of initial pain I put my arm around Marlowe and kissed her on the cheek.

'I love you,' I said, loudly and clearly.

'I love you too, Jessica Rabbit,' she replied, before dragging me back onto the dance floor.

The sound of the music coursed through my veins, the smell of sweat and cheap perfume lined my nose and grew intoxicating. I looked around at the crowds of people dancing by my side. We had descended into darkness and I was in the midst of a movement: a whirlwind of life and lights and love, a heady mix of passion and carnage. It was raw and terrifying and brutal. I danced until my feet stung and could feel the droplets of sweat down my back, in an attack of salty dew. I closed my eyes and drifted into the darkness of my consciousness. The colourful lights seeped through my eyelids, making light shows in the sky. The sway of the crowds took control of my body as I delved deeper into the sea of people and into the abyss of carefree abandon. In a vast haze of shots, dancing and dallying in the girls' toilets, we had been transported as two women who were once responsible, but had now been reduced to messy, beautiful creatures, clinging onto each other in the vain hope that one day, things would be slightly different. Better. Because it's not easy to be a girl: to have exactly the right amount of ambition, not too much, not too little, to be loving and sensitive and kind. To not wear too much make-up or dare go out bare-faced. To be just the right amount of female.

At the end of our night, we ran across to Victoria Station, the sight of daylight stinging my eyes. I looked over to see Marlowe laughing, her denim jacket caught around her elbows, her ice-white blonde hair resting over her mouth, straggling from an unruly ponytail. It was 2010 again and we were free.

WINTER

Chapter Fourteen – Trying to
Catch Water: Part One

Winter provides the city with a tricky path to negotiate: sleet, cold winds, slippery roads and painted windowpanes sealed shut with frost against the howling winds. It's a time when people gravitate towards one another in the chill of the cold nights, anticipating Christmas and New Year, celebrating a new beginning, reflecting on the one left behind. In this decadent time of merriment and overindulging, we were free to indulge in a few weeks of novelty and frivolous fun, when the coldness of the world outside counter-balances the warmness of the human spirit inside.

Amber awoke to a string of text messages from her boss, claiming, rather desperately, that he needed to talk to her. She looked at them: his last-ditch attempt for her had proved too little, too late. What was once an innocent flirt in the office had somehow developed into a regret on his part and judging by the subsequent messages and their content this was something that now bordered for him on embarrassment. She put the phone on her bedside table and rested her head back down on the pillow. It was funny how the one thing she feared most in the beginning, the possibility that he would leave his wife, had now ironically become the opposite. An impossibility. She knew she needed to draw some sort of conclusion to this mess herself. A decision originally fuelled by passion and anger had now been replaced by retribution and guilt. Those original fears had not come to fruition, which hurt her more than she had thought it would. Deep down she knew she had done the right thing, for him and for his marriage. But there were some things that she couldn't make any less painful for herself to bear. No matter how hard she tried.

That morning, she walked into work like any other day. The only obvious indication that separated this day from any normal day was that she was an hour early. It was 7.30 a.m. and she wanted to give herself enough time to pack some of her desk away should he, as she had expected, do the cowardly thing and ask her to leave. As ever, she had covered all possible outcomes with logic. But as she sat down at her computer she couldn't help but feel the practicality of it all was a cover-up for emotions that she felt stabbing inside.

There was a squeak as June, the lady who cleaned the office, wheeled her plastic mop bucket through the corridor. 'Good morning Amber,' she said, breezily.

'Morning June,' Amber replied, smiling for a brief moment.

She strode on towards her desk and opened her top drawer, pulling out a memory stick in preparation of transfering her client list. If things did get nasty between them, although her heart was crushed, she wanted to at least give her career a fighting chance. After all, she had spent over two years cultivating it. She clicked 'transfer' and waited for the file to copy. As she watched the turning wheel on the screen, her childish expectation that things were going to work out made her feel nothing less than a fool.

At 8.50 a.m. he came into the office. As planned, Amber sat and waited, her fingers twitching on her desk as she prepared herself for the inevitable.

'Amber,' he called from his office, 'got a minute?'

She nodded and made her way over to him, a strange sense of relief washing over her now that events were underway. He closed the door behind her and rested his hand on her shoulder.

'Don't,' she said, stopping him. 'People are already starting to talk so I'd rather we didn't add fuel to the fire.'

'Of course,' he said, complying. 'I sent quite a few messages yesterday but you didn't reply.'

Amber looked up at him from her chair. He was standing by the bookcase in a move that only further demonstrated his authority. Sit down and tell me to my face, she thought to herself. At least give me the benefit of seeing your eyes when you do it.

'I assume you've... taken care of things,' he said without looking at her.

'Yes,' she said. 'I was going to ring you, after. But then I just thought... well, what was the point. It wasn't going to change anything.'

He sat down in front of her and leaned back in his leather office chair. She watched as he ran his hands through his long grey hair. 'Christ, I feel like such a bastard.'

'Stop it,' she said. 'It doesn't matter... I mean... It *does* matter. But it's no one's fault.'

'I just wish I could've gone with you, Amber, but it was just…impossible.'

'It doesn't matter,' she said, feeling the repetition trip off her tongue like the habit she'd developed over the past few weeks.

'And financially…' he said, leaning forward.

'I don't need your money,' she said, taking a deep breath. 'I've handled it. Just go back to your wife. We've both made a mess of things here. At least one of us should be able to salvage something from it.'

'What does that mean?'

'It means that I am asking you to accept my resignation,' she said, looking at him defiantly. The move was spontaneous. None of this was planned but she had enough to heal without seeing the look of regret on his face every morning.

'Amber, don't do this,' he said.

'Why?'

'Let me look after you.'

'I don't need looking after.'

She paused as she reached the door of his office.

'It just wasn't worth it, in the end, was it?' she said, a lump forming in the back of her throat. She left before he could witness any more. She wouldn't give him the satisfaction.

I pulled the empty bottles of wine from the large silver ice bucket and dropped them heavy-handedly into the bottle bin. After spending the past three hours buttering him up, laying the foundations for a favour, I asked Guido if I could stay behind at the restaurant that night. I had just finished the dinner shift and had received a message from Amber saying that she needed to talk. I hadn't heard from her since Marlowe's dinner party so I was anxious to hear what she had to say. I had promised him, with utmost certainty, that I would lock up properly and post the keys through their letterbox on my way out.

'Is this for a date?' Guido enquired.

'I'm afraid not.'

I could see him mulling things over as he stroked his black moustache. 'I just don't think it's possible, Jess. What if you leave the grill on?'

'I won't be using the grill,' I said. 'I promise I won't create any potential fire hazard.'

'Let her,' Maria said, walking over with a cup of tea. Guido looked at her and then at me, sandwiched between two pairs of expectant eyes.

'Fine,' he relented. 'But you post the keys immediately after and any damages, you pay for.'

I leaned over and gave him a hug, which of course was shrugged off immediately.

On his way out, Guido had given me strict instructions on how to leave the restaurant in preparation for the next morning and as Maria tentatively led him upstairs to the private flat where they lived, I began lifting the chairs onto the tables before doing a final sweep of the floor. Before I could fetch the sweeping brush, Amber walked through the door, pushing it shut behind her. She still had her work clothes on and her cheeks seemed flushed.

'What's this?' she said, looking around.

'Private hire,' I said, smiling. 'Sit down; I've made us

some coffee. Obviously I don't know what's wrong and I don't have anything stronger to hand so here we are, this'll have to do.'

I handed her a mug filled with freshly brewed coffee and placed a sugar bowl on the table between us.

'Thank you,' she said, taking off her scarf.

'I don't know who's supposed to talk first,' I said. 'Biscuit?' I'd maneuvered four clumps of freshly baked biscotti from a glass jar onto a plate, and hoped that Guido hadn't counted them before he left.

'Jess, I did have an affair with my boss,' Amber said. 'But it's over now. He's still with his wife, as he should be, and it's over. The only damage appears to have been done to myself. I just wanted to apologise for how I handled things.'

'Right,' I said, sipping my coffee. I wasn't there to judge. You'd have to be sat on a pretty high horse at this stage to be dishing out morality.

'I know I haven't been coping with things too well and I thought you deserved an explanation.'

'Don't worry, the other night at Marlowe's was actually vaguely amusing.'

She laughed. My plan had worked – share a giggle and the problem is half solved.

'So now that I've got you here, why don't you tell me all about it?' I said, topping up our coffee from the pot.

She went on to tell me about her work: the mutterings in the office, the advances, and the stares. How he had told her that it felt wrong. How he so desperately wanted to go with her that day, but couldn't.

'He was right,' she said, nodding.

'Where?' I interjected. 'He wanted to go where?'

'He even offered me money,' she said, scoffing. 'Maybe it was just a demonstration of his authority.'

'Money for what?' I said, growing more and more confused. 'Amber, what are you talking about?' It was clear this wasn't one of her typical meltdowns, one of her innocent mistakes. Like the time she accidently unplugged our fridge-freezer to charge her phone. This was serious.

'It's all a mess. I quit my job. I think I've got enough on without seeing the look of regret on his face every morning.' She peered up at me, as a tear ran down her left cheek. 'It just wasn't worth it in the end, was it?' she said.

'Amber, you're going to have to be clearer and you're starting to scare me. What happened?'

'I got pregnant, Jess. And now... I'm not. So that happened and now it's not there anymore.'

I could hear her voice quiver and my heart stopped.

'I mean, it'll be okay,' she said, taking a napkin to wipe away a small tear. 'The hard part's done, right?'

We both sat there speechless, only the hum of the light above us breaking the silence.

'Why didn't you tell me? I would've gone with you.'

'For what?'

'To be with you,' I said.

'I was fine. I was on my own and it was fine.' I could see the barriers slowly building up again around her. As if the best way to function was to be on her own.

'Who was there?' I asked.

'A volunteer, who was lovely and sweet and kind. She actually held my hand the whole time.'

I wanted to get up and wrap my arms around her, protect her from her own sense of self and the accusations that I knew she would be thinking but instead I just sat there and listened.

'You know the worst part?' she said, almost laughing. 'Everybody else in the waiting room was so much younger than me. I felt ashamed not to have my life in a place that could withstand it, to have to resort to *this*. We couldn't have brought a child into that, Jess. It was just *impossible*.'

'Why didn't you tell me?' I asked.

'I think I was scared that you would look at me differently if you knew.'

'You're my best friend,' I said. 'How else could I possibly see you?'

I reached out across the table and held her hands within mine. She wasn't a talker, Amber. She got on with things. She wasn't one to pester you for your time or unleash heartrending secrets. But the time for her to talk had come and I was finally there to listen. I was right in my perception: the quiet girls, the ones who bear the burden alone – they are usually the strongest.

Trying to Catch Water: Part Two

The first frost had gathered and a thin, glittery mist had now blanketed the city. Sean had spent the evening having drinks with a musician called Henry, a man who had revealed himself to be by all accounts, a bit of a mystery. They had met on a gay app, a digital haven at this point in Sean's life, where work had rendered anything more serious, or time-consuming, a sheer impossibility. And to be honest, he didn't want the distraction. But rather than go home to an empty flat he had agreed to migrate north for a couple of hours to see Henry's studio in Kentish Town. Henry was twenty-five and the youngest man he had met on there. Up until now, Sean had been the young one and naturally migrated to the older, slightly studious type of man like a moth to flame. Paul had taken care of him and discouraged his, often, wild ways. The dynamics had proved perfect. After all, it's difficult to be a rebel when you've no one to rebel against.

Looking at Henry, he knew instantly that it wouldn't work long term, but a bit of fun in December never hurt anybody. Henry seemed a lot younger than his years with tanned skin and soft eyelashes. A drunken chatter could be heard from the pub on the corner as they walked down the cobbled street arm in arm where drunken people wearing tinsel and Christmas jumpers, a bit too confident in their post-mulled wine revelry, spilled out onto the pavements littered with beer cans and crisp packets.

'It's just up here,' Henry said, turning past a launderette and down an unlit alleyway.

Away from the safety of the crowds in the street, Sean paused. He barely knew Henry. And although there was something so completely disarming about him, and although they had spent the majority of the night getting to know one another, he couldn't hide from the sound of his own instincts. He hesitated.

'What's wrong?' Henry said, looking back. 'Scared or something?'

Despite his reservations Sean followed him inside, always the first to take the plunge and never one to resist a dare. After climbing up the fire escape and in through what appeared to be an open sash window, Sean took off his navy blue coat and carefully dusted down the back of it.

'Sorry,' Henry said. 'Gets a little dirty out there.'

'It's fine,' Sean said, hanging it over the corner of the door.

'Would you like a drink? Beer?'

'Beer would be great.'

While Henry went off to the kitchen, he looked around at the white walls and the piles of sheet music that scattered the floor.

'Sorry, it's a bit of a mess,' Henry said, coming back with two cans of beer. He was self-conscious, and quickly moved over to the chair which was covered in more papers. 'Here,' he said, moving them, 'you can sit down now.'

'Leave it,' Sean said, 'I'm fine standing.'

He glanced slowly around the room at all the cases covering the floor. Sean had never seen anything like it. He walked over to the row of instruments lined up against the wall.

'So what type of instrument do you play?'

'All sorts: jazz, mostly. Why, do you play?'

'No,' Sean said. 'I was more of a hard house, techno kid when I was your age.'

'Sit down, please,' Henry pleaded, gesturing an old brown leather armchair with a spring protruding from the underwire. 'Do you want something to eat?'

'Do you play all of these?' Sean asked.

Henry nodded with a mouthful of beer that he swallowed quickly so he could answer him. 'About eight or nine in total: it's really not that hard; they say once you know one the others come pretty easily. The difficulty is reading the music.' He looked over at Sean who was crouched down over a guitar. 'That's a Gibson,' he said, proudly.

'You know, I always wanted to play,' Sean said, running his forefinger over the strings.

'What stopped you?'

'Life?' Sean grinned. 'Back in New York I was in a band called The Blonds of Brooklyn.'

'But you're not blond?' Henry laughed.

'No, but I was eighteen and high...'

Henry nodded in understanding. 'Do you still get high?'

'Do I what?' Sean asked, thrown by his comment.

Henry laughed. 'It was a mind fuck. I thought that if I offered you a smoke and you immediately said yes then that would be proof.'

'Of what?' Sean said.

'That you're not talking crap,' he said, suddenly becoming one of the most intriguing men Sean had ever met.

He walked over to open a dented filing cabinet, pulling out some filters and a see-through bag of weed. After watching him roll it, Sean joined him and took a large drag of the slightly crumpled cigarette. In truth, Sean hadn't got high since his last year of college but looking at Henry and his light turquoise eyes shining, he couldn't find a reason not to.

Half an hour later, the pot had kicked in for them both sitting side-by-side leaning against the cold, white-painted wall.

'Doesn't toast taste much better when you're high,' exclaimed Henry, licking off the butter with his tongue.

'Uh huh,' Sean said, finishing his third slice.

They both caught a glimpse of each other at the exact same moment and broke into hysterical laughter. By now Henry had put on some loud jazz, a screeching, piercing attack on the ears.

'Hear that?' he said, waiting for a piano solo in the track.

Sean listened dutifully. 'What am I listening for?'

'Freedom,' Henry said. 'God, you can almost smell the prohibition.' He turned the cigarette lighter around and lit it against his thumb.

'Isn't there anything that scares you?' Sean said. All of this was a bolt out of the blue, even for him.

'Missed potential,' Henry said, taking another drag of the cigarette.

Sean had only come here tonight for a few beers and perhaps a quick lay, but in the meantime Henry had completely derailed him. Sean looked at his messy hair and spotted a hole in the sleeve of his jumper. The sound of the track had now faded and rather than sit in his curiosity any longer, Sean got up to leave, not wanting to get too drawn into the boy in the loft with a million guitars.

'You could stay?' Henry said. 'I can sleep on the sofa?'

Sean smiled and shook his head. 'No, I think I'd better get going.'

As he put his coat on and walked back over to the fire escape, Henry placed his hand on his arm. Sean pulled away gently, shrugging off his attempts. But as he lifted the window to climb out he did something even less familiar to him.

'I don't suppose you want to meet again tomorrow night, do you?' Sean said with caution.

'That would be great,' Henry said.

Just as Sean leaned in to kiss him on the cheek, Henry turned his face. There, under the sash of the window, their lips met. After a slight reluctance Sean kissed him back, fully and without hesitation.

'I don't think we should do this,' Sean said, nervously pulling away.

'Don't start something you can't finish,' Henry whispered.

It wasn't supposed to mean anything: just a prominent display of harmless fun. But there they were, two apparent strangers in the midst of the familiar. And he had never felt more alive.

Chapter Fifteen – And a Partridge in a Pear Tree

I could feel the car shudder as I uploaded a new picture onto Instagram. It was taken of myself and Amber decked out in reindeer antlers with a large blob of red lipstick on the end of our noses. So far it had received 107 likes and 36 comments. I wouldn't usually dream of putting on fancy dress, in the same way I wouldn't dream of wearing blue eyeshadow, but we had been ice skating at Somerset House and got a bit carried away in the moment. It was a Tuesday night and I was in the back of a taxi having spent the entire evening late-night shopping with Charlie. He had been picking out a suit to wear at a wedding that I wasn't invited to. In what could perhaps be seen as a role reversal for the stereotypical sexes, he had dragged me to the tailor to watch as he tried it on for the first time.

'I just don't know about the cut,' he said, while I attempted to colour-edit some pictures I had taken on my laptop.

'Charlie, I swear to God if I have to hear about that bloody suit one more time…'

I could hear my phone ringing in the bottom of my bag that was hooked precariously over the back of the doorframe as my cold, chapped hands struggled to grasp it.

'I can't remember if I kept the receipt?' Charlie said to himself as he rummaged in the bottom of the plastic suit bag.

'Hi, Cathy,' I said, finally retrieving my phone.

'Jess, I'm not disturbing you, am I?' she said.

'Not at all, what's wrong?'

'I've got a bit of good news. Saatchi are planning on exhibiting a couple of my pieces at a show they're doing on Christmas Eve. I know it's a time for families and all that but there'll be a few photographers there, mostly my age, and I wondered if you'd like to come along?'

'I'd love to,' I said. 'Thank you so much for thinking of me.'

'Fantastic, I'll put your name on the door…'

'Wait, Cathy?' I said, looking at Charlie who was still elbow-deep in his suit bag. 'Can I bring someone?'

'Of course. Does that mean I finally get to meet Charlie?'

'Yeah, maybe,' I said, still watching him. 'I think it would be good for him to see what I'm trying to do here.'

'In that case I'll give you a plus one,' she said. 'I'll see you then!'

As I hung up the phone I heard the front door slam. It was Amber. Against a constant barrage of noise, our flat had now turned into Piccadilly Circus.

'Been shopping too?' I said, hearing the rustling in the hallway. She'd been out all day and was carrying half a dozen carrier bags. 'Please tell me it's more exciting than Charlie's inside leg measurements.'

He looked up at me, put out for a second.

'Hi,' Amber said with reservation as she made her way into the kitchen. It was the first time they had seen each other since that infamous night at Marlowe's.

'Amber, what a pleasure…' Charlie said with a cocky grin.

I could tell she wanted to punch him but instead she glided slowly past him and offered him a drink. To the outside eye this would seem like a kind gesture, but I knew Amber, and she was indicating to us both that he was a merely a guest here.

'So what's in the bags?' I asked, trying to catch a glimpse.

'Office supplies. I've gone freelance.'

Charlie looked over at me before stating the obvious, 'Freelance by choice or…?'

'I quit my job,' she said, bluntly. She looked at me. 'You don't mind if I set an temporary office up in the living room, do you?'

I shook my head. 'No, not at all.'

'I'll be all right,' she said, half to herself. 'It shouldn't take too long to get a client base going.' She looked at me for approval and I nodded in support. She took a deep breath and collected all of her bags together. 'I'll be in the living room if anyone wants me.'

As I heard the door close I tried to avoid Charlie's gaze.

'Is she okay?' he asked, this time with genuine concern.

'She'll be fine.' I didn't want to talk about it because I didn't want to lie to him. 'Let's just look for this damn receipt.'

They say that nothing's ever perfect but we were certainly edging closer. Since my father was spending the holidays in the South of France with his latest girlfriend and my mother was on a cruise with the women from her book club, I had made the decision to spend Christmas in London. Now that she was freelance Amber had gained a little more time to herself and had taken both Christmas and New Year off to go and visit her family. Sean was nestled away in a cabin somewhere with Henry and Marlowe was at the in-laws'.

I had been offered the chance to spend time with my father, but had politely declined to spend the festive period eating shellfish opposite a woman only two years my senior. Consequently, that left me with only Charlie, a bottle of scotch and a pack of twenty-four mince pies. As he had made the unusually romantic gesture of inviting me out for dinner on Thursday night, I thought it would be the perfect chance to sound him out.

On a rare occasion such as this, I'd taken an increased amount of time to make the extra effort: I'd tidied my eyebrows, trimmed my fringe and painted my nails, both hands and toes. I looked down at the red gloss and could see a smudge on the left side of my forefinger. I licked my finger and rubbed it gently but the patch stayed there unchanged, permanent. It was never going to be perfect. It was always going to resemble me, in some way, pretending. It was as if the shiny outer layer that I'd taken so long in becoming, represented a different version of myself – an everyday form of fancy dress.

I had arrived at the restaurant twenty minutes early and sat at the table, confidently, slowly taking in my surroundings. I watched as the waiters were rushing to the tables, carrying trays of food and opening bottles of wine, as the sounds of 'Service!' bellowed from the bustling kitchen. Seated in my chair, on the opposite side of the expensive table, I couldn't help but feel like a fraud: I was one of them.

I watched Charlie make his way through the restaurant and he sat down in front of me with the grin of a teenage boy.

'What's that smile for?' I asked, intrigued.

'It's just James. He's sent me an e-card for Christmas and it is shall we say? Amusing.'

He turned to show me his phone as I watched a cartoon Santa swinging his hips at the top of a chimney, totally naked from the waist down.'

'I'll send that to Sean,' I said, laughing, 'that's something he'd appreciate I'm sure.'

'Anyway, come here,' he said, giving me a kiss, 'haven't had a chance to say hello yet, have I?'

His kiss lingered longer than it usually would. It never failed to catch me off-guard.

'So do you have a big family?' I said, as we made our way through two bowls of soup.

He shook his head as he brought the spoon to his mouth and slurped the liquid gently. 'You?'

'Just me. And my mum and dad. And his girlfriend.'

'How very European of them.'

'They're not still together!' I said, smiling. 'My dad's the successful businessman and my mum bore the brunt, I'm afraid. Both of them are away for Christmas so it's just me on my lonesome. You could join me?' I was sounding out the situation. Testing the water.

'Can I think about it?' he said, wiping his mouth with a tissue.

'Of course you can.'

I could tell there was something on his mind but as with any other argument we'd had in our history, I knew not to press the issue. Instead, I reverted back to our initial conversation.

'So what was your family like? Were they part of that stereo-typical tradition too?' I asked, my mouth running away with me. 'Who was the breadwinner?'

'Me,' he said, as a silence fell on the table. 'I was the bread-winner.'

I looked at him. I could sense that there was something he'd wanted to tell me but had been looking for a particular moment. Here it was.

'You know, the offer's still there of a homemade mince pie and a glass of sherry, if you change your mind?' I said, grinning. I was trying to make him laugh. Perhaps clear the air.

'You know, there's something I would like to tell you, Jess.' He looked at me, expectantly.

'Okay,' I said, softly. 'I'm here.'

After a heavy dinner and over two double measures of brandy, he talked about his family. How his mother was suffering from early-onset dementia at a home for assisted living in Cornwall, and his sister, Freya, was studying fine art in Florence. I reached my hand over the back of his hair and pulled his head into me. I could feel the weight released into my arms. I wanted him to know I was here to share the burden. Whether or not he took it would be up to him.

The next morning, I pulled back the covers and did the annual British winter jig, sprinting into the bathroom as my body shivered in the December freeze. I hopped from foot to foot, twisting the hot tap of the shower, waiting for the heat of the water to compensate. As the bathroom filled with steam and the power of the water blasted my skin, I looked out of the small bathroom window at the snow still falling outside, the small, delicate snowflakes floating through the air. There, on the other side of the shower curtain, the beauty of it falling made me forget the nuisance that snow can bring.

It was the day of Cathy's exhibition and as with most occasions in London where the snow exceeds two inches, public transport had descended into chaos. I pulled on my faux fur-lined winter boots and padded parka and decided to brave the elements on foot. I walked with my head down, my forehead shielding the rest of my face from the snowflake-laden wind blowing in sideways. With a take-out coffee in hand, trying not to slip on the ice disguised as snow, I arrived at the gallery just in time for the opening. A woman wearing a grey trouser suit, hair tight in a bun, greeted me at the door with a clipboard.

'Jessica Wood,' I said, and she highlighted my name.

'Are you related to Ronnie?'

'Nope. Don't think so,' I said, discreetly trying to read the list of names.

'And you've a plus one, I see?'

'Yes. He'll be here soon. I'll head in though, if that's okay?'

'Follow the red rope to the right and straight into the main room,' she said, directing me as she'd done to hundreds of people that day.

I could see the flashes from paparazzi as I made my way across the piazza. Once inside, the exhibition was enormous: glamorous models and old rockers mingled with waiters carrying trays of champagne. I observed huge prints on the walls from every photographer I could name, spanning the last forty years. I walked in awe through the portrait room and looked up at the main image, an eight by six-foot portrait of Janis Joplin holding a tambourine and dancing, her eyes closed, completely absorbed in the moment. The tiny silver placard by its side read, 'Janis Joplin 1969 (Cathy Abbott).' I stood back to gain the right perspective and felt a huge sense of pride swell within me.

So this was it, I was finally coming face to face with the basis of Cathy's stories, told to me over cups of tea on a Tuesday and Thursday morning. I still smiled at the fact that she was probably on LSD at the time. I walked right up to the image again to get a closer look.

'Jess,' Cathy said, creeping up behind me, carrying a glass and a leaflet of all the works on display. 'Not bad for an old codger, is it?'

'It's… incredible,' I said, not exaggerating.

'I like how they've printed it on glossy,' she said. 'Where's Charlie?' She looked around. 'I was hoping to meet him…'

I glanced at my watch. It was now half past one.

'He'll be here later…'

Although I tried to hide it maybe for a brief moment, it was too late. She had already seen the disappointment on my face.

'Fancy a bit of lunch after?' she said, smiling warmly.

'Sure,' I replied.

'Let me do a bit more mingling and I'll meet you out front at two thirty.' She sauntered off, champagne in hand.

I spent the next hour wandering around the gallery, its three vast floors of musicians, actors and singers captured throughout all decades of modern history. It was the perfect way to document time: real, raw and unapologetic. I knew that it was time to make a plan, perhaps travel to places that would scare me, meet people whose lives I wanted to capture. I had waited for the desire to buckle, like many of the plans I'd made in life, but this time, it was unwavering. I had to do this for myself.

'Jess, there you are!' Cathy said, waving at me from across the entrance. 'I want you to meet Vin. He's the in-house photographer at *Route* magazine,' Cathy said. 'Hugely talented.' He gave a nervous laugh.

'Nice to meet you,' I said, shaking his hand.

Vin was tall and broad and smelled of faint cigarette smoke unsuccessfully masked by peppermints.

'Cathy tells me you're looking for assisting work?' he said with his hands in his pockets.

'Yes, I'm just putting my portfolio together. Although to be honest, I wish I could just work with Cathy for ever.'

'Well,' he said, rubbing a hand through his wiry brown beard. 'I might have something for you over at *Route*. Why don't you email me some of your stuff and I'll give you a ring in the New Year should something come through? Anyway, Cathy, let me know if you need a hand with transportation once the exhibition comes down. I'd better get back to the office. Nice to meet you, Jess.'

I watched him walk away, through the piles of snow that had now gathered in the doorway: a stocky version of my ghost of Christmas future in biker boots and a camouflage jacket.

'You ready?' Cathy said, linking my arm.

'Yep,' I said. 'Lead the way, I'm starving.'

Lying on the sofa amid wet hair, chocolate wrappers and shame, I was watching Gene Kelly dancing on roller skates. I had indulged in a two-hour bath and twenty-minute pedicure, coming to the realisation that Christmas wasn't much fun when you spent it alone. I hadn't heard from Charlie since his no-show at the gallery and now had the option of moping and watching repeats of old sitcoms, or instead being proactive and making the most of the evening.

What eventually pulled me out of my stupor was remembering that my mum had given me her old cookbook before moving away. There was only one distinct smell of Christmas from my childhood and in a bid to recapture it, I sought out the recipe. I instantly knew what I was looking for. I pulled out a large plastic storage box from under my bed and searched for the A5 book adorned with illustrations of flowers, fruit and vegetables. The years that had passed had caused the colours to fade and the spine had begun to twist but that didn't matter, it still contained something far more special: the culinary memories of my childhood.

I placed it on the kitchen table and quickly began to flick through the pages. I could still smell the pastry mix as I pressed the book to my face. It was a distant memory of coconut and strawberry jam, sitting by the fire watching a Christmas film, first licking out the contents before completely devouring the pastry case. After passing through recipes for chicken and leek pie, Victoria sponge and sausage rolls, I arrived upon it in a ballpoint squiggle. It was barely legible in its messy scrawl, but it still represented so much happiness. I put on Amber's apron that she had bought specifically for juicing and flattened out the crumpled edges.

The recipe read:

Coconut tart

Short crust pastry as follows:
200 g self-raising flour
50 g lard
50 g margarine

Rub flour, lard and margarine together in a bowl until it
has the consistency of breadcrumbs. Add a little water
to bind together.

Roll out pastry and use cutters to make approximately
18 tarts. Place a small amount of strawberry jam into
each pastry case.

Cake mix as follows:
50 g margarine
50 g caster sugar
50 g self-raising flour
1 egg
50 g dried coconut

Cream margarine and sugar together. Fold in beaten egg
and flour. Add coconut.

Spoon mixture into each pastry case. Bake in 180 degree
pre-heated oven for 15–20 minutes.

Fifty minutes later, the sound of the smoke alarm rang out as I battled my way through the kitchen amidst the plumes of smoke. After wafting away the debris using an old tea towel, I was faced with eighteen round cakes the colour of coal and brittle-like charcoal around the edges. I slid them onto a cooling rack and broke one in two, tearing off a small piece from the inside. Despite the exterior carnage, it was sweet and warm and fluffy.

I could see through the window that the snow had begun to fall again on the street below, and for the first time that year, there were barely any cars on the roads. The snow had created a cold silence. I looked around at the empty room I was standing in and decided in a gust of Christmas spirit to put my ego aside and ring Charlie. He answered on the third ring.

'Hi, Jess,' he said, 'I was about to phone you. I'm sorry about today, I was swamped at work. How did it go?'

'It went well – it was a beautiful show actually. I'm just watching the snow from the sofa, it's really coming down out there…'

'You can say that again. I'm walking in it.'

'Is it as bad out there as it looks from in here?' I said, curling up against a cushion.

'Apocalyptic,' he said. 'I had to leave my car at work. Listen, Jess, I'm sorry about today, darling. I just couldn't get away.'

'It's really okay,' I said. 'How's work?'

'Busy,' he said, sighing. I felt the sound of his exhaustion travel through the phone. 'You?'

'I actually had a lovely night,' I said.

'Oh yeah? What did you do?'

'I had a two-hour bath, baked some tarts, well, attempted to and now I'm just about to watch a film.'

'So you're fine on your own then?'

'Yes!' I said, laughing. 'I'm fine on my own.'

'Well, that's a shame,' he said. 'Only I'm standing outside your flat and it's bloody freezing.'

I ran over to the window and could see him on the pavement carrying a small, freshly cut Christmas tree under one arm and a carrier bag full of food in the other. 'I thought we were spending Christmas together?' he said, grinning.

I buzzed him in and watched him climb the stairs, his feet buried in mounds of white fluff. Despite all the phone calls, the late nights, the work commitments, when I really needed him, he was there.

We stayed together for the next seven days. Of course it wasn't the same as my old childhood memories, but it was something different, something new. As I tipped the pile of burnt coconut tarts into the dustbin I looked over at the postcard that I'd bought from the exhibition gift shop. There it stood, pride of place on the mantelpiece above the flickering light of the television: a black and white image of Janis Joplin.

Chapter Sixteen – Going Against the Tide

I awoke early, my feet nestled beneath the covers, my eyes wide open in the sunlight of yet another frosty day. I ran the list of things to do through my mind, numbering them in order of importance. I could feel the swell of excitement sitting in the pit of my stomach, not overbearing or outlandish, just patiently. It wasn't the usual lull of post-Christmas excess either. It was a sense of urgency, waiting to be acted upon. I had the benefit of hindsight when reflecting over the previous year, and knew by this point that excitement doesn't come from a party or drinks or getting in at sunlight, though it had done for quite some time; it came from the feeling of knowing that I was exactly where I needed to be, or making appropriate ends to get there. This year, I wasn't going to get caught up in the expectations of it all or those around me, I wasn't going to focus on where the crowd was going. I was blazing my own path without excuse or apology. I was going against the tide.

Amber was tucked under her makeshift desk, typing with the intensity of a maniac. She was wearing an over-the-ear headset, listening to the soundtrack of Nineties R 'n' B that she claimed kept her momentum going. By the look of her, it was working.

She paused briefly to massage her neck before continuing, as if sitting a speed type test. On my side of the room I was binding together a new portfolio. I had promised myself that I would remain disciplined, and not get caught up in the nostalgia of the overused creativity of the right side of my brain, allowing the left, more logical side of my brain a chance to find its way through. I sorted the images into chronological order and fastened them neatly into my new, leatherbound display folder.

What lay before me on the living-room table like a treasure map of the soul, were street shots, portraits and some experimental work that I had taken just for fun on the side. It spanned eight months of progress. We were girl guides in a portacabin, crafting out our futures, attempting to hold things together with PVA glue.

'Cup of tea?' I mouthed to Amber as I walked across the living room before receiving a brief but enthusiastic thumbs up in return.

My phone buzzed on the kitchen table and I could see the screen flashing Charlie's name. I rolled my eyes and answered it.

'Charlie, I told you I was working today, what is it?' For a brief but very real second, I caught myself sounding like him.

'All right,' he said, amused, 'am I now the needy woman in the relationship?'

'I didn't mean to snap,' I said, softening. 'It's just important that I get this finished. Then I can start canvassing by the end of the week.'

'I've gone,' he said. 'I just wanted to hear your voice.'

'And that's really sweet,' I said. 'But you can also hear it tonight, when I'm finished.'

I heard a loud, throaty laugh as he hung up the phone.

The brief conversation had delayed my tea duty and Amber looked over at me with desperation.

'What?' I said.

'Don't say you're going to make one if you're not.'

'I'm making it now!' I tutted loudly.

I had made an intricate list from Google of all the agencies, magazines and publishing houses across London that used freelance photographic imagery in their work. My plan was to hand-deliver, hoping for someone to take the bait and maybe offer me an interview. I put the folder on my lap and ran my hand over the soft leather cover. Then I went to make the promised tea, returning a couple of minutes later with a freshly made brew.

'What now?' I said, as Amber stopped typing.

'That job's not going to find itself...' she said.

'I know,' I whispered, pulling myself up onto my feet.

I put on Amber's camel coat which I wasn't supposed to borrow, but fitted like a dream, and grabbed my keys in preparation to leave the house. I folded a small, white envelope and placed it neatly in the pocket. It contained a decision that I had been working towards tirelessly, but now, once the day had arrived, it felt sadder than I ever could have imagined.

'You look like someone's died,' Guido said, as I walked into the restaurant. 'And I've told you before, use the staff entrance!'

'She's not due to work,' Maria said, hitting his arm.

'I dropped by to give you this.' I handed them the small, white envelope. 'It's just my notice to say that I'm leaving. And

I wanted to thank you both for the last six months and helping me when, well, no one else would really.'

I handed Maria a small bunch of yellow flowers that I'd bought from a flower stall on the way with a thank you card slotted neatly down the cellophane wrapper.

'These are to say how much I appreciate both of you and what you've done for me.'

Guido gave me what I thought to be the tiniest inclination of a warm smile and turned his back to restock the wine.

'You're getting married?' Maria said, smiling.

'No, I'm not getting married.'

'Do you have another job?' she said, wiping a dry tea towel along the already clean counter.

'I'm actually hoping to find a job in photography.'

'She'll be back,' Guido said, carrying a crate of wine through to the cellar.

Once he was out of earshot Maria carefully put two coffee cups and saucers down on the counter. 'Got time for a coffee?' she said.

At that point Brenda walked through the door with her shopping trolley. 'Bloody kids, throwing snowballs at my window. If I catch the little bleeders I'll murder them!' she said before smiling sweetly. She pulled off her red beret, her fiery orange hair standing to attention. 'Espresso please.'

I poured coffee into three small cups, sat down on a stool at the counter, and for what could be the final time, the three of us gossiped about world affairs, love in the modern age and Brenda's arthritis.

*

'Four for a pound!' I heard a man in a tweed flat cap and navy blue wellingtons shout loudly from behind me. His sales pitch still rang in my ear as I turned the corner. I slowly walked through the stalls of Borough Market, the smell of freshly caught fish and foreign cheeses accentuated in the damp air. I navigated through wooden crates of produce as a runaway tomato squished under my foot. I was shopping for some food with which to make dinner that evening, a meal I was cooking for Charlie in a last-ditch attempt to spend some quality time with him before I delved into a hell of my own making, also known as the job search. Plus, it was an opportunity to reveal my new hairdo, a spontaneous decision I had made that lunchtime.

Two hours earlier I had been staring at my reflection in the hairdresser's mirror. I still didn't know if it was a moment of madness or an act of renewal but wearing a wafer-thin black gown with my long hair free from its ponytail, I immediately found myself apologising profusely to the hairdresser for its condition. I'd been busy, I lied. I told him there had been a personal problem and so, naturally, I hadn't been keeping on top of things. That personal problem being that I didn't have the money or time to waste forty-five minutes sitting on my toilet seat, my hair coated in a hair mask. I watched as he attempted to brush it through with a small plastic comb. Finally and with a slight look of disdain, he pulled my hair in front of my shoulders so we could both assess the damage.

'So how much are we taking off?' he said, in a question that sends shockwaves through every long-haired woman in the country. We both stared at the dry, brittle ends. 'Your hair's got great potential,' he continued, sounding like a teacher discussing an unruly pupil on parents' evening. 'If you took two to three inches off and had a quick blast with one of our protein treatments it really could look lovely.'

He was focused, willing me with his eyes to do it.

'Sounds great,' I said, too afraid to decline.

'It's going to look fabulous,' he said before whisking me off to get a shampoo, still unsure of what I'd agreed to.

About forty-five minutes later, I spun round in my chair as Stuart – we were now on first name terms – held a mirror up so that I could see the back. No longer was my hair down to my bra fastening but cut in a harsh, long bob, just touching my shoulders: no layers, no fuss; it was perfect. I thanked Stuart on my way out the door, clutching a bag of hair products that I had bought with best intentions and promised him that things would be different. This time, I would definitely use them.

Like many amateur chefs chasing the dream of a culinary masterpiece, I'd gone with an Italian theme. I had arms full of cherry tomatoes, fresh burrata and a plastic container of tiramisu, which I hadn't purchased from the market, but rather cheated and bought from the Italian shop around the corner, pre-made in a plastic container. I popped a tomato in my mouth just as I turned a corner, hearing a familiar voice from behind me shouting my name. It was Jack. I had known Jack since law school but hadn't spoken to him for at least four years. I tried to chew my tomato quickly, the seeds and juices spurting out in a frenzy. But despite my attempts at appearing less like an animal, he had already arrived in front of me, motioning me into some sort of greeting.

'Hi,' I said, putting my hand to my mouth as he half kissed the corner of my cheek. 'How are you? It's been… forever.'

He smiled, instantly transporting back to the policy and theories class that we'd both shared on a Monday morning.

'I'd say three to four years…'

'Marlowe's wedding!' we both shouted at the same time, before becoming equally embarrassed.

'Well, how the hell are you, Jess?' he said. 'You look… different.'

'New haircut,' I said, my mouth now firmly in control of the tomato. 'It's so good to see you.'

For some reason I felt myself blushing for the second time in under a minute.

'So what's new with you?' he said.

'Nothing much,' I said, shaking my head but at the same time still smiling like a buffoon.

'I saw online that you didn't graduate from law. It was a shame, Jess, it really was. What is it that you do now?'

My mind swayed between ex-waitress, unpaid assistant and hopeful photographer before settling upon the latter.

'Just trying to get my photography off the ground.' I took a deep breath, as my mouth lay in recovery from all the fast-paced tomato chewing.

'Listen, law's not for everyone: office politics, suits, not to mention the level of debate in the canteen – take someone's chair and you'll be sued,' he said, trying to lighten the mood.

'You look really well, exactly the same in fact.' I noticed his hair set in the same groomed style – 'Slick Rick' as my friends had once referred to him. Although nothing had officially happened between us, we had always dabbled in the odd flirt now and again.

'So, enough with the pleasantries, how's it *really* going?' he asked, suddenly staring right into my soul and catching me off-guard.

'Difficult,' I said, 'if I'm honest – hence the new hair.' I made the best of it. After all, he wasn't a therapist and we were already taking up too much room in the crowded walkway. 'Can we talk about you now, please?' I asked, my smile now straining.

'Of course! Hate to say it but things are good: great actually.'

'You don't have to apologise for your success,' I said, laughing.

'I'm hoping to make partner by the end of the year.'

'Okay, maybe rein it in a little… but no, seriously, I'm really happy for you.' I genuinely meant it.

Our attention was suddenly drawn to my hand, still resting on his forearm. I withdrew it immediately.

'You know what, I think you did the right thing, despite my outrage when I heard that you'd left: you actually stayed true to what you wanted to do. That must be quite brave, and it's inspiring actually.'

'Thank you, Jack, that means a lot,' I said.

'Although I did think you'd make a fine barrister,' he said, laughing. It was the same laugh I'd rather fancied in my first year.

I began to collect my bags together in preparation for an exit. 'Well, it was nice bumping into you,' I said, politely.

'Look, there's a partner over at the law firm who does quite a bit of litigation for Condé Nast. Do you want me to see if there's anything going in publications?'

'You don't have to do that, Jack,' I said, feeling the weight of the bags hanging from the end of my arms.

'No, I want to,' he said, insisting. 'I'm heading back to the office now. Why don't I drop him an email this afternoon and let you know if anything comes up? You still on the same number?'

'Same number,' I said, realizing only then that we were once incredibly close.

'Listen, I'm on lunch now, don't suppose you've got time for a quick drink? I know a great wine bar on the corner...'

'I really can't,' I said, shrugging my shoulders. 'Better get this lot home.'

'Well, Thursday, then?'

I looked away, hesitating. I wasn't sure if I was ready to hear about his steady rise to partnership.

'Come on, we haven't seen each other in years, Jess.'

'Okay,' I said, relenting. 'I'll see you Thursday!'

'And I'll be in touch on the job front. But no promises,' he said, calling back from his stride.

'No promises,' I shouted, watching him leave.

I waited as the spaghetti sank into the boiling water, transforming itself from hard to soft in the bottom of the pan. Dressed in my slippers and an apron, I looked like a sketch from an ideal home magazine, the dutiful housewife preparing an evening meal, but just like the spaghetti that was sitting there limply,

I was slightly sinking on the inside. My wrist twisted as I wrestled with a tea towel and bottle opener, trying in vain to open a vintage red wine that I'd bought on my way home from the market. I gave up. As I rinsed the salad leaves in the colander, I reflected on the coincidence of bumping into Jack. Jack, the man I hadn't stopped thinking about all evening.

'What's cookin', good lookin'?' Charlie said, taking the bottle of wine from me, before freeing the cork in one seamless pull. 'Bottle opener's a bit stiff, that's all.'

'Thanks,' I said, pouring it into the saucepan of tomatoes and chopped onions.

'Take a look at this, will you…' he said, throwing a brochure onto the table in front of me. 'It will amuse you, I'm sure.'

It was a copy of the company's in-house magazine, which included a feature-length spread on Charlie and the level of growth he had single-handedly brought to the company.

'They put me in a beige suit. Can you believe it?' he said, closing the fridge.

'Oh no, how awful,' I said, sarcastically. 'Well, I bet this has got the office girls swooning.'

I continued reading before arriving at a quote about how a stable home life can enable you to prosper. I looked down at my apron adorned with lemons and could feel a pang of nausea within me. With my career on the precipice I had developed an irrational fear of complacency: waking up at fifty, still wearing this apron. I went back to slicing the mushrooms.

'Did I mention that I bumped into my friend Jack from law school earlier today?'

'No,' he said, opening a can of beer.

'It was while I was at the market, just before I came to meet you. He said he knew a colleague who worked with Condé Nast.'

'They run our ads for the company from time to time,' he said. 'Amazing coverage. I tend to get an invite to their summer drinks party – a chance for all the top dogs to get together and discuss corporate lending.'

'Did you just refer to yourself as a top dog?' I asked, placing a bowl of salad on the table.

He nodded, grinning.

'Well…' I continued, 'they publish *Wired*, *GQ*, *Vanity Fair* and, of course *Vogue*. So hopefully that will lead to an opportunity.'

'Yeah,' he said, dipping a spoon into the saucepan for a quick taste.

'Anyway, I said I'd go for drinks with him on Thursday.'

'With who?'

'Jack,' I said.

'Okay. Great,' he mumbled, making a groaning noise of pleasure through a mouthful of bolognese.

The constant battle between old and new had dominated the past year, leaving me overwhelmed. As if destiny was a metaphorical race with no real winner. It was beginning to feel like a battle to fight this unseen force, built on the foundation of who was going to reach this invisible finish line first. But despite the pressure, it was up to me to provide the resistance. I had stumbled, almost fallen, into a new year and with it, it seemed, into an impending sense of longing.

In the comfort of a warm bed on that cold January night, I decided that anything I had planned to do the next day could wait just a few more hours. I looked over at Charlie sleeping next to me; the sound of his measured breathing a metronome against my thinking. On the cusp of a new year, I had started a ripple effect – maybe only a teardrop in a wave of change, something bordering on insignificant, or maybe it was a sign that this year was going to flood me.

Chapter Seventeen – Rah, Rah, Relationship

It had culminated in a tear-your-own-hair-out kind of moment, perhaps feeling like I was not quite understood. Relationships: the biggest irony being the 'relate' part, which can only ever really be gained by regular contact. Instead we are forced into an overkill of the mundane that will, ironically but inevitably, kill all elements of passion. In exchange for random acts of desire, the excitement of flirting, single identity and the question mark towards an unknown stranger, all still felt but no longer acted upon, we are given the stability that a relationship can bring. And it's no coincidence that these sacrifices are the very elements that we so desperately struggle to maintain. Despite inviting them into your mind, your heart and even into your bed, the temptation remains to descend the dangerous slope where you catch yourself believing that the grass might be greener, blocking out the possibility of what might still be out there. In a sexually charged game of cat and mouse, it can sometimes be hard to know when to stop running.

Despite the mornings growing somewhat lighter now that we were coming to the end of winter, I was still forced to wrap a fleece scarf around myself, while puffs of steam filled the air as

I panted. My face stung as the icy wind hit it, my feet pounding in time with the music. That particular morning I'd woken up alone and wanted to feel the resistance of a hill run through Regent's Park. Using the strength in my thighs I powered my way across, sprinting to its peak without stopping, an achievement that I hadn't quite been able to consider at the start of my training but after three runs a week, since the start of the year, I had finally built up the stamina to bear it. What began as an excuse to take my mind off the stresses of daily life – job, lack of job, finances, relationships – had now turned into a physical endurance test, a chance to push myself towards a higher level of fitness, both physically and mentally. And it wasn't going to be used as a boastful claim on social media. I didn't want to lose a few centimetres around the waist and thighs either. I just wanted to test my own sense of self: just to see if I could.

The buzzer sounded as I towel-dried my hair. 'Come in!' I shouted into the intercom as I pressed the button to unlock the door downstairs.

I had arranged for Sean to sit for a portrait: he needed a professional picture taken for his career and I needed to expand the genres of my portfolio.

'Well,' he said, as I opened the door, 'it's a good thing I didn't report you missing. Anne Frank had more of a social life than you.' He stepped over my running shoes, left out in the hallway. 'What's this you're doing, training for a marathon?'

'Kind of – besides the running, I've been under house arrest here all week. I've been trying to get fit by day and building my own website by night – both are taking forever.' I walked into the kitchen and boiled the kettle.

'Well, whatever you're doing it's working, girl, you look insane.'

'Really?' I said, pulling the milk from the fridge. 'I'm doing it more for stamina but…'

'Enough, Jess, I'm bored already,' Sean said, as he hung his shirts on coat hangers.

'How's work?' I asked, putting a freshly brewed cup of tea down on the table.

'Super busy…' he said. 'We've got the pre-season collections coming out soon so I'm up to my ears in shit. Great line this year, though.'

'Can I come to the show?' I asked, giddily.

'Sure,' he said. 'But leave the stud at home, will you? I've got enough to contend with surrounded by male models. Christ, it's hard to be monogamous…'

'Monogamous?' I said, almost scalding myself with my tea. It was as if I were a parent hearing a child use a curse word.

'Yes, Jess. If you actually gave a fuck about my life you would know that I'm now in one of those serious relationships you lot are always talking about.'

I smiled. 'Sorry, it's just hard being…'

'Unemployed,' Sean said, finishing my sentence.

'Yeah. How did you know?'

'Because, and I mean this as one of your closest friends, Jess, so that gives me a free pass to bash you from time to time. But first it was hard because you were single, then it was because you actually found someone to be with and now it's because you're frustrated with your career.'

'What's your point?' I was confused.

'There's always going to be *something*,' he said, bluntly. 'You don't always have to be striving for something all the time. Just take a minute to enjoy what today brings.'

'I know. I do! Well, I try to anyway,' I said, defensively. 'So how is Henry?'

'He's great. You'd really like him, Jess… I do.' Despite us being alone in my kitchen, Sean lowered his voice to a whisper. 'I'm actually thinking of asking him to move in…'

'Really?' I was genuinely surprised.

'Well, he's over most nights anyway so I thought why the hell not?'

He echoed the exact same words that Charlie said to me, the first time we had moved in together. But I wasn't going to bring that up now. I was going to let him enjoy his moment. Besides, he may have been passing his excitement off as nonchalance but I could see that it meant a whole lot more to him.

'Well, let me know a good night to come round. I really want to meet him.'

'I will,' Sean said, firmly. 'But hey, speaking of elusive boyfriends, how's Charlie?'

'Not so elusive. Why do you ask?'

'Because you only invite me round when things aren't going well.'

'That's not true and besides, everything's fine.'

'Fine?'

'Yeah, it's fine.'

'Look,' he said, sipping from his cup of tea, 'I know I give you stick from time to time but that doesn't mean you can't be honest with me.'

'I'm just finding it a little difficult to make time for everything at the moment – there's the website, the job applications… plus he's doing really well at work. It's just a bit…' I searched for the word I was looking for, '. . . insensitive, the way he flaunts it in front of my face sometimes. To be honest, it's really starting to piss me off.'

'To give him credit, it's not his fault that you're struggling, Jess, so don't take it all out on him, okay?'

'I bumped into this guy, Jack, who I went to law school with and haven't seen in a gazillion years. He has some link to Condé Nast. Anyway, I'm going for a drink with him tonight, so hopefully there will be something there…'

Sean looked over at me.

'Jobwise, I mean.'

'Is he attractive?'

'Some would think so, yes. Why?'

'Just asking.' He shrugged his shoulders but I could see he was fishing.

'It's a drink, Sean.'

'Just be careful, Jess. Remember how much you fought to get here.'

I watched as he took off his casual T-shirt and replaced it with a smart, freshly pressed work shirt. I began to set up my camera and tripod in the corner of the room as he sat down on the metal stool in front of the white backdrop. It was the thing I loved about photography so intensely. It was a form of honesty, where the participant had nowhere to hide. As I slowly cleaned the end of the lens with a dust cloth, I looked through and could see Sean's eyes looking directly back at me. I wasn't able to hide either. What I had thought to be just a harmless drink left me thinking it might be something more. Perhaps I had begun to doubt my own motives.

In a pang of guilt following my conversation with Sean, I had changed the meeting time with Jack from 8 to 9 p.m., leaving a small window of time within which to have a drink with Charlie. Despite the feeling of excitement with Jack, I knew that it was initial and fleeting. I was in love, and no amount of flirtation would change that. It *had* taken me a long time to get here and our relationship was one of my more solid investments. I wasn't about to throw it away now.

I stepped into the lift of Charlie's building and looked around at the stainless-steel doors. There was an unflattering mirror on one side, and a carpeted wall on the other. This lift had become the catalyst from the night we first met, for everything that had happened since: passion, kisses, tears, tantrums. It had been a cross-country run for the heart but up to this point always, always, followed by reconciliation.

'Evening,' I said, kissing him on the lips as he opened the door.

'Hurry up,' he replied, 'you're just in time for the big game.'

I slowly walked inside and closed the door behind me. I was wearing a tight black dress and the clutch bag that he had bought me for Christmas. In my eyes it was not exactly an outfit to collapse on the sofa and watch the game in. As he made himself comfortable, positioned exactly in front of the television, I went into the kitchen and poured myself a drink. He was out of wine, scotch and even vodka. All that was left was lager, one of about ten green glass bottles left chilling in the fridge.

'Could you get me another beer while you're there?'

'Yes,' I replied, searching his drawer for a bottle opener.

I walked back through to the living room and sat down next to him. As he watched the teams jog out onto the pitch I glanced down at my legs, my eye catching a small patch of faint blonde hair that I'd missed with the razor. Typical. I licked my finger and smoothed it over, not knowing what I was hoping to achieve by doing so. I pulled my dress down and crossed my legs, inspecting the rest of my handiwork.

'You look nice,' he said, not taking his eyes off the television. 'Special occasion? Oh God, I haven't forgotten your birthday or anything, have I?'

'Nope,' I said. My birthday was in a month's time, but if he didn't know it now, he probably wouldn't know it then either. I picked up a magazine that had been left on the coffee table and began flicking through. 'I'm going for a drink with my friend Jack. The guy I told you about from law school.' I exaggerated the word *friend* but wasn't sure if I'd over-egged it.

'Dressed like that?' he said, finally noticing me. 'I thought it was just a casual work thing?'

'It is,' I said, 'but I want to make a good impression. He might be helping me to find a job.'

We both sat in silence for the next ten minutes as he watched the game and I read my horoscope from the back page of the magazine.

'Right then, I'm off,' I said, briefly checking the time. 'I'll probably stay at mine tonight.' I kissed him delicately on the forehead as I walked past.

'Woah, woah, woah…' he said, jumping to his feet and pulling me back by my waist. 'At least tell me who he is?'

'I told you, his name's Jack, he's an old friend from college – but then you'd know that if you listened to me!'

I could suddenly feel my voice rising.

'Oh, I'm sorry, Jess. Sorry if I want to ask who it is that my girlfriend's swanning off with…'

'I'm not swanning anywhere…'

'Come off it, Jess, you're asking for it.'

For the first time in our relationship it appeared that *he* didn't trust *me*. 'This is about work,' I said, calmly.

'I'm sorry,' he said. 'I know. I just love you, Jess, that's all.'

'You're starting to use that as an excuse, not a sentiment,' I said, reaching for my clutch bag.

'What's that supposed to mean?'

'I just think we might be holding onto each other a bit too tightly.'

'Holding you back, you mean?' he said loudly as he watched me leave.

I could feel the door close firmly behind me as I stood on the other side trying to calm my breathing. I never did like confrontation and the uncomfortable feeling that I had been keeping inside of me for weeks had somehow crept out into the real world. Of course we'd had disagreements before, tiffs and squabbles, but they had always mended themselves with time. The only difference with today being, that this time, I wasn't entirely sure I wanted them to.

My argument with Charlie meant that I was now running twenty minutes late. I arrived through the revolving doors and looked around for Jack who I could see in the far corner, standing at the bar.

'Sorry!' I shouted, quickly walking over to him. 'Traffic was a nightmare.'

'No worries,' he said. 'I didn't know what you'd be drinking so I just got my own.'

'I think I'll just get an elderflower and soda,' I said, signalling for the bartender.

'You're not drinking?' he asked, surprised.

I took off my coat and slid it over the back of a bar stool. 'Yeah, why not,' I said, laughing. 'Go on then, I'll have a white wine.'

'Are you okay, you seem flustered?'

'I'm fine,' I said, 'I just ran here, that's all.'

I followed him over to a small round table towards the edge of the room.

'This okay?' he said, waiting for me to sit down.

'This is perfect. So, what kind of law are you practising now? I didn't ask before.'

'Hold your horses, dive straight into business, why don't you,' he said, laughing.

'I'm sorry,' I said, quickly. 'Just trying to play catch up, that's all.'

I felt my foot touch his under the table as I shuffled in my seat. I pulled my feet tightly back under my chair.

'Well, I was considering domestic but the thought of all those messy divorces and custody disputes really put me off. So now I'm doing quite a bit of community-based work. I'm actually working on some litigation with City Children's Hospital.'

'That should be fun,' I said, sipping my drink.

'Fun?' he said, with a smirk.

'Not fun, God no, course not. Just productive… *rewarding*! That's the word I'm looking for…'

I didn't know why I was so nervous. But it was starting to show. I re-aligned the straps on my dress, purely to give my hands something to do.

'So the colleague I mentioned, he said he'd be happy to put a word in for you at Condé Nast. But I can only put you in touch with the right person, mind you; after that you're on your own.'

'Wow, I completely forgot about that,' I said, faking a small laugh. 'But that's great. Thank you so much.'

'You just need to send through your portfolio and covering letter – all the normal stuff, really – and with any luck you'll get an interview at least.'

'Thanks, Jack, I really appreciate it,' I said. 'I hope it wasn't awkward asking your colleague? I hope I didn't put you out too much?'

'Nah,' he said. 'He's gay and I've got a feeling he fancies me.'

'How do you know that?'

'Tight trousers,' he said and I laughed, spluttering into my wine glass.

'You know, it's quite strange seeing you after all this time.' By now we had spent almost two hours reminiscing about our university days. My nerves had thankfully subsided, which I assumed was largely down to the three glasses of wine I'd had without dinner, and it felt nice to talk to someone who held a part of my past. We had a history together – something which only ever becomes of value as you get older.

'Do you drink scotch?' Jack said with narrowed eyes. 'You know, just to shake things up a bit...'

'Better not,' I said, looking at my watch. 'In fact, I think I should probably go.'

'A small one,' he said. 'Go on!'

I took a deep breath and relented. 'Okay, just a small one.'

He made his way to the bar. If this *were* a date, I thought to myself, it would actually be going too well.

'Well, cheers,' he said, as he sat back down.

'Cheers too!'

'You know, I have a slight confession,' Jack said, gently rubbing the sides of his glass.

'Oh yeah?'

'I don't know, I think I always felt slightly disappointed that we didn't ever get together.'

'Jack, I think that might be the scotch talking,' I said.

'No, don't brush me off like that. Listen, and tell me if I'm overstepping the mark here, but I just think we'd be good together. I was really glad when I bumped into you and look, I know this is going to sound pretty forward...' He pulled his chair closer to the table. '...I was wondering if you fancied getting some dinner sometime?'

He looked over as I stared down into my glass of whiskey. The ice cubes swirling amidst the liquor.

'Or not, Jess, but at least listen to what I've come here to say...'

I looked up into his big eyes, the sort of eyes that naturally expected me to say yes.

'Jack, I'm just not very good at this kind of thing…'

'I can see that I've thrown you through a bit of a hoop.'

'No, you haven't, it's me. I probably should have told you before, I don't know why I didn't really, but I'm actually in a relationship with someone.'

There was a pause.

'Oh right,' he said, shaking the moment off. 'Not to worry.'

He finished his scotch and looked over at the small, square television playing sports in the corner of the room. 'It's meant to be a good game. Do you watch sports?'

'Jack,' I said, gently. 'I'm sorry. I should've told you.'

'No, it's fine,' he said. 'I'm still glad we did this. Mind me asking who he is?'

'His name's Charlie and he works for Giles and Morgan.'

'Not Charlie Rainer?' he said.

'Yes…' I nodded, hesitantly. 'Why? Do you know him?'

'Isn't he the man who was quoted as saving the company's balls a year ago through a major share deal? He's basically the reason half the city's still got jobs.'

I pushed my untouched scotch to the side of the table. 'Well, I wouldn't know about that,' I said. 'He's just Charlie at home.'

'You must be very proud,' he said.

'This won't make it awkward between us now, will it? I'd hate it to…'

'Stop it, Jess,' he said, putting his hand on mine.

As his grip became a little too firm I pulled my hand away and reached for my bag. 'I really do have to go now,' I said, as I pulled the coat from the back of my chair. 'It was great to see you again, Jack,' I said, as he stood up to walk me out.

'Let me know how everything's going with the job hunt. I've got my fingers crossed for you.'

'Thanks,' I said, as I reached the doorway. I pulled my coat tightly around me as the cold wind seeped through the door. He leaned in to give me a kiss on the cheek and lingered, closely, next to my ear. 'Jack, what are you doing?' I said, softly.

'I just have this feeling that you want me to.'

I could feel his hands move in around my waist.

'Jack…' I said, as I pushed his hands away gently.

'Just say the word and I'll stop,' he said, putting his hand back around my waist.

'Jack, I need to go home,' I said, pushing him away a little harder.

He leaned in, this time kissing me hard on the mouth.

'Jack!' I cried. 'Jesus, you can't just lunge at people like that…'

'Fuck!' he shouted, as the bar fell silent.

I continued quickly through the door and out into the street but as I turned the corner towards the tube station I could feel my sandal slipping down around my ankle. I looked down at the gold, metal fastening, which had snapped in the struggle. I felt like a fool. I knew in my heart that I wanted a change: a new career, a new boss, a new in-tray perhaps, but there were some things from my past that I wasn't willing to change.

Some things were worth more than the flutter of butterflies or even a successful career. Some things you should value and cherish. Something like love. They say you can't chose who, or why, or how long for, but like a wake-up call, masquerading itself as a kiss, one thing's for sure: requited or otherwise, it's impossible to let go of and even harder to forget.

Our phase of familiarity had been naively confused with boredom. We were the film on the surface of forgotten teacups, left carelessly to go cold on windowsills; we had gone from sex in the morning to arguments in the evening and I didn't know a way to fix it. But I knew I had to try. In a frantic regression I had turned a wrong corner and presumed I had wanted more. But I didn't. In a quest for the whim of excitement, I had learned my lesson. I had flown too close to the sun and now I was left to repair my melted wings.

Chapter Eighteen – A New Chapter

I held my portfolio tightly in my arms as I navigated my way through the sea of commuters. I was surprised when I received the email. People always say they will be in touch when you are introduced to them at a party, but in reality they never really do. I clung onto the metal bar overhead as the train pulled away from the platform, my back pressed into the closed doors.

I had been invited to interview at *Route* magazine for the position of Vincent Campbell's photographic assistant and following one desperate phone call to Cathy and a quick search on Google, I had learned that he had made his name taking pictures of extraordinarily thin models for London's heroin chic scene of the Nineties. My role, should I be offered it, would be to schedule shoots, prepare equipment and assist in creative direction. Perhaps it was the lack of air on the stuffed train carriage, or the inability to eat breakfast due to nerves, but deep down inside, I felt giddy with excitement.

The magazine was casting for one of their spreads for the new season and I had consequently found myself in the waiting room amongst six of the tallest, most strikingly beautiful females I had ever had the misfortune of sitting next to.

A lady wearing a headset glanced up from her computer.

'Could you tell me where the toilets are?' I said, in a subdued voice.

'Turn right at the bottom of the stairs,' she said, politely.

I walked over to the door and pushed it lightly as two women chatting animatedly pushed past. I entered the empty bathroom and looked at my reflection in the small, round mirror above the sink. A strand of hair had escaped from my ponytail and pulled every time I moved my head. It wasn't a style that I would wear in my normal life but as Melanie Griffith had once said to Joan Cusack in *Working Girl*, if I wanted to be taken seriously, then I needed serious hair. I wiped the corners of my mouth to erase the pale pink lipstick I was wearing and took a deep breath before going back outside.

'Jess!' Vincent said, in a loud voice that boomed from the Gods. He wore his familiar dark green cargo jacket, and was sporting his usual bushy beard. Carrying what looked to be a sandwich and a large cup of coffee, he waved me up to the top of the tall flight of stairs.

'Morning,' he said, as I reached him. 'Thanks for coming in – it's really nice to see you.'

'Hi, Vincent,' I said, clinging onto the banister in an effort to disguise my trembling hands.

'Call me Vin,' he said. 'Why don't we go into my office?'

He led me through an open-plan office filled with light grey desks and rows of computers. Keyboards clicked to the ring of telephones. It was a glimpse into the office in its natural state: people making their way to the photocopier, others standing over their desk, glued to their phones, cups of coffee in hand. I didn't feel like Jess who worked at Guido's or Jess who had dropped out of her law degree. I was in the unfamiliar but that had somehow brought me a sense of home.

'Reception was pandemonium, wasn't it?' Vin said as we entered his corner office. I sat down in the small wooden chair opposite his big leather recliner. 'Do you want a coffee?'

I shook my head, knowing that one more coffee that morning might send me completely over the edge.

'So let's have a look at your portfolio.' Famous images that he'd taken of equally well-known faces lined the walls either side of me. I laid my folder out on the desk in front of him. He glanced over my file, my eyes fixated on him. I was listening for sounds, movements, body twitches, anything that would indicate his impressions.

'So, here's the thing,' he said, finally. 'I've been looking over your CV and was struck by a bit of a gap between your first job out of university and, well, now really. Why was that?'

I prepared to give a rehearsed speech about life lessons and personal development, but as he sat there awaiting my answer, I decided to go with the truth.

'I think I got a little disoriented, to be honest,' I began confidently. 'Maybe, I'd lost my way a bit. But having spent those few months putting together my ideas I'm definitely ready to move things forward.'

I looked down at my lap, at my notebook resting gently on my knees. 'I just want to work hard. And be the best that I can be.'

'A professional rest, I'll call it,' he said, rubbing his beard.

I nodded as he made some more notes on a piece of paper.

'But can I just say, Vin,' I continued, 'I am willing to learn and I know that the skills that I do have, as varied as they may be, well, I will use them all to help in any way that I can. And all I ask in return is that you show me how to be a better photographer.'

My brain was screaming at me to stop talking, but my heart had run away with the story. I knew that I had gone out on a limb, but with a CV that equated to tap water in an office full of Evian, I knew I didn't have a choice.

He put his pen down. 'It's hard, Jess, I know. But I'm not going to beat around the bush with you, I'm giving it to you fair and square: judging by your portfolio, you've got great vision and a lot of potential but you've simply got to raise your game if you want to work in this industry. It's competitive and I don't want to see you broken by it all.'

'I'm ready, Vin,' I said, defiantly.

'Then you're going to have to prove it. I was interested in working with you when we met at Saatchi's. I've since read your application and your work is different to any of the other applicants I've seen. Your work has substance, but you've still got a long way to go,' he said, leaning back in his chair, exhaling loudly. 'It's just tricky...'

'Vin,' I said, getting his attention. 'Please just give me a chance. I want to prove to you and to myself that I can do this.'

My eyes met his across the table. I had to remind myself to blink.

'Then let's give it a go, shall we?' he said after a pause that went on for decades.

I could feel my tight grip loosen on my notebook, removing my hands from the sweaty fingerprints that remained.

'Thank you,' I said. 'I won't let you down.'

'Let's see you a week on Monday?' he said, flicking through the diary on his phone. 'That will give us both time to get organised and in the meantime I'll send things over to HR.'

'That sounds perfect.'

'They'll email you over all the paperwork, rules and regs of employment, that kind of thing. But, for now, welcome to the team.'

He held out his hand for me to shake.

'Thank you, Vin,' I said.

'It's been a long old road for you, I can tell. But hopefully this will mark something new.'

'This really means a lot to me, Vin,' I said, as he walked me out of his office.

'I know,' he said, 'Trust me, I've been there myself.'

Everything about that afternoon was typical: the weather, the noise of the traffic, the impatience of London, but one thing had changed – I was finally moving in the right direction. I had left the magazine and was now walking through the backstreets trying to find a quiet spot away from the bustle, in order to make a very important phone call. As soon as I was out of sight of the building and of any future colleagues who may be able to see me through an office window, I pulled out my phone to ring Cathy.

'Guess what?' I said as she answered.

'What?' she said, expecting my call.

'I got the job as Vin's assistant!'

'Oh Jess, that's brilliant!' she said, screaming wildly. 'When do you start?'

'A week on Monday,' I said, my excitement being egged on by her energy.

'Jess, I'm so happy for you. I feel like a weight has lifted.'

'Me too,' I said, smiling. 'And it's a real chance to move forward. I'll be working with him every day so something's bound to rub off. I saw his pictures of all the famous actors and politicians on the wall. It's unbelievable the people he's met.'

'He's the best,' she said, effortlessly. 'Does that mean I lose you then?'

'Kind of,' I said, cautiously, 'but if you need any help with anything, I can always come round on a Sunday?'

'I'm joking, Jess,' she said. 'Darling, just go for it! Listen, I've got to go, I've got the dog barking at me for lunch. But congratulations, that's fantastic news.'

In a post-adrenalin haze, I walked back onto the main high street and through the crowds of busy shoppers. Something sitting quietly inside of me was now able to come to the surface, finally able to show people what I believed I could do. And after all the pre-race nerves had faded and the finish line had been crossed, there was only one person that I wanted to celebrate with.

'This is not exactly what I had in mind,' I said as Charlie passed me a pint of cask ale from the bar. We had somehow found ourselves in a traditional English pub, under an arch of Union Jack flags and standing beside a bust of Queen Victoria. 'They've got pie and peas on the menu,' he said, grinning. 'But I might start with a pint of sausage rolls...'

'Splash out,' I said, looking at the menu.

'So, I'd like to say a few words in honour of my incredible girlfriend…' Charlie said, lifting his pint in a toast.

'Charlie,' I said, smiling before playfully hitting his arm.

'No, seriously, Jess. I've seen how hard you've worked for this and I couldn't be more happy for you.'

I wiped the residue of beer froth from the top of his lip and kissed him.

'I love you,' I said, 'and I love you even more for supporting me.'

'I do have a bit of news of my own,' he said, facing me. 'They're considering me for a promotion at the company. It would be the same hours but more responsibility – that's why things have been a bit chaotic lately.'

'Charlie! Why didn't you tell me?'

'Because nothing's definite and I need it to be before we discuss things.'

Just when I thought I knew all there was to know about him, he would go and do something to remind me that I didn't.

'Well, I think that does deserve a toast,' I said, drinking from my pint, 'to my new job and your promotion.'

He reached his arm around me and planted a heavy kiss on my cheek. It had been a turbulent flight but we had finally landed. In the midst of the furor I had somehow kept my balance juggling my career, my relationship and my friendships: all the fibres of my so-called life. I had twisted and twirled them through each day, one at a time, and managed to turn an unexpected corner. Hopefully, moving myself on into a better future.

I'd become one of the head bobbers, the marching band of young professionals who lined the pavements each morning, walking to work in the rising sun. It was Monday morning and my first day working for the magazine. I had arrived at the office before Vin to make a good impression, and I watched diligently as the other workers started their day. I was fresh in their world full of Monday mornings, office meetings and group emails. I carried the papers from Vin's in-tray and laid them on his desk next to a brief that we would be working on that day.

'Morning, Jess,' he said as he arrived, clutching a handful of stencils and a coffee.

'Morning,' I said, turning on his computer.

'You've got the meeting with the art director at 9.30 and coffee with Will from marketing at 11.00. I've put everything in your online calendar but just to remind you.'

'Very good,' he said, pausing, before hanging his coat up on the back of the door. 'So I'm afraid I'm going to have to throw you in at the deep end today. We've had a last-minute shoot come up with Gracie Andrews at Alexandra Palace so we need to head over there straight after lunch.'

I wasn't sure I'd heard correctly. I knew Gracie Andrews from the cover of many fashion magazines, one of which was currently housed next to the taps of our bath at home.

'What do you need me to do?' I said, opening my notebook.

'I need you to pack up the lenses and the tripod, though I doubt we'll use it. And then I need you to do the inventory so we don't leave any equipment behind.'

I quickly scribbled everything down in handwriting illegible to anyone but me. 'On second thoughts…' Vin said. 'Do the inventory and then speak to Kate about booking a van. We're going to need some wheels to get us over there.'

I nodded, picking up an inventory form from a tray on his bookshelf while desperately trying to remember who Kate was.

One hour later, and deep in the contents of two equipment bags, I got a phone call from Amber.

'How's it going?' she said. I could hear her typing at the desk in our living room.

'Good. It's a bit… overwhelming, at the minute,' I said, looking down at the array of cables sprawling the carpet in front of me.

'Fancy a drink after work?'

'I can't,' I said, running my hands through my hair. 'I've got my final evening class on technical lighting to go to.'

'Sounds riveting,' she said drily.

'I'll see you at home later.' I put my phone back in my pocket and checked off the lenses one by one. You can do this, I thought to myself as I pencilled down their names in size order, you've got this all under control.

As I began setting up the equipment for the afternoon's shoot on a set far bigger than I had expected, I lifted up the camera and walked it over to the markings. In the meantime, Vin had knelt down beside Gracie, talking her through the storyboard. She was sat, elegantly, in hair and make-up surrounded by a team of people pulling and poking her into place.

'That's great, Jess,' Vin said, jogging back from Gracie's corner. With my assistance he checked the height of the camera on the tripod and moved a few errant cables out of the way with his feet.

'Do me a favour, would you? Go and tell Gracie we'll need her in ten.'

I walked back through the vacuous room that had quickly been converted into our studio for the day.

'Gracie?' I said, approaching the crowd. 'Vin says we'll need you in about ten minutes.'

'That's cool,' she said, assessing me. 'I've not met you before, are you Vin's assistant?'

'I'm Jess. I'm new,' I said, as I turned to walk away.

She held out her hand to shake mine. 'I'm Gracie. It's nice to meet you. You know, we all love Vin here. You're pretty lucky that you get to work with him.'

'I know I am,' I said, smiling.

'Massive problem,' Vin said as I stepped back over the cables. I could see he had been on the phone and was pacing around the camera.

'What's happened?' I said.

'Tony's assistant's stuck in traffic on the other side of the Thames and it's very doubtful he'll get here in time.'

'Who's Tony?' I whispered, crouching down beside him, unzipping the lenses from their cases.

'He's the lighting technician.'

'Well, I can assist you both,' I said, quietly. 'I've almost finished a course at night school. I at least know my way around a bulb or two.'

'Good job,' Vin said, as he walked off. 'Go and see Tony, I'll shout up if I need you.'

I walked over to the lights and began setting up the tripods.

As the house lights dimmed and the music got louder, we were finally ready to start shooting.

'This lighting is fucking magnificent,' Vin said, snapping away as Gracie turned around to face him. 'What'ya think about that, Jess?' he said to me, laughing.

I looked at the laptop that was connected to his camera and gave him the thumbs up as they flashed onto the screen. They were beautiful.

'Vin,' I said as he was in between shots.

'Shout up, Jess?'

'Well, you know that you said if I had an idea I should come to you?'

'Yep.'

'Well, I've thought of another way you could shoot it.'

He smiled briefly, and nodded for me to continue.

'The backlight looks amazing against the shape of the dress,' I said, carefully. 'But if we lit it from the front we would also get the texture. And that's what interests me most about this fabric.' I trailed off, and turned to Tony for a second opinion.

'We could rearrange a third light somewhere over here,' he said, waving to the side.

'Let's do it,' Vin said, as I handed him the camera.

I quickly ran over to the equipment bags and pulled the extra cables from inside a zip wallet.

After asking Gracie to stand a little more to the left and gesturing carefully towards the wall, Vin crouched down and shone the lens up, causing a flare of the artificial light against the black quilting on her dress. 'Fucking brilliant!' he said, clapping. 'Okay, that's a wrap everyone, thanks so much for your help today.'

And just like that it was over. As soon as they heard Vin's voice, two assistants wrapped a huge puffer jacket around Gracie and helped her into a pair of sheepskin boots.

'Start packing all this away and I'll take a look at the laptop,' Vin said to me. 'Then we'll head back to the office and see what's what from today.'

I opened the silver cases and began curling the cables around my elbow. I loaded up the memory card onto the laptop and could see over 1,000 images from that day alone. As I downloaded them into a folder, I could feel Vin breathing over my shoulder, his eyes transfixed on the tumbling imagery.

'Guess I got a little snap happy towards the end there, didn't I?' he said, meticulously watching them flash by.

'They look amazing,' I said.

'Jess, I need an honest opinion, not a fan. Now tell me properly, what are you seeing?'

'I think the ones at the beginning are quite weak. In my opinion, you need to focus on the close-up section. They're more obscure and a little different.'

'Thank you,' he said, without looking at me. 'Much better.' He was scribbling a list of numbers on a piece of paper before handing it to me. 'I saw a lot of potential from you today. I want to see you apply yourself and work hard because not too long from now, you could be the one running the show, d'ya hear?'

I nodded.

'Now read me back the numbers of the shots that I flagged;

I need them to be shortlisted before we take them back to the office.'

I glanced at the piece of paper and secretly let out a smile. He had just given me a mini pat on the back; in Vin's world, encouragement.

'Jess?' he said, impatiently.

'Sorry.' I pulled open the paper and began reading the numbers out slowly. '0011,' I said, working my way down the list with my finger. '0069, 1082, 1024…'

Chapter Nineteen – The Deep Blue Sea

We were approaching spring. If rain were to fall now, it would be torrential. A moist heat that threatened thunder had hung in the air for days. It was just before sunrise and I was on my way to the local swimming baths in need of a quick swim before the day began – exactly the same way I had begun most mornings these past few weeks. I had grown to rely on the feeling of weightlessness that the pool gave, a welcome respite from the rigor of a new job. I pulled on my red swimming costume and tiptoed across the cold tiled floor to the edge of the communal pool. I dipped my foot in first to test the water. It was cold, but not bitter. I tied up my hair and spontaneously dove sharply into the pool, submerged.

As the sun rose across the pale blue water, all the things I was unable to do each day without worrying or overthinking seemed secondary: it was bliss. I swam fast and hard, powering my legs through the otherwise tranquil water, pushing, gliding and kicking my way through. In a matter of minutes I'd reached the other side and came up for air in a welcome blast of oxygen; I felt light and then heavy again. A gasp of air hit the walls of my lungs as the water trickled down my face. The short sprint had taken my breath away.

*

The sounds came and went softly. It began with metal pans clattering in the kitchen, the distant noise of the television, the irritating high-pitched voice of cartoon characters, all unforgiving to tired ears. A smell of burning toast slipped quietly under the door as Marlowe's head re-emerged from underneath the bath water. She ran her forefinger along the white bathroom tiles, moist with condensation before slowly sinking back beneath the water, faint bubbles rising from her nose as she went. Because the noise seemed to fade beneath the surface and she could forget about everything that waited for her on the other side of the bathroom door. She watched as a yellow rubber duck sailed passed her hip and down towards her feet at the far end of the tub. It stopped briefly, getting caught up in the bubbles, spinning slightly from the weight of the current. She reached out and pushed it, gently sending it on its way, watching its hard, orange beak turn gracefully as it bobbed past.

'Mars,' George said through the door.

She tipped back her head so that the water covered her ears, playfully going in and out of earshot, a childish rebellion that she had reverted back to in recent months.

'Marlowe,' he repeated, this time trying the door handle.

'Yes,' she replied, her head fully breaking free from the water.

'Is Elsa allowed eggs?'

'What?'

'Elsa, she grabbed a bit of my scrambled egg and before I knew it she'd chucked it in her mouth. What should I do?'

'It's okay,' Marlowe said, 'she eats eggs all the time.'

'Oh,' he said, quietly. She could tell from the tone of his voice that he was getting irritable. 'Well, how long are you going to be in there because I have to leave in thirty minutes and I've not started packing yet.'

'Where are you going, again?' she asked, lifting her body from the water and rubbing her feet dry on the bath mat.

'Luxembourg. We talked about it, remember? Look, Elsa's getting really fidgety and she says she only wants you.'

Marlowe sat down on the cream marble floor and gently began rubbing the towel through her wet hair. Her arm collapsed beside her in defeat. She pulled in her knees and hugged them tightly under her chin.

'Mars?' George said, banging loudly on the door.

'Coming,' she said as she stood up to open the bathroom door.

'Why are your eyes bloodshot?' he asked, still doing up his tie. 'You look like you've been crying.'

'Shampoo,' Marlowe said, as she squeezed past him.

It had been a relatively uneventful Thursday and I was currently on all fours in Charlie's kitchen. We had decided, in a moment of madness, to deep clean the kitchen, an optimistic idea that was quickly followed by regret as soon as we had emptied the cupboards. Surrounded by an inexplicable amount of tins of beans and packets of dried pasta I looked over at Charlie with a rather regretful look on my face.

'Why did we start to do this?' I said, wringing the sponge into a bucket of warm, soapy water. 'I've never met anyone in my life who doesn't own a mop.'

It had actually been my idea to get rid of his cleaner in favour of being responsible for our own mess. We were keeping things real, taking care of our own duties, together. His side of the bargain was that he was meant to be spraying the surfaces. When I say spraying, I mean drinking a beer from the bottle with one eye on the sport coming from the television in the corner of the room. As I picked up the bucket of murky water to empty it in the sink I could feel my phone vibrating in my jeans pocket.

'Charlie, will you get that?' I shouted to him. 'My hands are wet.' I lifted up my arms decked out in yellow rubber gloves, carefully cowering from the dripping bleached water.

After a lot of giggling on my part amid several risqué manoeuvres, his cold hands reached into my jeans pocket and pulled out my phone. He answered it. I tried to get his attention, signalling him to help me pull off my gloves. But he batted my hand away playfully.

'Hellooo?' he said in an overly British accent.

I rolled my eyes, stupidly believing that he might actually be able to do something with a hint of sincerity.

'Oh hi… yeah, sure, just a minute,' he said, handing me the phone. At that point his face dropped. 'It's George,' he said, covering the phone with his hand and whispering. 'I think he's crying.'

I pulled off the gloves and gave them to Charlie who quickly threw me a tea towel on which to dry my hands.

'George,' I said, putting the phone to my ear.

I waved to Charlie to turn down the television, my ears trying to compete with screams of cheering sports fans.

'It's Marlowe,' he said. 'I'm at the hospital.'

The journey was a bit of a blur. Charlie had offered to drive me as I pulled on my boots and wrapped a large cardigan around myself. We drove in confusion, a million questions coursing through my mind about how and what and why.

'Well, what did he say?' Charlie said as he wove in and out of the traffic.

'He didn't say anything,' I said, my voice shaking, 'just that we needed to get to the hospital tonight.'

'Did he tell you how she did it?'

'Pills,' I said, looking over at him.

After a short journey that I couldn't even remember, he pulled up onto the kerb outside the hospital. I opened the door to jump out.

'Ring me when you can,' he said, before driving away.

I quickly ran up the concrete stairs two at a time and pushed against the revolving glass doors. Too slow for a hospital, I thought to myself, too slow for people who needed to rush through.

'Sean,' I shouted, as he stood talking to the receptionist. I ran over to him. 'What happened?'

'They said it was a mixture of paracetamol and vodka. George and her parents are with her now. The doctors say she'll be fine.' His neck was flushed and blotchy. 'I just can't believe it.'

I rubbed my hand across the top of his back to comfort him. I couldn't believe it either. At that point, Amber flooded in wearing a hoodie and leggings, her wet hair still hanging around her shoulders. 'How is she?' she said, in a fluster, 'have you heard anything yet?'

'She's going to be fine,' Sean said, 'that's the main thing. Luckily, George found her and was able to call the ambulance.'

I followed them through to the hospital lift. We'd been here before. The rush to the hospital, hearing my heart beat in my chest, facing the possibility of losing someone, permanently. Not some subsidiary problem that can sometimes seem important, but a tragedy. My feet felt weak from under me. It took all of my strength just to stand.

The three of us sat side by side on the waiting-room chairs. As I walked over to the vending machine to buy us some tea, I couldn't help but think how such a monumental car crash could have happened within my best friend's life and how I could've remained oblivious to it. Why wasn't I her shoulder to cry on, why wasn't I there when she had thought this through? I should have been providing the late-night phone calls: listening, caring. Over the past few months I had been lost in a whirlwind of happiness, within the confines of a new job and relationship. And while I was celebrating success, concerned only about proving my worth, she was struggling to keep her head above water. I felt a wave of shame as I waited impatiently for the hot water to fill the plastic cups.

'Here,' I said to them both. 'I got us some tea.'

As I sat down I could smell the clinical, sterile air of the hospital, the squeaking sound of the nurses' shoes as they did the rounds.

'I just still can't believe we're here,' Amber said, fidgeting in her seat. 'How long are we going to have to wait?'

'As long as it takes,' I said, gently.

It was half an hour, which felt like a year, before we all stood up in unison as Marlowe's parents walked into the waiting room.

'Thank you for coming,' her father said, despite all the torment, still maintaining a politeness. I walked over to her mum and put my arms around her, her weight resting heavily in my arms. She smelled of faint floral perfume and stale tears.

'She's in room number thirty-one,' she said. 'She's tired and obviously needs to get some rest but I'm sure she'd appreciate some company.'

Her father shook his head as he sat down, slowly coming to the realisation of what had happened to his daughter.

'Amber...' I whispered as we walked down an endlessly long corridor. 'I don't understand...'

'I do,' she replied. 'She's been miserable. But not in my wildest dreams did I think it would come to this.'

We slowly turned the corner and arrived at room number thirty-one, knocking lightly on the open door. The sight of her in her hospital gown was the first thing to hit me.

'Hi, guys,' George whispered, getting up from his chair.

'Don't get up for us...' Sean said, as he walked over to Marlowe, lying so perfectly in the bed.

'No, it's fine,' George replied. 'I need to go and speak with the doctor.'

I sat down on the chair next to Marlowe, my eyes focusing on a thin, clear tube going into her hand attached to a bag of liquid that hung above our heads.

'I'm so sorry,' I said to her, quietly, as I pushed the blonde hair from her forehead. She was still weak and pale and I could tell she had been crying.

Amber sat silently in the chair opposite. I could see her staring at the monitors, the monotonous bleeping cutting in and out of the silence.

'Thank you for coming to see me,' Marlowe said, trying to sit up.

Sean looked around at the wires, the clipboards and the jug of water before stopping at Marlowe, her once-glossy exterior now faded and tired. He got up and perched on the edge of her bed.

'Right, lady,' he said, looking her directly in the eye, 'this stops now, okay? If you have problems you come to me, do you hear?'

'I'm sorry for worrying you all. I just… I just couldn't…'

'We know,' Amber said. 'You don't need to explain anything. We are all here and we love you. That's all that matters now.'

'I think it's time we had a proper chat about all of this, don't you?' I said, sternly.

The three of us sat back down and faced her. This time, we were all here, and we were listening.

'It all started months ago. I just reached the point where I didn't know who I was anymore. Everything just got so…'

'Just say it, Marlowe,' I said, holding her hand.

'. . . heavy,' she continued. 'I can pinpoint exactly when it happened. One day I was young and excited about my future and the next I just didn't seem to care, about any of it. I mean, I had Elsa on the promise that we'd both be raising her… well, it didn't work out like that… and I'm not blaming her, of course, she's my absolute world but I just felt so… alone.' She pressed a tissue to her face as if to form a barricade against the tears.

'I suppose I just bottled it all up until I was ready to explode,' she said, welling up again.

'What do you need us to do, Mars?' I asked, feeling embarrassed that I didn't already know.

'I don't think there's anything you can do,' she said, smiling at me. 'He's cheating on me, Jess.' Her comment silenced the room. I discreetly looked over at Amber who had a face like thunder. 'I found out a few weeks ago. Some woman called Samantha… if she's the only one.'

'How do you know?' I asked, stunned.

'His phone accidently synched up with the computer,' she said. 'I've read every text message, every email, seen every picture. He doesn't know I know and I don't want him to. So you can't say anything.'

'He should be lying in a hospital bed,' Amber said, angrily, 'not you.'

'But why are we here, Mars, what pushed you to this?' I asked, softly.

'Well, a few months ago at the dinner party, the one where you brought Charlie and Amber…'

'Shagged her boss and then drank the guilt away…' Sean said, rolling his eyes.

Amber looked over at him as Marlowe let out a small smile.

'Well…' she continued, 'I don't know, maybe it was having you all there and meeting Charlie's friend James… but…'

'Just say it,' Amber said, holding her other hand. 'You don't have to be the sensible one all of the time.'

'Let her rip!' Sean nodded.

'It was exciting and a bit of fun,' she continued. 'I couldn't remember the last time I'd had that effect on someone. I suppose it was the thrill of flirting and mixed-messages and sexual tension. I'm still young and I'm starting to sound like a fifty-year-old. Sometimes I wonder where my life went. I forget that it's still in front of me.'

'I think it's only natural, Marlowe, to have these feelings,' Sean said. 'But excitement and passion, they wear off, you know. That's something we've all got to face some day.'

'It's true, Mars,' I said, nodding in agreement. I leaned back slowly into the plastic chair. 'I'm sorry,' I said, shaking my head. 'I should've known.'

'This isn't anybody's fault but mine,' Marlowe said. 'I don't know much right now but I do know that. I've agreed with my parents to talk to someone about it, a professional, who can help me figure out a way to navigate through it… somehow. After all, I'm far too young to feel so hopeless.'

'You're not hopeless, Marlowe,' Amber said. 'If anyone can take that crown this year it would be me.'

'Or me…' I said.

'Either of you,' Sean said. 'But not you, Mars.'

I looked over at my friends as we all sat there, our silence broken only by the sound of the nurse entering the room.

'Now, I've just got to run a few tests,' she said, in a faint Irish accent. 'Nice to see you've got your friends with you.'

'I think we had better leave you both to it,' Sean said.

'I'm sorry for being such an idiot,' Marlowe said as we collected our things and made our way out of the room. 'If I knew you were going to abandon your plans on a Thursday night I never would have done this…'

'Oh please,' I said. 'I left Charlie watching sport and he's probably on the sofa right now, sitting in his pants.'

'And I've turned over a new leaf since I started the business,' Amber said, proudly. 'So you've really only interrupted my tax return.' She leant over and whispered quietly into Marlowe's ear, 'There's a new man on the scene. For real this time, no playing games. His name is Mitch and it's even verging on something serious.'

Marlowe squeezed Amber's hand as she left.

'But give the poor guy a year,' Sean said drily, 'and he'll probably be where you are now, Mars. Tied to a drip... can't go on...'

And in the darkest way possible she laughed, we all laughed. And despite the coldness of our surroundings, it was the warmest thing we'd done together in a long time.

As the others left I walked over to the bed and kissed her forehead. 'You're not on your own,' I whispered to her. 'Remember that.'

'I hope she's going to be okay,' Amber said, linking arms with Sean.

'She'll be fine,' I said, as we piled into the large silver lift and descended to our own lives. 'She just can't do it all on her own.'

I hugged them both goodbye as they got into a taxi and made my way to find the nearest tube. As I walked through the night air I thought about something that had occurred to me in the lift. It seemed that true friendship was just a continuation of relays, passing the baton of help back and forth depending on which one of you needed it. Suddenly, a persistent car horn pulled me from my thoughts and stopped me in my tracks. I turned to see a black car parked against the kerb outside of the hospital. It was Charlie.

'Well, I didn't know if you had your phone on you,' he said, winding down the window. 'So I thought it best to just wait here.'

I climbed into the car and could feel the warmth of the dashboard heater across my face. And just like that the car pulled away and we drove back to our home and back to our ordinary life. I reached over and held his hand: uneventful and even mundane at times. How lucky we both were.

Sean arrived home to find Henry in the midst of cooking up spaghetti bolognaise. A bottle of red wine was already left open on the side and the sound of music could be heard from the kitchen.

'In here,' Henry shouted, turning down the radio.

Sean gave him a small smile and began taking off his coat. Secretly he had gotten used to the idea of Henry being there when he got home.

'You okay?' Henry said.

'Relieved.'

'How was she?'

'Not good,' he said, wrapping his arms around Henry's shoulders.

Henry sighed. 'It's just hard for some people, I guess… life.'

'Yep,' Sean nodded, taking a spoonful of the tomato sauce on the stove. 'Hmmm… delicious,' he said, holding out the spoon for Henry to try. Their relationship was always so physical, so tactile. But in the light of what had happened, Henry pulled away.

'So tell me about it then...' he said.

'I don't know what to say. It's awful. She took an overdose. And we didn't even notice as to why: not us, not her parents, not even her husband. And that's it. Full story.'

Henry nodded. 'Have you ever been in a serious relationship?'

Sean hesitated and then nodded.

'Who was he?'

'His name was Paul.'

'And you're not together anymore?'

Sean smiled. 'Obviously not.'

'Come on,' Henry said. 'I want you to tell me about Paul.'

'You know, you are looking so… good right now,' Sean said pulling Henry's waist towards him.

'Stop that,' Henry said.

'Stop what?' Sean said, defensively.

'Stop using sex to get away from actually talking to me.'

Sean was overwhelmed. After the day he'd had he wanted to keep things light and have a little fun, but here he was under a wave of questions from Henry. All of a sudden he felt trapped. How was a mere fling, standing up to him in his kitchen, probing a little too deeply, trying to knock him off his perch.

'What do you want me to say?' Sean said, stuttering. He could feel his neck reddening.

'I want to know you, Sean. Like, really get to know you.'

'Henry,' Sean said, exasperated. 'I like you but this is all just a little too much for me right now. I don't know. Maybe you should just go home.'

'You want me to go home?' Henry said.

'Yes.' Sean undid the top buttons of his shirt so he could breathe. 'I think that would for the best.'

Henry looked at him, stunned.

'Well…okay,' he said, turning the light off from under the pan on the stove. 'If that's what you want.'

As Henry began putting on his coat Sean looked over at him. He actually cared. And it was terrifying.

'Wait,' Sean said as he reached the door.

Henry turned back to look at him.

'So what do you want to know?'

'I want you to tell me about Paul…'

As he looked into Henry's eyes, Sean relented. After all, it was harder to let someone in than to push them away. For the rest of that night they sat together at the kitchen table, eating bowls full of Henry's spaghetti bolognaise as Sean told him about Paul, the fact he died far too young in a car crash, about his love for navy blue jumpers and dachshunds. For the first time, Sean was underwater, submerged in the thought of somebody new. But maybe, he thought to himself, it was finally time to stop fighting the tide and just give in to the strength of the current.

SPRING

Chapter Twenty – The Magical Hour

Up to that point, I suppose complacency had kept us going. Without the ability to see behind closed doors we marched on, glazed over the cracks, lost each other in various distractions, as if we hadn't bothered to look closely enough at what was really there. She was there – and if it hadn't happened, we may have looked up to find one day that she wasn't. They should be called unwanted necessities. Of course we don't want these things to happen, but in the greater scheme of things it's somewhat necessary to pull you back to life.

It was officially spring, and the events of the past few weeks had forced us to look at our interior priorities. In a landslide of miscommunication on our part and an emotional decline on others', we knew the tonic lay within each other as we attempted to pull our friendship from the wreckage. Together, we had entered the Magical Hour, the mysterious aftermath that follows in the wake of something terrible. I knew that life, however fragile, might just be the seamless effects of magic. An extraordinary force that works its way into our lives, influencing what had happened, bringing with it a sense of purpose – it already existed inside of us, all we had to do was listen:

To the heart: the beating of the want inside you.

The brain: the thought behind the desire.

Belief: the possibility in the unseen.

Our want: the motive behind the struggle.

Our will: the strength to endure it.

Their personality: the elements that make up the person.

Our awareness: the consideration of everything around.

The signs: the glistening markers that pinpoint the way.

The physics: the law of effort and time.

The attraction: the force that drives us there.

Our love: and all the things we live for.

'What's with the luggage?' Vin said as I dumped a large black bag next to my desk.

Since the infamous night several weeks ago, Marlowe was now living at her parents' country retreat in the Cotswolds, an idyllic paradise in the English countryside, just two hours from the heart of London. And so we were embarking on a mini-break, away from the everyday stresses of the city. It would be a chance to sit around, in conversation, away from the clicking of keyboards and incessant bleeping of mobile phones.

'I'm going to the Cotswolds with my friends for the weekend,' I said. 'I'm going straight from work so I had to bring my bag in case we ran over.'

'Very nice,' he said, still focused on his computer. 'Love the Cotswolds. Bit pricey but great in the summer.'

'We're staying with Marlowe's parents. They have this huge house with a tennis court and a pool, although I doubt we'll get a swim this time of year.'

'Thought they lived in Chelsea?' he said, as he chewed down on his biro.

'So you do listen to me?' I said, surprised. 'No. Well, they do, but this house is for weekends and holidays.'

'Jeez…' Vin said, exhaling loudly. 'In the Cotswolds?'

I nodded.

'Don't they have a son for you?' he said laughing.

I rolled my eyes as I sat down at my desk.

'How is she now, your friend – Marlowe?'

'She's fine. Baby steps. She's been taking some time out since… that night. It's funny how nothing changes and then *everything* changes,' I said, switching my computer on. 'So, what's the plan for today?'

I cleaned the whiteboard with a cloth to signal the end of the week and pulled out a marker pen to prepare for the next one.

'I need you to start editing those charity photos that I did.'

I nodded, with maybe a hint of trepidation, knowing that I hadn't been given such a level of responsibility before.

'What?' he said. 'What's that look for?'

'You mean, get them ready for you to edit?' I said, double-checking that I hadn't misheard.

'No,' he said, sipping his coffee. 'You do it.'

I stood looking at the memory stick and all it represented. It was more than an edit. It was blind belief in me.

'If that's okay, Jess?'

'Yes, it's fine, I was just confused because you normally edit them but… if you want me to do it, that's fine.'

I transferred the images from his hard drive to my computer and watched as they popped up one at a time.

'These are really powerful,' I said. They were taken from the magazine's clean water project, a series of black and white imagery documenting his time in Rwanda: women carrying water in large containers, children playing in the sprinklings of a new fountain.

'Don't ever let anyone accuse you of being frivolous because you work in fashion,' he said. 'There's a lot of money in it and with that, a lot of influence.'

'What was it like?' I asked. 'In Rwanda?'

'Without sounding like a do-gooding wanker,' he said, 'it totally changed my life. Seeing what other people have to contend with when they wake up each day makes my morning commute look like a trip to Disneyland.'

'Well, they're incredibly moving,' I said, slowly creating a shortlist for the editor to choose from.

'Bit different from girls wearing dresses made from bubble wrap?' He laughed. 'Like I said before, work hard and you could go a very long way here, both personally and professionally.'

I studied a close-up picture of a little girl smiling, carrying fresh water in a large blue bottle. She was wide-eyed and beautiful. The expression on her face stayed with me for the rest of the day.

That evening I called Marlowe from the taxi to tell her that we were on our way. Together, we had achieved the unachievable. From all four corners of London we had arrived at the station on time and had departed Euston just after rush hour.

'Are you sure your parents won't mind us all staying?' I said as I watched muddy pink pigs rolling in fields through the window.

'Bit late to be asking that, isn't it?' Sean said from the back seat of the taxi sandwiched between Amber and Henry.

'Not at all!' Marlowe said, breezily down the phone. 'I think they'd be glad of a new set of faces, to be honest.'

From what I could gather, her parents now spent their days relaxing in the gardens of their country home, a place I had been desperate to visit since I had seen the photographs from Christmas 2007. They still said things like 'jolly good' and, more importantly for us, still celebrated slightly older traditions like cocktail hour. I stretched my legs out in the footwell in front of me and looked out at the road as we sped on through. I made a mental list of everything in my head: my friends were well, my relationship was happy and to add a cherry on top of the already rich cake, I was desperately beginning to love my job at the magazine. As part of a new exercise that I had promised myself, I took a moment to be grateful.

We pulled up to the large wrought-iron gates that had been left open in anticipation of our arrival. I had told the others that it was just a short walk to the house but as we stood at the foot of the driveway I could see it was longer than the average street back in London.

'Great idea to ditch the taxi, Jess,' Sean said, dragging his case.

'Can you stop moaning?' I said. 'I've never been here before. Just stop and look around you for a second...'

'So, what did her parents do again?' Henry asked, relatively new to the group and still piecing us all together.

'Her dad was a journalist and writer,' I said, 'and her mum…'

'Was *the* party girl of the Seventies. Apparently she once dated Jagger,' Amber said, finishing my sentence before throwing her large bag over her shoulder.

After a steady walk up the driveway in which Sean moaned, Amber scrolled through her phone and I chatted to Henry, we eventually arrived. The large red brick house was decorated like a wedding cake with yellowy cream coving. I broke into a small jog as I saw Marlowe standing by the door. She smiled and waved at us, clutching a small mug of tea.

'It looks like one of those pictures from the front of a biscuit tin,' Henry said, slightly shocked. At that point Amber noticed Sean and Henry's clothes, all burgundy, both knitted, twinning outfits in the setting sun.

'What's with the jumpers?' Amber said, looking at them both.

'This is what happens when you have the same dress sense – fashion happened,' Sean said, drily.

'Hi!' Marlowe cried, running barefoot across the lawn. 'I'm so glad you all came.'

'Mars, this is Henry, I don't think you two have met yet,' Sean said, making the introductions.

'Hi, I'm Marlowe,' she replied, giving him a hug. 'Make yourself at home. My dad's out the back and he's got the gin and tonics waiting.'

'You look really well,' I said as we walked up to the house.

'I feel really well,' she said, as I linked my arm through hers. She was wearing a smile that I'd not seen in months.

Once inside, we carried our bags up the wooden stairs to

our room. I was sharing the attic with Amber, while Sean and Henry were led to the pool house.

I sat down on the fluffy white bed linen of our covers. 'Double bed,' I said, bouncing my knees on it.

She smiled. 'Hurry up, Jess, I could murder a G and T...'

I began to sort out my toiletries bag and picked up my mascara wand to freshen up a bit. 'Can I borrow your hairbrush,' I asked, 'I've forgotten mine?'

'You know,' she said, handing it to me, 'I don't know why we haven't done this before. Why did we have to wait for something so terrible to happen for us all to get away together?'

'I know,' I said, 'perhaps it's just a way of reminding us not to take things for granted. It's a shame it took something so drastic for us to realise it though.'

I smiled at her limply as I reapplied my mascara. I wondered if the guilt had hurt her too.

Having changed out of our work clothes and freshened up a bit, we walked down to end of the garden where Marlowe's parents sat on sofas next to a pale blue swimming pool.

'Jessica, it's so nice to see you. It's been far too long,' her mum said as she got up to greet me. She wore a large cream floppy hat and light blue trousers. Marlowe's dad handed me an overwhelmingly large glass of gin and tonic. It seemed she had put our chance meeting at the hospital out of her mind, and I let her.

'Nice to see you again,' I said, looking for a vacant seat.

'Sit next to me on the sofa,' she said, as the others seated themselves on the white wicker furniture around us.

'I suppose she's told you about the situation with George?' she said, quietly, so that no one else could hear. Her small hands clutched a large glass of white wine, the contents swirling as she spoke.

'Yes,' I said. I was still unsure of the full story and didn't want to put my foot in it before I'd spoken with Marlowe.

'I know you may not see it, Jessica, but I believe they are truly meant to be together, and I'm her mother. I wouldn't say it unless I meant it. I just think that the both of them got a little complacent with things. And it can't be easy having young Elsa. I mean, I do my best to help them but it's quite difficult with her father travelling with his writing.'

'I don't know what to think,' I said as I peered down into my glass. 'But I have offered to help a little more too. I don't think they were the only ones who had got complacent. I could be accused of that too.'

She smiled at me and stared off vaguely into the distance.

'So do you have a nice man at home too?'

'I do,' I said, smiling.

She took a sip of her wine. 'I just don't want to see her do anything stupid,' she said. 'Something she may later come to regret.'

I watched as she sauntered off with the cook to talk about the evening meal, leaving an opportunity for me to have a private chat with Marlowe.

'So how are you?' I said, pulling a chair towards her.

'I'm fine,' she said. 'Pretty humiliated, but fine.'

'Why are you humiliated?'

'I just feel like a bit of a walking liability – as if I'm being watched all the time.'

'People are just worried about you, Mars, that's all.'

'I know,' she said, reaching for her glass of sparkling water. 'It's just bigger than that, you know.'

I put my hand over hers, which was resting on her knee. 'I know,' I said, gently.

'I've been seeing a therapist twice a week and they said we're okay to drop it down to just once.'

'And how do you feel about that?' I said.

'I'm happy if they are. To be honest, until I get to the root of the problem there's not a lot of point in talking about anything anyway.'

'Have you spoken with George yet?' I asked, tentatively.

She shook her head. 'No. I just want to spend as little time in London as possible. You know, I'm pretty lucky having all of this, I may as well take advantage of it.'

'I think you're doing the right thing.'

'I don't know,' she said, waving to Elsa who was playing handstands on the grass with Henry and Sean. 'He just doesn't love me anymore.'

'I'm sorry,' I said as she wrapped a grey cardigan around her.

'I'll be a divorcee... that'll make my parents proud,' she said, surprising me with a small smile. Or submission.

'And as for this,' I said, lifting my extremely large gin and tonic, 'I don't know how your parents manage to get anything done. I'd be in a permanent state of shit-faced.'

Marlowe laughed. 'Tell Amber to go easy,' she said. 'I don't want her puking on my mum's white tablecloth.'

*

As I was currently housing three double gin and tonics and only a handful of salted peanuts, I was counting down the minutes until I could finally eat something. After a quick catnap and a change of outfit, I made my way down to the dining room for dinner and what I suspected would be more gin and tonics. The table was laid for the seven of us, with three down each side and a place setting at the head for Marlowe's dad. I deliberately sat myself next to Marlowe and poured myself a drink of water, my mouth suddenly dry, existing halfway between hunger and potential hangover. Henry sat the other side of me and politely laid the linen napkin on his lap.

'I feel like I'm on a film set,' he whispered quietly in my ear. 'I'm too scared to touch anything.'

'I know, me too.' I smiled at him in reassurance as everyone else piled into the dining room.

'Got any brandy?' Amber asked as she took her seat.

'No, we don't,' Marlowe said, quickly.

To a soundtrack of old jazz music, which Henry loved and the rest of us tolerated, we made our way through the smoked salmon starter.

'So how are things going with Mitch, Amber?' Marlowe said once the plates were cleared.

'Who is Mitch?' her mother enquired.

'Amber's new boyfriend,' Marlowe said, smiling.

'Yeah, he's fine,' she said, swilling the remainder of her salmon down with a glass of white wine.

'Mum, Amber's acting coy because she isn't the relationship

type,' Marlowe said. 'There I was tied down by twenty-three while she was out gallivanting.' She turned to Amber. 'I really lived out my twenties through you, you know.'

'That's what I was there for,' Amber said, 'to journey out and report back.' She raised her glass sarcastically.

'Nothing wrong with that,' Marlowe's mum declared. 'Always best not to let the grass grow under your feet, darling.'

'Not exactly the advice you gave to me, Mother,' Marlowe said, under her breath.

'Can I ask something?' Sean said, as the main course was brought out. He had noticed the pictures of the London party scene from the Seventies halfway through his starter but had waited until a convenient time to get up and take a closer look at them. 'What exactly was it like in London at that time? I hear so much about it in terms of design and musical references, but what was it like, to actually *be* there?'

Marlowe's mum laughed. 'You want to know our secrets?'

'Well, yes,' Sean said with a smile.

'I will tell you this,' she said, laying down her knife and fork carefully, 'everything is better with hindsight.'

Marlowe's dad nodded strongly in agreement at the end of the table.

'Don't get me wrong,' she continued, 'the parties were fabulous, the people – by gosh they were characters… particularly the politicians…' she said, slyly. 'But I think sometimes you reserve a fond part of your mind for what has been. You don't actually remember it as it *really* was.'

'I completely agree,' I added.

'I always think that we'll look back on these years, when

we're old…' Sean said as he shot Marlowe's mum an apologetic glance. 'Older…' he said, quickly correcting himself. 'What will we think of ourselves and the way we reacted to things? You know, the choices we made.'

'Only time can be the judge of that,' Marlowe's dad said. 'There are no shortcuts in life.'

By now it was raining heavily outside and we could see the water falling down through the large glass doors overlooking the garden.

'I love being warm indoors when it's raining outside,' Amber said.

'Me too,' I said.

'Makes me fancy a brandy.'

'No, Amber,' Marlowe said, sharply.

One chocolate fondant and a cheeseboard later, we were making our way nicely through their vintage case of Barolo from the wine cellar. After numerous conversations about family and careers, the slightly tipsy chatter escalated into drunken party tricks.

'I don't have any,' I protested.

'Me, neither,' followed Marlowe.

'Amber, why don't you show them yours?' Sean shouted, clearly having had slightly too much to drink.

'Yes! Show us!' Marlowe's mum shouted, herself getting a bit too excited.

'Okay,' she said, sliding from her chair.

She proudly clasped her hands together and slowly began to contort her whole body through the small circle she had created with her arms before climbing back through again. Everyone watched in disbelief.

'That's quite marvellous,' Marlowe's mum exclaimed as a small round of applause shook through the table.

'I'm told it's better when she's naked,' Sean said, before she hit him hard on the arm.

'I can speak the alphabet in German,' Henry said, proudly.

'Take it away, boy!' Marlowe's dad boomed.

Henry stood up, and after clearing his voice, recited each letter word perfectly.

'Woo!' Sean cried afterwards, as Henry took a small bow.

'Let's open another bottle, I think…' Marlowe's dad said, proudly. 'It's towards the left in the cellar… mind your head on the doorframe, darling, as you go in.'

Shortly after Marlowe left, on the crucial hunt for more wine, there was a knock at the door. We listened intently in silence to the conversation taking place in the hallway, trying to work out the identity of the mystery caller.

'My gosh!' Marlowe's mum said from the hallway. 'Look at you, you're dripping. Get inside before you catch cold.'

We all watched the door waiting for an answer when in walked George, completely drenched, despite wearing a waterproof dark green rain mac.

'Hi, George,' we all said, pretty much in unison.

'Hi,' he said, inspecting the table of half-eaten cheese and red wine stains. 'Sorry to interrupt,' he continued. 'I didn't want to ruin the party or anything…'

'You're not interrupting anything, son,' Marlowe's dad said from the head of the table.

At that point Marlowe returned carrying another bottle of Barolo. 'Found it!' she said, lifting it in the air before quickly laying eyes on her husband.

'What are you doing here?' she said, as her face dropped.

'I need to talk to you,' he said, clearly not knowing the extent of how much she knew.

'Let's go upstairs,' she said. 'You should take a shower first.'

We didn't see Marlowe or George for the rest of the evening. They were busy having a heart to heart in the conservatory, and by midnight the rest of us had decided to call it a night.

As I lay in bed next to Amber, I thought about how fun the whole evening had been, just the seven of us in the middle of nowhere. For the entire evening, and accidently, we hadn't looked at our phones or gadgets once. The evening had some-how consisted of only company and conversation, with the only source of entertainment being Henry's ability to recite the alphabet in German.

'Amber?' I whispered in the darkness.

'Yeah,' she said, half asleep.

'I had a really good time tonight,' I said, stretching my legs out under the covers.

'Me, too,' she said, mumbling, 'but get your feet off me, they're freezing.'

I smiled as I pulled the covers around me. We were at a sleepover and I was seven years old again. For the next forty minutes I listened to Amber sleeping soundly by my side. If all we really have is the here and the now then maybe Marlowe's dad was right, maybe the choices we all make with the best intentions might never come to fruition: only time would tell.

But I did know that our weekend in the Cotswolds with friends and family and too much gin had re-established the equilibrium and re-set the levels of our friendship, to move forward together, not pretending as if nothing had happened, but as if *everything* had happened.

Chapter Twenty-One – Once Upon a Time...

Our initials were thrown together in gold calligraphy. The 'C' and 'J' making their own shape as they combined. They slotted neatly together as the swirls of the ink branched out and off to the side. It would have made my heart stop at one time, to see our names so closely entwined. We had been invited to a financiers' ball, an event that Charlie's work held every year in the City but this was the first time I had been invited. As I fingered the shiny, gold engraving and stuck it to the fridge using a red chili fridge magnet, I couldn't help but feel apprehensive. It had started as only a tiny feeling; a small bean of suspicion that had been planted in my mind a few weeks ago but now had somehow grown into a stalk of certainty. I'd tried to stifle it and thrown myself into work, building a solid foundation of my own person, should history again repeat itself. It was a strange way to live, always feeling on the outskirts of your own life.

It was a modern-day fairytale, although I hadn't heard from Prince Charming for days; messages were read but not replied to, telephone calls were made but left unanswered. He'd gone through these periods before, something that I'd grown to accept, but this time, it was different. Thanks to a steely determination on my part, I now had a safety net: a job, a place to go to, a part of my life where he didn't exist.

It was Saturday night and Amber was holding me hostage over drinks at a bar in Shoreditch, a cocktail sanctuary for the young and carefree in the heart of East London. She was standing next to me, top to toe in beige. The type of girl who could wear double beige and not look like she was naked from afar and if she did, probably wouldn't care. I, on the other hand, was here to blow off some steam and forget about my current situation. I was now able to relish in the ability to buy my own drinks and even pay for an indulgent taxi-ride home, but it was still a relatively new feeling. I was still getting used to being that girl. There was still a glimmer of optimism surrounding the progress I'd made in the world and although Charlie had been distant during the past few weeks, I couldn't help but fight the feeling that I was slowly losing the will to care.

'It certainly sounds like he's lying,' Amber said, trying to locate her bankcard in her purse, 'and you think he's lying or you wouldn't be asking my opinion.'

I took our drinks from the bar and held her phone while she looked for it.

'I just don't really know what to think, Amber. It doesn't add up. He works late every night, leaves early every morning and to be honest, I've barely seen him in the past three weeks. Yes, I've been working late too but, I don't know, something's different.'

'I don't get it, Jess. I've watched you for the past year going through the whole pretending-to-be-someone-you're-not routine and then you got him and you got the job you wanted, and you still aren't happy? Yeah, he's dark, mysterious with a touch of the bad-boy about him. But you knew this all along.'

She was right. I reached inside my bag to check my phone. Nothing.

'You've done well to last this long,' she said. 'It's hard to keep things together, Jess, really hard. Look at me and Jay.'

I was taken aback. Amber hadn't mentioned Jay since they'd split over two years ago and it was the first time I'd actually seen Amber happily ever after. She picked up her cocktail to take a sip as his name lingered heavily in the air.

'But then again, people do change,' she said, quickly correcting herself. 'Hell, you've come this far, why give up now?'

'I'm not saying I'm ready to end things. I just want to know what's going on. What if it's another girl? He's tied to his phone morning, noon and night and he always comes home later than he says he will. He's invited me to go to some financiers' ball with him next Friday night, but it's hard to talk when you're surrounded by bankers.'

'Wankers?' she said, above the loud music.

'No, bankers,' I said, correcting her.

'Same thing,' she said, shrugging.

On the outside I was fighting for the cause but inside I couldn't avoid the realisation that maybe it all just wasn't worth it.

'They might just be friends or work colleagues,' Amber said. 'Or maybe she's one of those exes who won't go away and you have to be polite so they don't come and piss on your garden. But honestly, Jess, you're starting to sound like his wife: a dangerous territory without a ring on your finger. I'll mention it to Mitch and see what he says…'

'Don't, Amber…' I said, as I followed her back to the table.

But it was too late. The only thing worse than confiding your worst fear to a friend was to read the look on her new boyfriend's face that said I belonged in a loony bin for jealous girlfriends. Amber had only been seeing Mitch for a couple of months. They were still in the first throes of passion and he was likely to side with her for fear of upsetting the apple cart. As they sat together, knee-to-knee, it was apparent I was on their seventh, possibly eighth, date and as a result I thought it best to do the honourable thing and give them at least ten minutes alone.

I escaped to the loos where I could check my phone again and mingle with the other women who inhabited the toilets, preening like exotic birds in an aviary. When women are comfortable in the privacy of such confidential surroundings, there are no limits to the short-term bonds that are formed. There is no more hospitable a crowd, more complimentary or welcoming than the Snow Whites and the Sleeping Beauties of the ladies' bathroom, especially when they've had a cocktail or five with their girlfriends. Their entire world could be falling down around their ears but they would still demonstrate the power of a steady hand to apply their liquid eyeliner in a mirror. It's honest, it's raw and offers a sense of community like no place else. I checked my teeth in the mirror for red lipstick and made my way back down the staircase, carefully navigating the way in five-inch heels.

'She thinks he's cheating on her. What do you think?' Amber blurted out as she reached for a bowl of nuts on the table.

I sat down, still drying my hands on a piece of tissue, adjusting my chair.

Mitch sat back as if taking in the audience before speaking. 'I know you by now, Jess, and you do have the tendency to overreact at times...'

'She does, yes,' Amber chipped in.

This was supposed to be fun drinks on a Saturday night, not a seminar on my personality.

'But if it were me,' he continued, 'I would never stop making the effort. It's definitely important to put that extra time in.'

I smiled, humouring him. He was clearly giving me advice in the hope of being Amber's future long term but, as he would soon learn, it's hard to keep the effort up when real life comes into play; it's not all just sleepovers and cocktails on the weekend. But I still couldn't resist in taking the bait.

'Look, Mitch,' I could hear myself out loud, saying his name like it was a question. 'I'm not talking about effort; it's more a question of monogamy, something I'm not prepared to compromise on.'

'But he lied to you before, didn't he?'

His question hit me like a bullet between the eyes. I shot Amber a glance: she'd told him.

'I'm just saying,' he replied, 'if he wants to, he will. Remember that.'

But what about what I want? I thought, as I looked at the two of them kissing each other for slightly longer than I would usually be comfortable with. I had reached my limit. It was time to go home.

At the crossroads I glanced up at the signs, waiting for

the red man to turn green and I felt my eyes well up, which surprised me. I had been lying to myself for a while, losing myself in the throes of a new job: arriving early, staying late, soaking up the opportunity in the hope of proving my worth, but there was no mistaking one fact: I didn't need him anymore. I wanted him, yes, but I didn't need him. I wiped the uninvited tears from my eyes that had annoyed me by running down my face, ruining my carefully applied eye make-up.

Away from the main road and the glares of passersby, I slipped down a side street where the upheaval of the last few weeks came flooding out. It was happening again. But this time, I didn't need the idea of a man in my life to be dangled in front of me like the top prize – making sure I played my cards right and was the girl he wanted me to be. It was one game too many. In the privacy of a shop doorway, I just finally let it all go.

I battled with the brackets of my fold-out table/makeshift desk and tried to get on with the paperwork laid out in front of me. I had been working at the magazine for four months now and although it was long hours on shoots, it was proving to be the only form of stability in my life.

'Morning, Jess,' Vin said as he arrived in the office.

'Morning,' I said, handing him a coffee.

Our mornings had evolved into a routine like clockwork.

'Can you send me those pictures from the shoot in Camden when you get a minute?' he said, sitting down to his desk.

'Sure. They're on a hard drive in my bag. I finished them at home last night.'

Vin had increased my responsibilities and I was still pinching myself at the fact I was being paid for doing something I would gladly do for free. Having proved myself to be a diligent student, he even listened to my opinion when selecting his final prints. We were operating as a team and the office had become a place I had to drag myself away from to even attempt to retain a semblance of a normal life.

I looked at the clock, shortly after lunch. It was the financiers' ball later that night and I still needed to convince Vin to let me leave an hour early. Charlie had texted me to say he was picking me up at 7 p.m. As I wiped down the whiteboard to signal the end of another week, I pictured the black ball gown waiting for me in my wardrobe.

'Vin, can I talk with you about something?' I said, as he closed his laptop.

'Is it about next Wednesday's shoot, because I think that location is terrific.'

'No,' I said, tentatively, 'it's not about the shoot.'

'What's up, Jess?' he said. I could tell by his face that he was in a good mood.

'Vin,' I said, getting straight to the point. 'I'm so sorry to have to do this and believe me, I know how presumptive this sounds, me sort of still being the new girl and all…'

'What is it?'

'It's just that I'm going to an event with Charlie tonight, a ball,' I said with a hint of embarrassment, 'and I need to talk to him about something beforehand. It's quite important so I was wondering if I could perhaps leave an hour early to give me some time to get ready?'

'Paint your nails, that sort of thing?' he said, teasingly.

'Yeah, something like that,' I said.

He began to tidy his files away on his desk and stood up to put his coat on.

'Jess,' he said, 'why are you asking me like a girl on work experience? This is your job. If you feel you need to leave early, then leave early. You've done some incredible work these past few months and if you think you need personal time, then by all means, take it.'

I stood there, hesitating. In all honesty I wanted to pour myself another cup of coffee and get a head start on the next week's work. But I had already bought the dress and promised Charlie. Something inside me still didn't want to let him down.

'And don't worry about the others, I'll write it off as an hour in lieu so you won't need to bother with it looking like a favour. I know what the gossips around here can be like.'

'Thank you, Vin,' I said as I took down my coat from the peg. 'I appreciate it. I'll see you on Monday.'

'Yeah, don't be late,' he said, smiling.

Two rushed hours later, I stood in front of my mirror in a floor-length black gown, my hair scraped back in a blow-dried ponytail, face painted, primed and ready to go to the ball. If princes did exist, then mine was running thirty minutes late, currently stuck in traffic south of the river. A balmy sheen ran across my forehead as I tried my best to cool down. It was a swift turnaround, but I had made it all the same. As I fastened my necklace and applied one last wipe of lipstick I heard the horn pip from the pavement outside. I looked out of the window and gave him a small wave; maybe I could try and be the girl who ignored the signs, try and be the girl the slipper fit.

We arrived an hour later and drove up the long driveway to the country mansion flanked by fir trees either side. The lights in the car park lit up the partygoers who spilled out through the large open double doors that framed the entrance to the ballroom. Charlie held my hand tightly as we walked towards a large crystal chandelier that hung over the dance floor where a group of Charlie's colleagues had signalled us to join them.

'Jess,' James said, kissing me on both cheeks. 'How are you?'

'Good, thanks,' I said, smiling hard.

'Great turn out, Charlie!' a man wearing a bow tie, shouted as he passed us by.

Charlie nodded to him and let go of my hand. He twisted his cufflinks and pulled down his shirt cuffs, a sign I'd grown to recognise that he was nervous. I reached down and squeezed his hand in support as I searched for a waiter with a fully stocked tray of drinks. From the start, I was out of place, a mismatch, but if all I had to do was show up and laugh heartily at a few jokes to show him I still cared, then that is what I would do.

'I've missed you,' Charlie whispered in my ear as he leaned in to nuzzle my hair.

'I've missed you too,' I said, quietly.

'Sorry for not being around much,' he said, 'work's just been crazy lately.'

'I know,' I said, throwing him a lifeline, 'and I'm sorry that I've had to work so much too. I just need to put in the extra hours until I've settled in.'

He held my hand and kissed the back of it. 'I'm proud of you,' he said, 'and I'll always be here.'

'Charlie…' I went to speak but was cut off by a group of black suits that swarmed back around us.

'Waheey… Rainer. How are things?' a big, plump, blond man squashed tightly inside his suit pushed between us, knocking my champagne as he went. 'Nigel's got some gear out back if you're interested? Looks like this is going to be a pretty crazy night.' He stopped as he noticed me.

'Hi,' he hesitated.

'Ah, not tonight mate,' Charlie said.

'Is this the Mrs?' he said, to Charlie more than me.

'Yeah – this is my girlfriend, Jess,' he said. 'Jess, this is Stu.'

'Pleased to meet you,' he said, holding out his pale, slightly plump hand for me to shake.

It didn't take long for me to realise that the plan for the evening seemed to revolve around taking out our weekly stresses on the bar bill. I could see James struggle through the crowds, heading our way with two double shots of tequila. My mouth winced.

'We're going to miss you, Charlie, you bastard,' Brian said, handing them to us before violently slapping him on the back. Charlie's smile faded as he saw my confusion.

'Are you leaving your job?' I said quietly, assuming it would be yet another one of my comments missed.

'Yeah, he's off to greener pastures,' James said. 'Look at you two,' he laughed. 'Inseparable.'

Brian walked away from his bombshell remark, leaving me to get splattered with the debris.

'Maybe we should get some air?' Charlie said.

He took my hand and led me outside, squeezing our way

through the crowds in the doorway. We continued all the way to the car park, my mind racing like a freight train. I was right, was all I could hear myself think, I was right about everything.

'Look, Charlie,' I said, as we reached a grassy verge. 'I'm not sure what all of this is about but maybe you should just be honest. I'm a big girl, I can take it.'

'What do you mean?' he said, turning to me.

'I haven't seen you in weeks. You ignore me when I try and talk to you. You start work early, finish late… so, if you're going to tell me that there's someone else, then you can just tell me. I'll be okay.'

And that's when I noticed, for the first time in weeks he wasn't on his phone, he wasn't distracted by an email or text, he was actually listening to me.

'Is that what you think?' he said.

'Well, what am I supposed to think?'

'Jess, I love you.' He loosened his tie and undid his top button. 'But you're right, there is something. I just didn't want to tell you sitting here, on a wall, in a car park.'

I looked at him as he gathered his thoughts as I fought the lump in the back of my throat. It was only then that I knew. I didn't want to lose him.

'Well, you know, Giles and Morgan were in trouble at the start of last year, don't you?'

I nodded, my eyes still fixed on him.

'And how they gave me the opportunity to get the company back on track. By the end, I'd reduced their plummeting figures quite dramatically.'

'Charlie,' I said, calmly, 'this is all work talk, what does it have to do with us? Wasn't that over a year ago now?'

'Around the time we split up,' he said.

'I see.' I could see the timeline of events falling into place in my mind. The reason for our break-up wasn't his unhappiness, as I had predicted. It was a far more complicated reason than that.

'I sold off half of the shares at a premium rate and then bought them back cheaply once our stock price had plummeted. It was the only way to get the job done.'

'Isn't that illegal?' I said.

'It's not illegal, Jess. It's unethical… at most.'

It might have taken twelve months but there on a wall in a car park, the past was starting to make sense.

'So what now?' I said, confused.

'They want me to do the same in New York.'

I could slowly feel my heart begin to pound inside my tight dress. 'You're moving to New York?'

'The office were putting pressure on me to make a decision but I was just waiting for the right time…'

'But you *have* made the decision, haven't you?' I said.

He nodded.

'And when were you going to tell me?'

'Well, I didn't want to tell you like this… standing out here…'

'When were you going to tell me, Charlie?' I could feel my voice rise.

'You've got it wrong, Jess.'

'You lied to me, Charlie. You told me that you wanted to be here with me.' I could feel my breath getting tighter by the second.

'I'm sorry,' he said.

'So why did you bring me here and make me go through all this if you knew that you were leaving?'

'Jess, can you let me speak, please...'

'What more do you want from me, Charlie?'

He took hold of my hand and I looked into his eyes that were wide and expectant. 'I want you to come with me, Jess,' he said, still holding my hand. 'I want you to come *with me*.'

I'd hung onto every word that had been fed to me through fantasy, recalling the countless stories I'd been told as a five-year-old girl. In folklore where unicorns grazed and dragons hid in caves, I imagined a perfect world, a house made of gingerbread and a handsome prince to catch me should I fall. I'd been fed the concept for as long as I could remember, giving up all logic and reason for the dangerous thrill of *believing*. But in a different tale, depicting the realities of *real life*, in usually a very complex situation, it seemed there was now a new story: the little girl who had an invitation to the financiers' ball, who had an inkling she was being lied to but was left with a question of earth-shattering proportions: a choice between love and financial independence. They hadn't made that into a children's tale yet; perhaps it would prevent young girls from believing.

Chapter Twenty-Two – Pushing Through Purgatory

Things in life that are sent to test you:
Slow walkers on a crowded pavement.
Noisy eaters in a quiet restaurant.
Not enough time to sleep.
Not enough money to eat.
Broken minds.
Broken hearts.

When a jury is asked to come to a verdict, there are usually twelve of them, and they have a spread of evidence laid out before them to guide them towards a final decision. I, on the other hand, had no one to deliberate with. I was on my own. Scared to tell others for fear that their reaction might cloud my judgment, I'd borne the burden of the news alone over the days that followed and I was still no clearer in reaching a decision.

As I heard the familiar chatter coming from the kitchen, I smiled safe in the knowledge that certain things, for now, remained exactly the same. It was barely light and my limbs lay heavy under the warmth of the duvet as I rolled over into the sheets that had grown too comfortable. I'd spent a large portion of the night wide-awake, trying to conceive of a way in which things could work. But each potential decision spelled out an ending: a resignation from my job, my relationship or the concept of home that I had only just been introduced to. Instead I would start the day as usual. Eat Breakfast. Get dressed. Go for a run. Maybe. Not think.

The smell of scrambled eggs, fresh coffee and petty arguments hit me as I walked into the kitchen. Amber was sitting in her dressing gown, flicking through a magazine as Charlie stood over the cooker wafting the smoke from a pan of eggs.

'Morning, beautiful,' he said as I sat down across from Amber.

'Jess, please tell him that the pan is mine and if he burns it, he can buy me a new one.'

'Charlie, if you burn the pan, again, then this time you need to buy her a new one,' I said, trying to stay impartial. She shook her head dismissively.

'So, what's the plan for today, Amber?' I could see her itching for an argument with Charlie, so I tried my best to keep her distracted.

'I'm going to meet with a man about running some traffic through my new website,' she said, 'and then off to the bank for a meeting. Why, what are you doing?'

'Work,' I said, putting my phone in my bag. 'And if we don't get a move on, we'll both be late. Charlie!' I shouted as he rinsed the pan in the sink, a hiss of steam coming from it.

Amber rolled her eyes before going back to her magazine.

'What?' I asked, defensively.

'It's like you're married.'

Charlie had wanted me to tell her yesterday, and the day before that, but it was a conversation that could only begin once I knew how to finish it.

'Amber, I was thinking, and feel free to say no if you want to...'

'I don't like the sound of this already,' she said into her coffee cup.

'Maybe the three of us could have dinner with Mitch? I want to get to know him more before...'

'. . . you move to the other side of the world,' Charlie said, finishing my sentence to Amber's confusion. Luckily the comment was brushed off.

'Okay, I'll see what he says,' she said. 'I know what you're like when you get a bee in your bonnet. What about tonight?'

'Works for me,' I said eagerly, as Charlie pretended he couldn't hear us. 'Works for him too – you're free tonight, aren't you? To meet Mitch?'

'My excitement is at fever pitch,' he said, deadpan.

'Just don't make it into a big thing,' Amber said. 'Just a casual dinner... very low maintenance...'

'Low maintenance?' Charlie laughed. 'Involving Jess?'

'Why don't we go to that new clean-eating place?' I said, 'the one with the blue lampshades off Wardour Street?'

'Fine by me,' Amber said.

'Clean-eating?' Charlie mouthed, before seeing that I was not amused. 'Fine, I'll have a steak or something before I meet you. Come on Jess, we'd better go, it's almost 7.30.'

I kissed Amber on the top of her head. 'See you later!' I said as I left.

Outside on the concrete steps, things were definitely getting a lot warmer. I took a big breath of fresh air and exhaled it slowly. It was a clear sign that spring was here.

'So have you given it any more thought?' Charlie said, landing on a question I had so far been avoiding.

I hesitated, knowing I needed to be slightly diplomatic with my words. 'It's just a difficult situation at the moment,' I said. 'What with Marlowe and everything, I can't exactly leave her without knowing she'll be okay.'

'I know it's a difficult situation, Jess, but I'm not asking you to move to the moon. It's a once in a lifetime opportunity for us.'

'And it's also a massive decision that you're asking of me. I just need a bit longer to think about it, that's all.'

'Well, time's passing,' he said, as we reached the point where we went our separate ways.

'I know it is,' I said, kissing him goodbye.

I arrived at my desk at 8.05 a.m. I was retouching the latest shoot when Vin arrived: it was a beauty piece on face creams for which Vin had taken pictures of models with their faces being hit with white liquid. I counted them out in my head slowly as I heard the sound of Vin approach the office.

'Morning,' I said, as he burst through the door with four rolls of paper.

'What time did you get here?' he said.

'Around eight. I did something to the shots from the face cream launch. It's a bit different but I hope you like it.'

He leaned over my shoulder to get a closer look.

'And I saved a copy of the originals just in case you hate it…'
I said, double-clicking each one to enlarge it on the screen.

I tried to gauge some sort of reaction but he continued to stand there in silence. As what would usually happen in this instance, I filled the void by talking.

'I thought they would look more effective in black and white and by increasing the exposure with the spotlight from above hitting the cream, it makes it glossier, cleaner…' I trailed off, still waiting for his verdict.

'Good job, Jess,' he said, breaking into a smile. For the first time, I caught a glimpse of his teeth, which were tobacco-stained and crooked. 'Run a print off and I'll take them to Rebecca and see what she thinks.'

I stared cautiously at the work in front of me. Rebecca was the editor of the magazine and someone who I had only ever stared at from afar in the lift. I pressed 'print' and quickly made my way to the machine outside to wait for the copies.

'Just so you know,' Vin said, as I made my way out of the door, 'we're having the people upstairs look into getting you a space of your own somewhere. We're really impressed with the work you did on the pictures from the last issue.'

'My own office?' I said, surprised.

'Not really, Jess,' he said, bringing me quickly back down to earth. 'Might be more like converting the paper cupboard into a little space for you next door. What are you doing for lunch? Fancy grabbing me a sandwich?'

'Sure,' I said, nervously twiddling three small memory cards in my hands. I wondered if my face showed any of the questions going through my mind. 'I'll nip out at twelve.'

For the remainder of the morning I waited for the ruling. The jury had been out for the past two hours and I hadn't seen Vin since he left to have a meeting with the magazine's editor. As I looked over at his large wooden desk surrounded by piles of reference books, I couldn't help but picture what it would be like to be in his shoes; for people to have enough trust in your vision to let you call the shots.

Before I knew it I was clutching an egg mayonnaise sandwich sitting neatly on a cold bench in the public square at the end of the road. A paper bag containing a beef and mustard baguette and a packet of cheese and onion crisps for Vin sat at my feet. Somehow, buried beneath the will to forget about it all, I had to weigh up the decision. And it wasn't just about work. It was about my life. For the past year I had built up some semblance of a home, a group of friends, a career. It was everything I knew: it was *me*.

And then I thought about him, or rather, life without him. It was the first time I'd allowed myself to think about it. For the past few weeks I had been hiding behind Marlowe, behind humour, behind anything that would give me more time to arrive at a decision.

Without him, what would any of this mean? He was the person I rang when something went right, or wrong, the one who would put himself forwards to bravely sample my cooking or laugh at a joke that wasn't very funny. He was on my team. But either way, whichever choice I made, I was going to lose either my job or my relationship. A new job was nothing in the scheme of things, when you compared it to something like falling in love. But if that was the case, then why did it feel like everything?

*

That afternoon, I distracted myself by re-organising the drawers in the left hand side of Vin's desk. I pulled out old highlighters, paper clips, a cereal bar that had gone out of date six months ago and a shatterproof plastic ruler that had shattered. I delved my hand towards the back of the bottom drawer as the end of a drawing pin slipped under my fingernail, piercing the skin.

'Damn it!' I shouted, sucking the droplet of blood before it could seep any further.

'Everything all right?' Vin said, popping his head around the door. He was still clutching half of the beef sandwich that I'd bought for him over an hour ago.

'You know, you really should keep on top of these drawers,' I said, 'it's an Aladdin's cave of crap in there. I just cut myself.'

'Righto, boss,' he said, smiling. 'Well, if you're done giving me a bollocking, I've got something to show you.'

I followed him into the small room next door that was once used as a darkroom for film development. A cobweb hung from the exposed light bulb that swung from the ceiling in the centre of the room. The exposed pipework had gathered dust and the small patch of grey carpet I stood hesitantly upon felt loose beneath my feet.

'Since things went digital,' he said, 'they've used this for storage but… welcome home.' He pulled on the dangling light cord that still turned on a red light bulb outside. 'I know it needs a lick of paint but there's a small window behind those filing cabinets, and once we get those moved and a desk brought in I think it will be grand.'

'Is this for me?' I said, looking around.

'Well, we've got a lot on later this year. I need you to have a decent space to work in. When I showed your images to Rebecca, she loved them. We both think you deserve something of your own.'

'Vin…' I said, hesitantly.

'Yeah…'

'Thank you,' I said, 'window or no window – it's perfect.'

I stood there doing all that I could not to slump to the floor. With my insides crumbling, I watched as he closed the door behind him, leaving me under the buzzing of a flickering fire exit light. I looked out of the small window partially covered by the filling cabinet and rested my head against the silver steel doors. Right there, listening to the sounds of the city below, I was caught between matters of the heart and the head; making the decision between a relationship or a career, love or a promotion, a living or a life.

I arrived at the restaurant to see Amber and Mitch talking intimately across the table. He said something under his breath which made her roar with laughter, before hitting him sharply, and I almost didn't want to disturb them.

'Jess!' Amber shouted as she saw me.

I waved and shimmied my way through the tightly packed tables.

'What do you think about Ko Lipe?' Amber said, expecting me to know what she meant.

'Where?' I said, sitting down.

'Ko Lipe,' Mitch said, as if saying it twice would make a difference.

'It's an island in Thailand,' Amber explained, still scrolling through a holiday website on her phone. 'Mitch was just saying how we should get away for a few days before the summer rush hits.'

He leaned over her shoulder to get closer to the screen.

'They turn the electricity off at midnight,' he said, proudly.

'And that's a good thing?' I asked, tearing into a piece of bread.

'I think so,' he replied. 'Are you and Charlie thinking of going away? Actually, why don't you come with us?'

'Yeah, why not!' Amber said, eagerly.

'I think Charlie would probably need electricity. Sorry,' I said, with one eye on the door of the restaurant.

'Speaking of which, where is he?' Amber asked, 'I'm starving.'

I looked down at my watch and could see that he was over half an hour late. I checked my phone: no messages.

'Let's order some starters,' I said. 'I'm starving too.'

It was typical Charlie. The odds were that he had forgotten where we were meeting and was probably in the back of a cab trying to decipher from a string of texts exactly where he was supposed to be. As a phone signal was completely absent in the restaurant, I made my way outside to give him a quick courtesy call. I shivered standing in the pavement and put my phone to my ear trying to get past the short rings.

'Hi,' I said, as he answered, 'just so you know we have a table at the back and there's no phone signal so perhaps ring the restaurant itself if you get lost, saves me spending half the night out here on the pavement.' I laughed.

'What? Where are you?' he said from the end of the phone.

'I'm at the restaurant with Amber and Mitch. I texted you about it this afternoon?'

There was silence on the end of the phone.

'Let me guess, you forgot,' I said, rolling my eyes. 'Well, get over here now and you'll probably make it in time for mains. I mean, I can wait if you won't take too long only, well, everybody's starving.'

'Jess…' he said. 'I'm not going to be able to make it.'

This time, I was the one who was silent.

'Why not?' I said, quietly.

'I'm sorry, Jess. I'll make it up to you. I promise.'

Through the window I saw Amber and Mitch sitting before two untouched starters.

'Okay,' I said, 'not to worry, I'll see you later tonight maybe.'

'I miss you,' he said as I hung up the phone.

Although his withdrawal wasn't exactly a bolt from the blue, and despite the fact that it would have been a regular occurrence less than a year ago, I had grown to believe that things had changed. But as I heard the sound of my heels clicking against the hard wood floor as I made the slow walk back to the table, I realised the actuality of the situation. It was all so unsurprising. After all, it wasn't Charlie's behaviour that had changed, but rather the way I was reacting to it. Gone were the needy text messages seeking constant reassurance, gone were the million phone calls, the anger followed by disappointment. They had all been replaced by acceptance. It seemed that without me providing the wall at which he threw his excuses, he was unable to do just that: he was unable to let me down again. The only behaviour to have changed that night was mine.

I wandered over towards an expectant Amber and Mitch.

'There'll only be the three of us,' I said to the waitress as she filled our glasses with wine. 'Looks like Charlie's not coming.'

'He's not coming?' Amber said.

I shook my head as I sipped my wine. I could feel her eyes on me as I crossed my legs under the table.

'So how's work, anyway?' I asked. 'All things on track with the business?'

'Not really,' she said, in an unexpected U-turn to the conversation. 'I just came here from the bank, actually...'

'How was it?'

'Not good, Jess. It seems that the business isn't really taking off as I expected. There are a lot more overheads than I had planned that, long story short, my incomings aren't funding.'

Mitch reached his arm around her.

'Can't you get investors to help you?' I said.

'No. That's the reason I went to the bank, but until I show at least twelve months' profit, no one is going to look twice at me. It's all gone a bit tits up really.'

'They will, Amber,' I said, trying to lift her spirits. 'Just give it time. I scrolled through the website the other day, it looks amazing. I even bought a make-up bag.'

She smiled at me from across the table and rested her head on her hand.

'But there is a silver lining in all of this,' Mitch said, pulling up the sleeves of his black jumper.

His behaviour implied that he was on the cusp of announcing some big news.

'Mitch has asked me to move in with him,' Amber said. 'And I said yes.'

'In Ruislip?' I said, knowing full well she hated it there.

'God no,' she said, as Mitch watched us exchange glances. 'I said I would like to live with him... but not in Ruislip. So we're moving somewhere south of the river, near Sean actually.'

'That's great news,' I said, still having to remind myself that Amber was in a serious relationship.

'And it'll give you the chance to save some funds until the business gets itself going again,' Mitch said, reassuring her.

'Do you mind?' Amber asked, scrunching her nose.

'Not at all!' I said, knowing that at this stage it would be a bit rich of me to feign disappointment in her.

After Mitch had left to use the gents, Amber was finally given her opportunity to interrogate me with the questions she'd been sat on for the past half hour.

'So Charlie's a no-show,' she said, rolling her eyes.

'Yeah,' I said, too tired to reel off excuses. 'Go on, let rip. Just say what you have to say...'

'He's unreliable,' she said, bluntly.

'Amber, I have to tell you something.'

She lowered her wine glass. She wasn't the only one with some big news.

'Charlie's asked me to move to New York with him.'

I watched her reaction as her eyes sharpened, trying to come to terms with the news I had just delivered.

'What? When? How?' she said, confused.

'He's been offered a job out there and, well, he wants me to go with him. Just keep it to yourself as I haven't made up my mind yet. And, as you know, I'm not good with too many opinions clouding my head.'

'New York, Jess, what the hell?'

'I know,' I said. 'I know it's a big decision.'

'Well, what are you going to do when this happens in New York? Sit and have dinner by yourself?'

'I don't know, Amber, don't start.'

'Sorry to interrupt,' Mitch said, sitting back down at the table. 'What have I missed?'

'Charlie's got a new job,' Amber said, as I looked at her, praying she would end the news there.

'That's great!' he said. 'Isn't it?'

'Yeah, it's great. So when are you guys moving to the river?' I said.

'We're thinking sometime in June.' Mitch's eyes suddenly diverted to the restaurant door. 'Here he is!' he said, getting to his feet. 'Thought you couldn't make it?'

I turned around to see Charlie, shirt open at the collar, hair flopped to the side.

'I'm sorry,' he said, smiling. 'Meeting ran over…'

He slid under the table and leaned in to kiss me.

'Well done on the new job, mate,' Mitch said. 'I'm chuffed for you.'

'Thanks, mate. I didn't want to be a complete let down,' he said quietly in my ear.

'You're not a let down…' I said. 'You're not a let down at all.'

His hand over mine sitting in the centre of my lap, drew my attention to what he represented; my elbow, followed my wrist, which followed my hand to join his fingers – all laying half a foot away from a quietly beating heart.

'Put your hand in my pocket,' Charlie said, smiling.

'Not a chance!' I said, hitting his arm.

'I'm being serious, Jess, put your hand in my pocket.'

I slipped my hand into his jacket pocket and could feel a set of cold, metal keys.

'I picked them up today. We're almost there, my darling.'

I watched across the table as Amber talked to Mitch about their new home, the girl who was once *my* home. Sliding from purgatory and on towards the future, I had somehow found my answer.

Chapter Twenty-Three – Seeds of Change

There is a certain safety in waiting for the right time, the right circumstances, the right number in your bank account, the right dress size. But in a decision caught between the ambiguity of a dream and the purpose of what is real, it is important to look to *who* is actually there, *what* is actually there and *how* you're going to strive for that destination called happiness. Sometimes our present inadvertently becomes our future and I had chosen to focus on what was right there in front of me rather than the concept of what might be. I had chosen what was real.

Once I got to my desk I saw that Vin had signed off the photographs from my last shoot and so I was able to begin planning the next one. I pulled open my notebook and started picking out possible locations. I searched the Internet for the next forty-five minutes, scouring everything from manor houses to private beaches along the coves of southern England but it all now felt like a distraction from something far bigger that was waiting in the wings for me. My mind struggled to focus, so I turned to procrastination instead, rearranging my pencil pot, trying to find my strawberry lip balm, then photocopying some papers with which to begin work on my storyboard. I drew six large boxes across the centre of the page and reached over to retrieve a black marker pen from inside my desk drawer.

'How's it going in here?' Vin said, smiling. 'Jess, I was thinking you could help me plan the editorials for Fashion Week? It's not until September but I want to get a jump on a few end of year projects. What do you think?'

'Sure,' I said as he walked off. 'Wait, Vin... no,' I said, quickly standing up from my chair.

'What's the problem?'

'Any chance I could talk to you at some point today?'

'Yeah, 'course,' he said, chirpily. 'Is this a standing in my office type of chat or let's sit down over lunch type of thing?'

'The latter,' I said.

'Well, why don't we meet downstairs at 1.30 p.m.? We can get some lunch.'

'Thanks,' I said, with a nervous smile. 'I'll see you down at reception.'

I sat back down at my desk and continued to fill in the boxes. As I drew out the different shapes in thick black lines, I remembered briefly the days I spent doing this for Cathy. Looking through her archives of pictures, I would arrange her work in a similar way. I had worked so hard to get here over the past twelve months, and still couldn't quite believe that it would all soon be changing.

Vin met me at 1.30 p.m. prompt for a meeting I had been dreading all morning. As we passed from the reception area to the pavement outside I hastily suggested a salad bar around the corner and led him to a small table for two by the window.

As he read the menu I searched his face for any indication that he knew what I was about to do.

'You're acting weird,' he said to me without looking up.

'Sorry,' I said, perusing the white card for a salad. But I couldn't eat. I couldn't even look at the options.

'I'll just have the small Caesar salad,' I said to the waitress.

'Bread?' she asked.

I shook my head. Vin followed by ordering a quinoa and avocado salad and we both watched as the waitress left us alone.

'Okay,' he said, 'something's wrong: just a salad? No bread? Jess, I've seen you eat three slices just for breakfast.'

'Vin,' I began, before fidgeting in my chair.

'Jessica,' he responded mockingly, his husky voice accentuated.

'I don't want this to come out the wrong way, and I don't want it to seem in any way that I'm ungrateful…'

'Oh I get it…' he said, cutting me off.

I stopped talking immediately. Was it that obvious?

'You want a pay rise? That's what this is all about. Well, to be honest, Jess you didn't have to take me out for lunch to ask that. We could have just spoken about it back in the office.'

'It's not a pay rise,' I said. 'Vin, I'm leaving.'

I looked at him for a reaction, feeling the sense of discomfort rise around my flushed throat.

'You're leaving?' he said. 'You got another job?'

'No, not exactly, I'm moving to New York with Charlie.'

I couldn't have felt like less of a disappointment. For the first time with Vin, I'd lost all words.

'That's a shame,' he said, rubbing his short beard. 'That's

a real shame, Jess. You know I was really pushing for you to make progress here…'

'I know you were, Vin. And I'm sorry.'

He rubbed his hands across his face and exhaled deeply. 'Okay, well, thanks for letting me know, I guess. If you want I've got a few contacts in the magazine world over there that I can look up? But you'll need a working visa. Do you have one?'

I nodded. 'Well, not yet but Charlie's work are sorting it.'

'Of course they are… golden boy, eh? Fuck me…'

We both grinned, which turned into shared laughter.

'Thanks, Vin,' I said, softly. 'Thank you for giving me this opportunity.'

He looked down as our meals arrived: a selection of leaves, edible flowers and green herbs. His expression changed instantly.

'No offence, Jess, but now we've got the convo out of the way, any chance I can go and get a full English or something? I can't last the afternoon on grass clippings.'

I laughed and nodded. 'Go!' I said, 'I'll see you back upstairs.'

I sat there in the café as the waitress came back over. 'Was everything okay?' she said, noticing the two untouched plates.

'Everything was fine,' I said, collecting my belongings.

And it was fine. It wasn't brilliant. But it wasn't the worst either: it was *fine*. I spent the remainder of the afternoon pulling down images from the wall in preparation for the next project. I ran my hand across the cream, painted plaster dotted with stray Blu-Tack, and began measuring up for the new ones: mostly from Vin's collection, some from the archives.

Later that afternoon I was given a black office chair on

wheels from the resource department and created a makeshift bookshelf from a stack of crates pushed aside in the corner of the room. I stood in the doorway to take in my progress. It certainly didn't have the grandeur of Vin's office but it was definitely my own space, if only it wasn't so temporary.

I picked up my bag and turned off the light bulb, which still hung bare in the centre of the room. Usually my exit had a hint of relief, the ending of another working day – a chance to relax before the start of a new one. But today it was tinged with sadness. I decided to take the stairs down to the ground floor, pausing to sit on the top step to change my work shoes into trainers. I looked down through the gap in the railings to the floors below, cascading metal in a cold, hollow stairwell. I felt empty.

I had arranged to meet Marlowe after work under the street sign on Carnaby Street. Unusually for an activity after working, I arrived on time and could see her white blonde hair bouncing above the shoppers in the distance.

'Sorry!' she said, catching her breath. 'Tube was a bloody nightmare. I've come from my parents' in Chelsea, which is a nightmare to get to on public transport, but never mind... here now!'

'Fancy a coffee?' I said.

'Yes,' she said, 'but can we get it to go? I want to have a quick look at the make-up counter in Selfridge's and it always gets busy late afternoon...'

Armed with two double shot, tall, skinny cappuccinos, we walked down the wide pavement together, navigating our way through the people. It was busy on both sides of the pavement, filled with suits in a rush, dawdling tourists and teenagers, lingering on their way home from school.

'Thank you for coming all this way to meet me,' I said, linking my arm through hers.

'You're welcome. Any excuse to get out of the house. How is everything? You said you wanted to talk.'

'Things are good,' I said. 'More importantly, how are you?'

'Oh, I'm getting there,' she said, looking out at the pavement ahead. 'I don't know, after everything that happened, I'm just sort of cruising through normality now. Know what I mean?'

I nodded heavily. 'Yep, normality's pretty good sometimes.'

'As for George, he thinks that everything should be fine now, pleads that it's over, begs me to forgive him...'

'And have you?'

'In all honesty, Jess, I don't think I care enough to stay mad at him. That's pretty sad, isn't it: my husband had an affair and I don't care enough to even be angry. Can I tell you something that makes me sound like a completely bad person?'

'Fire away...'

'I'm just a lot happier without him. Is that terrible?'

'No, Mars, that's not terrible,' I said. 'In light of what's happened, I'd say that's actually pretty reasonable. But listen, I have some news too. Charlie has been offered a job in New York and I'm going to be moving there with him for, well, the foreseeable future really.'

She stopped walking and turned to face me.

'Wow,' she said. 'That's some pretty big news.'

'But before I sort the specifics, I need to know that you'll

316

be okay if I go, because if you need me here I can stay. I can even delay going out there and join him a bit later. That would be no problem.'

'Jess,' she said as she put her arm around me. 'Don't worry about me. For the first time in a long while, I feel like things are making progress. So please, don't delay your life just for me. Go with him and be happy.'

'I just need to know that you'll be all right, that's all.'

'And I will be. I am.'

'Looks like I've run out of excuses then…' I said, laughing.

'Jess, I'm sorry I let you down.'

'No Mars, I'm sorry I let *you* down,' I said as I hugged her tightly.

I put my arm through hers as we continued our walk through Oxford Street. Side-by-side, with our heads down against the wind, in a desperate search of a make-up counter where we could fix the mascara that had fallen down our faces.

Still wearing my work clothes and carrying a bottle of Côtes du Rhône, I arrived at Sean's studio at seven-thirty. I knocked three times on the wooden door and stood back, waiting for some sign of life. A few minutes later, a sharp buzz signalled my entrance. A beautiful, blonde girl, who I hadn't seen before, smiled as I walked through to reception. She took off her headset and laid it down on the pad of paper in front of her.

'Can I help you?' she said, politely.

'I'm here to see Sean. I think he's still in the studio.'

'Yes, that's right – studio four,' she said, pointing to the lift. As the doors to the lift opened I could see him through the glass wall, alone at a desk, surrounded by several ring binders and three mannequins. He was deep in concentration, lost in his own world. I pushed the door lightly and crept in trying not to disturb him.

'Jess…' he said. 'Thanks for coming all this way to see me.'

'Fancy a glass of red?' I said, tiptoeing in. 'Before you get too excited, it was £4.99 from the off-licence, I'm sorry, I'm a terrible friend.'

He looked up from the desk and smiled. I reached in my coat pocket to retrieve the bottle opener I'd borrowed from work's kitchen and sliced the foil top cleanly open.

'Jess, I have some news,' he said. 'Only I need to tell you before it spills out and I don't think I can keep it in any longer.'

'Me too,' I said, smiling.

'You go first,' he said, sharply.

'No, you…' I said, sitting down.

'It's really not a big deal, but me and Henry, well, we're engaged.'

I stood there open-mouthed as he took the wine bottle from me.

'Are you serious?' I said. 'When? How?'

'Henry proposed to me this morning when we were getting ready for work. And I said yes.'

'I can't believe it, Sean. That's fantastic news, Sean, I'm so pleased!' I reached out to pull him into me.

'Now, don't go making a big deal out of it. It's just some news that we want to keep low-key. That's all.'

'I'm really happy for you, Sean,' I said, smiling.

'So what about you? Are you getting promoted? Preggers?'

I shook my head.

'Well, spit it out, Jess. If we're both engaged you can't just leave me here hanging.'

'Engaged?' I said, smirking. 'Why on earth would you think I was engaged?'

'Because you said you had some big news. Obviously my first thought was that you had split up but you came in smiling so…'

'Christ no, I'm not engaged. Charlie's been offered a job in New York.'

Sean looked at me before taking a deep breath. 'And…'

'I'm going with him.'

He put down his wine and wiped his mouth on the back of his hand. 'You're sure this is what you want?'

I nodded.

'Then I think it's a fantastic idea. Honestly, Jess, I'm thrilled for you.'

He topped up our wine glasses that were already full and held mine out for me to take from him.

'Thank you, Seany,' I said, quietly. 'That means a lot to me.'

'So you'll come back for the wedding, right?' he said, taking a sip. 'You're not going to be one of those Brits that moves and develops an American twang.'

'Of course not,' I said, grinning. 'Sean,' I hesitated, 'you're not doubtful or bothered that I'm going with him, are you? You're honestly happy?'

'Babes, I'm an incredibly selfish person and of course I want you to stay, but trust me, you'll regret it if you don't spend the next few years with the person you love. Just make sure you come back for the wedding, okay.'

'I will. I'll have to if I'm maid of honour. Now, I know Amber will want to be centre-stage but you have to be honest with yourself, I think I'd be better at the job.'

'I'll hold a casting,' Sean said, reaching around my shoulder. 'Now pass me that bottle of wine.'

I arrived home just as Amber was putting the kettle on and sat down at the kitchen table, slowly massaging my neck before breaking into a yawn.

'You look knackered,' she said, bluntly. 'Go and get in the shower and I'll make us a cuppa.'

I went into the bathroom and ran a hot shower. I could feel the water beating down on me, pummelling my back as I stood beneath it. My bright red hands tingled as I reached for a towel, wrapping it around me as I took a moment to breath, perched on the edge of the bath. After forcing myself to open the door and brave the cold outside, I towel-dried my hair and walked into the living room wearing Amber's large cream woollen jumper. It was the jumper that had seen us through illness and break-ups, long days and short ones. It had seen us both through lost jobs, heartbreaks and hangovers.

'So you heard from Sean?' she said, tucking her legs beneath her against the edge of the sofa.

'Yeah, can you believe it?' I said, sitting down at the other end, like two bookends propping the sides up.

'Jess. About the move, are you sure you don't mind?'

'Of course not – I don't think I'm in a position to mind.'

'Don't tell me you're going with him…'

'I am, yes,' I said defiantly. 'Please don't start…'

'Jess, you can't. What about your job?'

'It's a job, Amber, it's just a job.'

'But how? Jess, you can't give up your life for him.'

'Who said anything about giving up my life?'

'Oh, come on, it will be just the same old stuff but in a new location. Him at the office and you eating dinner on your own…'

'Well, I've thought of it more as starting something new: I'll get a new job and live in a new home.'

'Oh, you'll just stroll into a photography job in New York, will you?'

'Okay, now you're starting to doubt me, Amber, and, believe me, I do that enough myself already so please, right now, just be a friend.'

'You mean this, don't you?'

'Of course I do.'

'This is crazy!' she said, half laughing, half lost for words. 'Give me one reason why this is such a good idea.'

'No,' I said, calmly. 'I don't need to. Why must I offer an explanation for every single little thing that I do. I would like you to support me, Amber… but I don't need you to.'

We sat there in the weight of what had been said.

'I'm sorry, Jess,' she said. 'I shouldn't have flown off the handle. Obviously, I'm happy for you and obviously I want you to stay. But you love him. And he loves you too because, believe me, Jess, neither of you would still be putting yourselves through this if you didn't. It seems to be the only thing that makes you both stick.'

Through all the frustration, I suddenly realised she was right.

'Amber...'

'What?' she replied, pushing her cold feet under my legs to warm them.

'You talk a lot of sense sometimes.'

She reached out gently to play with a loose thread on my jumper, twirling the cotton in between her fingers.

'It's all about to change, isn't it?' she said.

'You know what, Amber, I think it already has.'

I looked over at my friend, my partner in crime, my comrade. And if I'd learned one thing about relationships, romantic or otherwise, it was that the evolution was exactly the same...

First you need to plant it, and then you watch it grow...

Chapter Twenty-Four – Seek Happy Nights to Happy Days

A pendulum was swinging straight through our world, measuring the passage of time before a new phase would take over. Endless anticipation: days that turned into nights, nights turned back into days. It was a sign that we had quite possibly succeeded in the unimaginable: we'd built a happy life together, just as friends.

After a morning of procrastinating, in a half-hearted attempt to gradually pack up some boxes, I had been left sprinting through the crossroads outside Euston Station. It was the launch of Sean's first menswear collection as Jack Saunders' head designer and we were all invited to witness his debut show for them. As I ran down the escalator towards the Victoria line, out of breath and overheated, I could feel my hair damp on the back of my neck just as the tube doors closed behind me. I had arranged to meet Amber outside the venue and although it was only a short walk from the station, my four-inch heels were beginning to test me.

'Sorry I'm late,' I shouted to Amber, who stood in a grey shift dress on the phone to a potential client. I waited for her to finish, fighting to close my clutch bag in a tangle of lip-gloss, hair ties, chewing gum and bankcards.

For a short time, the imminent finality of goodbye could be forgotten, pushed to the back of our hearts and minds because on this night, we were going to celebrate. It was the dawn of a new era for all of us and in this newly designed trajectory, we had given ourselves up to a night filled with love, denial and happiness: a wave of feeling that defied the day that was going to inevitably happen, where our hearts could take over heads and love could triumph sadness.

'Here's your pass,' Amber said, putting her phone back in her bag. She handed me a plastic slip on a piece of rope: our backstage ticket to inside Sean's world.

'So did this place used to be a church?' I said, as we walked through an old rose garden hemmed in by a black iron fence.

'Isn't it beautiful...' she said, gazing up at the old stone architecture.

'Have you spoken to Sean today? How's he doing? Is he nervous?'

'Nah, he's fine,' she said, gliding past the red rope, 'he's going to be absolutely fine.'

We stood in a huddle backstage, patiently waiting for the show to begin. Sandwiched between Amber and Henry I looked down through the sheer white curtain as the collective chatter of voices fell silent. The lights dimmed as I held my breath, chewing on a piece of gum that had long ago lost its flavour. I closed my eyes as a loud, heavy bass ripped through the open space.

As the first model took his first stride onto the walkway, I could feel my heart beating in my mouth, seemingly pulsating to the sound of the music. In a spectacular vision of what life looked like through Sean's eyes, the models filed out one by one. I peeked through the curtain at the front row, a strip of young men, caught up in taking pictures for social media. Amber's eyes glistened in the orange haze. A sudden surge of pride crossed both of our faces – he'd done it.

As the crowd dispersed, we made our way through the models, photographers and make-up artists to find Sean, buried within carnage of congratulations. After posing for photographs with the models against a lit beige wall he came over to us and took a large gulp of my champagne.

'Needed that,' he said, as I watched the beads of sweat drip across his brow.

'That was incredible,' Amber said, kissing him on the cheek.

'Watch your lipstick…' he said, as she rubbed it off. 'I thought it went well, overall. Good press turnout too which is great.'

Sean was never one to overindulge in self-adulation. He kept things succinct and professional, at times, even with us.

'Sorry to interrupt…' A tall man with a grey beard strode over to us and we three stood aside to let him through. 'My name is John Warner and I'm the CEO of Grosvenor Menswear.'

'I know who you are,' Sean said, quickly. 'Thanks so much for coming, I didn't know you'd be here.'

Following the serious look on their faces, myself, Amber and Henry casually stepped away and distracted ourselves by perusing the rack of clothing hanging on the rail next to us; trying to be nonchalant while at the same time straining to listen.

'I'd like to get you in for a meeting to discuss some options,' John said. 'I was really impressed with the collection.'

'That would be perfect,' Sean replied. 'I would love to.'

'Why don't you give my office a call on Monday morning?' he said as he handed Sean a business card. 'And congratulations again, very strong work indeed.'

'Wow,' Sean said. 'I wasn't expecting that.'

'That's fucking epic,' Henry said, kissing him. 'I'm so pleased for you.'

'Hold your horses,' he said, shyly. 'I'm not there yet. And, well, a lot of this is down to you too. You were the one who made sure I ate when I had to work late and you cleaned my flat so that I could sleep in on a weekend.' He stopped for a moment. 'I really couldn't have done this without you.'

Henry lifted Sean's hand that he was holding and kissed it.

'That's all very lovely, but what did he say exactly?' Amber said, getting to the point.

'I have to call him on Monday. Let's just wait and see what happens then, shall we?'

Amber walked me outside to the rose garden where she could catch up on her emails and I could have a ten-minute respite with my shoes off.

'It's bloody perishing – I think *spring*? When did it get so windy?' She turned her back on the wind to pull her hair from her lip-gloss.

Through the window I could see that Sean and Henry had found a moment alone and were laughing together at the pop-up bar.

'I'm so glad they found each another,' I said, smiling.

'I'd stand back or they'll see your nose pressed against the window.'

'Well, what do you think?' I said.

'About what?'

'How it's all turned out for us.'

'I don't know…' she said, taking a deep breath of the cold air before shuddering.

'You do know,' I rebuked, wagging my finger at her. 'You *always* have an opinion.'

'What do you want me to say, Jess? That Sean's blissfully happy and you're leaving us to set up home with a pretentious, knicker-dropping arsehole?'

I laughed from the shock. I couldn't help it. 'Don't hold back on my account,' I said.

'I'm sorry. A pretentious, *former* knicker-dropping arsehole.' She broke into a small grin, which in some way redeemed her.

'Amber, just admit it, you don't like him.'

'I'm going to miss you, that's all,' she said, for the first time looking genuinely upset. 'But in all seriousness, Jess, I wanted to thank you for how you handled me through the… difficult time I had earlier this year. You were a good friend, my only friend really…'

'Amber, you're welcome,' I said with a warm smile. 'Always welcome.'

'No one puts up with me like you do,' she said, with a grin.

'You're right. It's been a tough job. First it was no carbs, then it was sugar-free… then it was only eating food harvested within a mile of here, when we live in Central London!'

'That was a dietary experiment that went wrong…'

'And clogging up our U-bend with your homemade yoghurt…'

'All right – so the roads been a bit… rocky.'

I smiled at her. 'Wouldn't have had it any other way though.'

'Wouldn't have had it any other way,' she agreed.

We made our way back inside where Amber went back to being the girl that didn't care and I followed behind, pretending I wasn't scared of leaving.

'It's been a pretty special night, Seany,' I said, perching myself on the stool next to him, 'and as for him…' I said, pointing across the room to Henry, 'he's pretty special too.'

'You know Grosvenor Fashion is a big deal,' he said nervously. 'I'm actually pretty petrified.'

'I know,' I said, 'but don't go in there feeling the need to prove that to them, just let them see it for themselves.' I rested my head on his shoulder. 'You need to go and mingle with all these people and I need to go home and pack.'

'I know,' he said, briefly stopping for a moment. 'There's an after-party in Knightsbridge if you fancy it, later?' 'One more party for the road, eh?'

I laughed at the familiar look in his eye, the twitch that said he needed a wingman. It was going end up in a landslide from the heights of success to the depths of debauchery – one messy, beautiful landslide.

'I'll go for you,' George shouted to Marlowe from the shower. To our surprise, she had convinced him to join us at the after-party. Standing in their bedroom, in her tights and underwear, she studied her reflection in the full-length mirror. After losing herself for nine months in a depreciating whirlwind, she scooped her hair up into a high ponytail and brushed out the edges of her eyebrows. As she pulled on a red dress that she'd found in the back of the wardrobe, she closed her eyes to the soundtrack of George moaning from inside their en suite shower.

'I mean, I don't mind coming, I really don't,' he said, mid-shampoo, 'but all they talk about are themselves… and then men… and then themselves again: it's all so… unimportant. It's just not really my scene, I suppose.'

Marlowe didn't reply; instead she wiped her hand against the condensation of the mirror thinking about how her 'unimportant friends' were the only thing that had held her together this past year. She walked back into the bedroom and carefully placed her jacket on the bed next to the contents of her handbag.

'Don't you agree?' George continued. 'I honestly don't know how you can enjoy standing in yet another pretentious club buying overpriced drinks while having the eyes of the room on you. Everyone just stares at each other. Quite frankly, it makes me feel uncomfortable.'

Marlowe got up and walked around to her side of the bed. 'You don't have to come with us, darling, if you don't want to.'

She smiled at him as he came into the bedroom, a smile that took all her energy to muster.

'No, I'll come,' he said.

They sat side by side in the back of the taxi as Marlowe watched the lights of the city whizz by. She thought about George, the man sitting next to her, his affairs and her supposed blindness to it.

'George,' she said, boldly and without apology, 'I want a divorce.'

He gave her a look of desperation. 'Sorry, what did you just say?'

'I'm leaving you. I actually made up my mind several weeks ago so I don't know why I've only just got round to telling you. I know about Samantha,' Marlowe said, calmly, 'and how you two have been seeing each other and I've just reached the point of no return really. I'm not even angry, honestly. I genuinely think it's for the best.'

The car jerked to a halt as it pulled up outside the bar. Without looking for his reaction and completely independent in her own train of thought, she got out of the car and slowly walked inside.

I stepped through the crowded bodies on my way back from the toilets and could see that Marlowe was yet to arrive.

'How long shall we wait?' Amber whispered from behind me.

I checked my watch. It was 10 p.m.

'A bit longer, hopefully she'll be here in a minute.'

Sean was talking to Henry on the dance floor and as Amber had cozied back up to Mitch on the sofas, I walked over to Charlie who was waiting for his drink at the bar.

'What are you ordering?' I said, my lips nestled into the back of his neck.

'I thought I'd get a bottle to toast Sean and his engagement,' he said, reaching around my waist.

'I love you, you know that,' I said, as I slowly made my way down his neck. 'And thank you for loving my friends.'

He turned around and kissed me softy on the mouth.

'Pipe down, guys,' Sean said, interrupting us. 'No heavy petting around here.'

'Well, Sean, Henry, congratulations!' Charlie said as he passed back two bottles of champagne and a handful of glasses.

'With this toast, we would officially like to welcome Henry to the family,' Amber said, holding up her glass.

At that point Marlowe ran over with George in tow following directly behind. 'Sorry! Sorry we're late,' she cried. 'Did we miss the speech?'

'No, 'course not,' I said, handing her a glass of champagne.

'You didn't say she was bringing him…' Amber said to me under her breath.

'Shhh,' I replied. 'I know he's a complete dick, but the least we can do is tolerate him for one night. Please be on your best behaviour, Amber. Do it for Sean.'

'I will,' she said, 'Scout's honour.' I laughed as she crudely licked the rim of her champagne glass.

'I was hoping I'd bump into you again,' James said into Marlowe's ear as she leaned across to kiss Charlie. 'I've got something for you back in the office.'

'For me?' she said, smiling.

'I was gifted some original prints from Dianne Cagney as a thank you for my work on the billboards. There's a dusty pink one that's from her latest collection, something… Sahara, I think it's called. Anyway, as soon as I saw it I thought of you.'

'Well, where is it?' she said.

'It's currently bubble-wrapped sitting on my office floor. I'll get a courier to drop it off for you on Monday.'

'Or I could come and get it?' she said, before quickly looking away.

'Whatever works.' James nodded, trying to sound as equally relaxed about the whole thing.

'Mars,' George shouted, 'your mum keeps ringing my phone: take it outside and see what she wants, will you? It might be something to do with Elsa.'

'Thanks again, James,' Marlowe said, as she took the phone onto the roof terrace.

I had initially followed Marlowe outside to see if she was okay, but once I was at the edge of the terrace, I quickly got sidetracked by the view below. I looked out over the rooftops of London glistening in the darkness: flats, houses, offices, all dotted about like fairy lights, lighting the way across the sky. I perched myself on the arm of a bench to take it all in. There was one other person that I needed to say goodbye to: London, for she had been witness to it all. I could hear Marlowe talking in hushed tones as she hung up the phone and slid it back into her bag.

'You all right?' I said as she turned to go back inside.

'Yeah, Elsa's just restless and won't sleep unless one of us is there. But as I keep saying, she needs to learn. Apparently that makes me a bad mother. Jess…' she said, starting to speak before stopping herself.

'What's wrong?'

'I'll tell you later,' she said, quickly. 'I need to take this phone back to George.'

'I can't believe you're leaving, you total cow,' Amber said, grabbing me around my neck. I had gone back inside in an attempt to find Marlowe but had somehow found myself on the dance floor instead.

'My hair, Amber,' I cried, as she attempted to spin me around.

'Sean, it's your job to clean the oven now she's gone,' Amber said, laughing.

'Yes, Sean,' I shouted. 'Please do run a cloth over her place every once in a while. I can't make it back every Saturday morning to clean.'

'And we'll come and visit,' Henry said. 'I've always wanted to see where Sean was born.'

'You're welcome any time, either with Sean or without him. You're my friend too, now.'

I smiled at him as Sean reached down and threw me over his shoulder. In a blurry, twisted haze, I could feel the world spinning quickly around me.

'Put me down!' I giggled before sinking back to the floor.

'Nice undercarriage,' Sean said, 'firm to say the least…'

'I hate you, you total bastard,' I said, playfully hitting his arm.

'But I can bet you'll miss me the most,' he said, grinning.

It was the first mention that night. A vivid reminder of all that I was leaving.

'Can I tell you a secret, James?' Marlowe said on the terrace, taking an extra-long drag of her cigarette.

He nodded as he exhaled a plume of smoke into the night air.

'I think I just ended my marriage. Sorry,' she said, immediately apologising. 'I just haven't been able to tell anyone and they're all so happy in there. I didn't want to put a dampener on things.'

'When did you leave him?' he said, calmly.

'About two hours ago, in the car, outside. I've wanted to for months, but I guess tonight was just a confirmation. It feels good in a weird way.'

'Can I tell you a secret?' James said, coyly. 'I haven't smoked since I was seventeen. I only suggested coming out here because I needed the chance to get you on your own for a minute.'

'James—'

'I know, before you say it,' he continued, 'you're still officially married and obviously that ruled out any ideas I may have had when I first met you, but I have to tell you: I can't stop thinking about you. I haven't been able to stop thinking about you since that night at the party. I even have a fucking painting with your name on it resting against my desk. Every morning you're there and every time…'

'James, I left my husband less than two hours ago and he's standing the other side of those glass doors.' Marlowe looked at him. 'I may not want to be with him anymore but I'm still married, as you said yourself. And besides, I'm not the easiest ride at the fairground. For the past six years I've existed only inside a marriage. And now you're asking for spontaneity? Things like this don't happen to girls like me.'

'I just don't know how he could've done that to you… it's just beyond me.'

Marlowe stubbed out her cigarette in an ashtray on the wall. 'I think we'd better go back inside,' she said, picking up her bag.

'Marlowe, wait…'

'I can't, James,' she said. 'I just can't do to him what he did to me.'

I could feel my feet throbbing under the bed covers as I tried to recover from a long night of dancing. I lifted them up one at a time in an attempt to relieve the sting from the newly formed blisters on the back of my heels.

'Charlie,' I whispered. 'Are you awake?'

'No,' he said, his face nestled into the pillow.

'You are!' I said, giving his cheek a slight tap.

He smiled gently but his eyes remain closed.

'Look. At. Me…' I said as I pressed my forehead against his.

He took a deep breath as he slowly opened his eyes.

'Any regrets?' I said. 'Before we leave tomorrow?'

'About you? Never. Not even for a second, not even for a moment…' I could feel his cold hands stroking the inside of my leg. 'Not for a day… or a week… or a month…'

'Or a year…?' I whispered, kissing his neck…

As I felt the weight of his body wrap around me I knew that this was where the struggle had ended. It had been twelve months of many different nights together, all the different kinds of nights, culminating in the here and the now.

I once thought that true happiness would be fireworks and celebration. I'd grown into thinking it should be shouted loudly from rooftops. But on that particular night, on the eve of a great adventure, I realised that true happiness was quiet, determined and strong. Whether you've decided to break free on your own for the first time, or lying, peacefully, next to the person you love.

Chapter Twenty-Five – Rainbows

My mind drifted in and out of sleep, halfway between real life and a faraway land. We were in a hurry, running across the forecourt of the tarmac towards an airplane. I could feel the floor crack beneath my feet as I jumped over the split and skidded, breaking free from the rubble. My legs felt like jelly and were powerless. I could see the tip of the wing. I could see the hordes of people boarding but they couldn't hear my shouts. They couldn't seem to hear my screams. Terror shuttled back and forth as the whole place felt just ten degrees out – only half an inch to the left – from exactly how things were supposed to be. I looked down towards my suitcase and noticed my hand: a hairline cut striped across my palm, which bled slightly as I twisted it. I looked up and had finally made it to the steps of the door as the sound of footsteps pounded behind me. My feet skipped up them two, three, four at a time, but the more I ran the steeper they got. How could I reach the door of the plane if I couldn't climb high enough? If I couldn't run.

I woke up with a start as I tried to regain my breath. My eyelids flickered in the morning sun as I felt the roof of my mouth with my tongue. It was dry and heavy, heaving in a gasp for air or water, anything that would ease the stiffness and quench the thirst. Beads of sweat from a disturbed night's sleep itched my forehead as I stretched my body out in release. My arms lay heavy above my head, my neck still damp from the nightmare. I took in the seconds, one at a time, slowly bringing myself to reality, returning me to the world that I knew.

It was just a dream.

It was just a bad dream.

I lay there watching the sunshine through the curtains casting bright, pale shapes onto the bed covers. I was tired and could smell fried egg coming from the kitchen as Charlie prepared his usual 'Saturday Sandwich'. Only it wasn't Saturday and I still had to begin my last day working for the magazine. I pulled off the bed covers with one giant tug and wrapped my towelling dressing gown around me.

'You're cutting it fine, aren't you?' Charlie said as I walked into the kitchen. 'Still, who cares if you're late on your last day, eh?'

I poured myself some coffee – my neck stiff from an active night's sleep.

'I had the worst dream,' I said, rubbing it gently, 'I've woken up feeling exhausted.'

'Was I in it?' Charlie said, as he looked over the frying pan at a congealed mass of eggs and bacon.

The 'Saturday Sandwich' was an invention that he had created which consisted of all the foods sitting in one's fridge that could be considered a breakfast item. In an array of dairy products and processed meat, it was usually bacon, egg, cheese and tomato all melted together and toasted between the bookends of a white bun. I had put it in the same culinary category as a Friday night kebab: it had its purpose, and was usually only appetising when either drunk or nursing a hangover.

As I watched him plate up the breakfast in his navy blue dressing gown, the decision that was once a distant concept had finally come to fruition.

'Are you all packed?'

'All packed,' he said, discarding the fat from the bottom of the pan.

'Don't tip that down the plughole, Amber will kill you…' I said, tapping the pedal bin open.

'I also made you some food to take to work, it's in a box in the fridge.'

'It's not another sandwich, is it?' I said, prising open the plastic container.

'No smartarse, it's actually a salad.'

'So what are you doing while I'm at work today?'

'I'm going to send the last of the boxes with the courier and then go past the office to collect our tickets…'

'What time's our flight again?'

'11:30 p.m.'

'11:30 p.m.,' I repeated out loud.

'I just thought it best to get a night flight. I have back to back meetings as soon as we get there and this way, I'll get a full night's sleep.'

'No. That makes sense,' I said, putting my packed lunch in my bag along with a token gesture of fruit that very rarely seemed to get eaten.

'So,' he said, leaning against the cupboard, 'does it feel a bit strange yet?'

His hair flopped over his face as he quickly ran his hand through to tame it. For a split second he reminded me of the Charlie I first met, exceptionally well groomed but a little straggly in the morning. It was endearing – a sight only reserved for me.

'Come here...' I said as I wrapped my arms around him. 'I could never regret any decision when it comes to you.'

He kissed me on the end of my nose and then again on my mouth.

'I'll make you happy, Jess,' he said. 'I promise.'

My feet pounded the pavement as I entered the last stretch of the commute, making my way towards the double doors for what would be the final time. As usual, I turned the corner and sprinted towards the lift, holding the doors open with my foot for a man running late behind me.

'Thank you,' he said, as he wedged himself in.

I smiled at him and pressed the button for the fourth floor.

I could see that Vin was already at his computer and knocked lightly on the door. An array of crumbs sat on the chest of his black T-shirt, a remainder of his breakfast, but for the first time, a breakfast that I hadn't been texted to collect for him. It was usually an extra large coffee and pain au chocolat, which I left on his desk each morning at 8.00 a.m.

'Where did you get the breakfast from?' I asked. 'Cheating on me with another assistant?' I smiled as he brushed the crumbs off, maybe a little embarrassed. 'Well...' I said, quietly,

'I'll get going then. Is there anything I can get you before I start work? Another coffee? Some toast?'

'No, I'm grand,' he said as he turned to his computer. 'Oh and Jess,' he added as I turned to go, 'you know, I haven't told anyone that you're leaving. I'm not rushing to fill the position so I thought it would give me some time with head office to mention it only after you've gone.'

'Scared they won't compare?' I said, smiling.

'Yeah, sure, Jess,' he said with a snort, 'because it's really sparse out there finding creatives in London.'

'Yes, but will they collect your coffee each morning?' I joked.

'Just get back to work,' he said. 'I want those shots at Emmer Hall finished before you leave.'

'Righto!' I said, closing the door behind me.

'And Jess,' he said, as I turned back *again* into his office, 'if you leave before I've had a chance to say bye and stuff, I just want you to know that the offer still stands, if you need any contacts once you're settled out there, don't hesitate to give me a bell.'

'Thank you, Vin,' I said. 'I really appreciate it.'

I smiled at him, knowing that this small exchange was as close to a goodbye as I would get. But it was enough. I walked into my refurbished cupboard that I had briefly referred to as my office, sat down at my desk and turned on my computer.

It's okay to be nervous, I thought to myself, as I made my way through the shots from Emmer Hall. I was eating a banana, slowly munching my way through the morning, a trait which provided a distraction from all the arrangements that were coursing through my mind – mainly logistical, carefully curating a mental list of things that I still was yet to pack.

I looked around at the walls of my office and at the images that I'd stuck against them: a few portraits from Cathy, the few shots I'd taken of Gracie in my first week of work and a picture of a traditional punk that Vin had slyly taken one morning on his way into work on the tube. I pulled them all down and slid them into my bag. I scribbled a note of thanks for Vin, signed off with a small 'J'. By the time he sees it I'll be gone, I thought to myself.

By late afternoon, the butterflies in my stomach that I had managed to settle had begun to flutter again. I gathered up the rest of my belongings, leaving a few items of stationery for my successor and turned back at the door to take one final look. The past few months had felt like a dream. A makeshift desk and two rusty filing cabinets represented all that I had worked for, so little in value, but undoubtedly worth so much to me.

I took a deep breath and pulled the door closed behind me. After twelve months of storm clouds, it was finally time for rainbows.

'Charlie?' I shouted, as I stepped over three large boxes in his hallway. I dropped my keys on the small table by the door and walked on through into the kitchen. The rooms were completely bare, with the very few things we weren't shipping, packed neatly to be collected for storage. As I attempted to find a kettle I heard the front door slam behind me.

'Well, today was a bit of a disaster…' Charlie shouted, from the hallway.

'Really?' I replied, 'what happened?'

'Nothing important, had to go back into work, didn't I, just paperwork stuff, nothing you'd understand.'

'You could try me?' I said, as I heard him turn on the shower.

I walked over to the window and looked down at the people below. It was a sight that I'd seen over a million times before, but only now did I seem to truly appreciate it. As I gazed out across the fairy lights, I struggled to comprehend all that I was leaving. I didn't want to think about it. I couldn't face the memories. I pulled out my phone buzzing loudly in my pocket to read the lit-up message. It was Vin:

Like I said, anything I can do to help. Safe flight. V x

'So,' Charlie said, pulling a jumper over his wet hair, 'what's for dinner?'

I laughed. 'You tell me. We've got a choice of dry cereal or the remainder of your bread bin.'

'We'll get something at the airport.' He shrugged. 'I picked up the tickets today; they're in the black wallet next to my coat.'

I reached over and pulled them towards me. As I flicked through the pile, a jagged corner ripped and sliced through the edge of my finger. 'Shit,' I cried, sucking it in frustration.

'All right,' Charlie said, 'sit down. Let me see.'

'Everything's just a total mess!' I said, sharply.

I held out my finger. It throbbed deeply as if it had its own heartbeat. He kissed it.

'Well, I'm glad we got that tantrum out of the way,' he said, trying to make a joke.

'I've had a really shitty day, Charlie.'

'Okay, Jess, I'll play the game. How was your day?'

'Awful, actually. I quit a job that I love, that I fought really hard to get and I let Vin down in the process, the one man who believed in me…'

He raised his eyebrows at me.

'. . . enough to hire me,' I backpedalled, 'you know what I mean…'

'Oh really?' he said, standing to his feet. 'The one man who believed in you?'

'I'm sorry. I didn't mean it like that… it's just hard to let go.'

'Well, quite frankly I preferred it when you worked at that shitty little restaurant. At least you smiled in those days…'

I looked at him. It was if the bubble of my existence had been popped.

He walked over to me and put his arms around my shoulder. 'I'm sorry. I think this move has just been a lot for us to get our heads around. I didn't mean to belittle you like that. I promise.'

'I know,' I said, quietly. 'This just isn't as easy as I thought it would be.'

Deep down I knew he was right. Of course there was a time to fight, but there was also a time to concede, when the fighting becomes just a means to an end, but not the actual end. I finished packing up the rest of my belongings and held firmly onto my tongue for the rest of the evening. Instead I focused on all the ways I should be grateful, too scared to let in all the reasons I should stay.

'Bloody holidaymakers!' the driver uttered as he swerved his way through Heathrow car park. 'Take up the whole bloody road, don't they...'

'We're at an airport,' I whispered to Charlie, 'what does he expect?' I reached down into my bag to check my passport and phone were still in the pocket where I'd left them. 'Did you pack an adaptor plug?'

'I packed six,' he said, smiling. 'Will you just relax, please?'

'And what about the keys to the new flat? Do I have a set of those too?'

He rummaged in his hand luggage and pulled out a set of three keys on a gold key ring. 'Here: they're all yours...'

'Brilliant,' I said, calmly. 'I think that's it then.'

I sat back in my seat and took a deep breath as Charlie squeezed my hand in reassurance.

'It's going to be fine,' he said, smiling.

'Terminal 3,' the driver shouted as he pulled the car to the side of the road.

'Where did this wind come from?' Charlie said, putting his coat on as we stood on the pavement.

I looked up at the glass building as we made our way through the large glass doors and on into a sea of check-in desks.

'I think this one's ours...' he said, waving me over.

I stood, fidgeting with my bag in a queue that seemed to go on for miles. As we reached the front of the desk I stood back as he handed over two large suitcases and one box.

'The rest we'll carry on,' Charlie said as he handed over our passports.

'One way?' the man behind the desk said.

'One way,' Charlie replied, confidently.

I browsed the rows of sunglasses in duty free as Charlie sprayed on a selection of aftershaves. They were the kind of products that were bought on a whim, on the verge of a holiday. But the tone of our mood had a different feel from one of excitement. It actually bordered upon fear.

He squirted me with a dark green bottle of what only could be described as musty grass clippings. 'Charlie, I'm not going to sit with you on the plane if you smell like a used car dealer.'

I didn't know if it was the sandalwood, or the mix of floral undertones but after a few minutes of spraying perfumes, I felt a wave of nausea suddenly wash over me.

'You ready?' Charlie said, shoving his carrier bag of duty-free purchases into his rucksack.

'Yep,' I said, smiling, 'you lead the way...'

We walked across the carpet as I tried to match my feet on the printed pattern: it was a calming technique that I'd learned as a child and a way of distracting me from my churning stomach. As the navy blue diamonds guided our way through the rows of fixed chairs, I looked up at the screens and could see our flight was now boarding.

'What wrong?' Charlie said as I gradually slowed down to a halt.

'Nothing,' I said, 'I'll be okay. I just don't like flying.'

I took a deep breath, put one foot in front of the other and carefully focused back onto the carpet.

'We're in first class, Jess, it's just booze and films,' Charlie said, looking back at me as he strode ahead. 'You'll be fine, just hurry up.'

'Mind if I just nip to the loos before we get to the gate?' I said as my stomach lurched for the second time.

'Yeah, but be quick, Jess,' he said, impatiently. 'I can already see a queue boarding ahead.'

I ran into the toilet and slammed the door behind me as a hurl of white liquid shot out my mouth and down into the pan. I could see my red nail polish move in and out of focus as my hands clung to the bowl through the weight of my retch. My stomach contracted again as I hung my head over the basin. But it was dry. I was empty.

After five minutes of calm on the toilet floor and a quick swill of water at the sink, I made my way back out into the waiting room.

'Get it together,' I said to myself as I walked back over to Charlie who had a sense of urgency written across his face. It became clear from his expression that if I didn't quicken the pace slightly then we were going to miss our plane. He jogged on ahead as my legs slowed from under me; my vision, strained, reverted back into a blur.

'Charlie,' I said, as I heard him turn around. 'I'm sorry, but I can't do this…'

'What do you mean?' he said, getting agitated. 'The flying? Jesus, Jess, it's fine, just hurry up will you…'

'Charlie, I mean it, I can't do this. I can't get on that plane… with you.'

He crouched down in front of me as I looked into his eyes.

'I don't get it, Jess,' he said, becoming more and more confused. 'You said so yourself, you wanted a new life.'

'But this is *your* life.'

'Don't be silly,' he said, pulling on my arm. 'Just get up, we're going to be late.'

'Charlie...' I said, reaching out to stop him. I could feel my legs fold to the ground again, my chest tightening as I struggled to breath.

'Get up, Jess, you're being ridiculous,' he said. 'People are starting to stare.'

'No, that's just it, I'm not being ridiculous, Charlie. I'm not your silly little girl anymore. That was a role I was given... but didn't once ask for.'

His eyes widened in despair. I looked over at the flashing neon light. 'The gate's about to close, you should go...'

'And you want to stay here?' he said, finally losing his patience with me. 'Right here on the airport floor?'

I nodded firmly. 'Charlie, you're going to miss the plane.'

And finally, he did as instructed, turning back for a brief moment as I pulled myself up to my knees.

'Miss, are you okay?' I heard in the distance, as a man from the gate ran over and quickly knelt down in front of me. 'Where are you trying to get to, Miss?' he said, his hand rested between the edges of my shoulder blades.

'I'm not trying to get anywhere,' I said, pulling myself to my feet, gently. 'I just want to stay right here.'

Chapter Twenty-Six – Human Nature

I tried to hold the sky up as the

clouds
   fell
   down.

As I climbed to my feet, pressing firmly into the ground below, I was foggy, aching and exhausted. The juggernaut of the past few weeks had faltered and I had fled, or returned home, which one it was, I was yet to decipher.

Throughout the past few years, a turning sphere that I had called my world had gathered pace. And I was strapped to it. Without gravity, I was being hurtled towards my future where life goals, ambitions, stable relationships and predicted accomplishments had passed me by and within this interchanging construct known as my 'formative years,' the parameters of what I was yearning for had now irreparably changed.

For the first time I wanted something that was within me. I wanted things in black and white, less fuss, no mess, no nonsense. I wanted to surround myself with people who had tried and failed: gold medalists at making mistakes, people who stuttered before they spoke, a little unsure, a little shy, but there, present, showing up regardless. I didn't want a glossy exterior. I didn't want things to be perfect.

I wheeled my carry-on across the squeaky marble floor and headed back to the familiarity of a place called home, all the while my heart convincing my brain that everything would be all right, while my brain convinced my heart not to cry: here I was. A few milestones light of what I'd hoped to achieve but hovering in its place, the divine possibilities of tomorrow. Soaring through the clouds of expectation, I sought truth and though it may not have been as people had expected, I was standing on a chequered carpet of subtle life lessons I had so invaluably now learned.

There are many things that can deny the world of real truth. The sound of fake laughter, a convenient relationship, heavy make-up, gossip, the polite group chuckle after the delivery of a bad joke or the smell of body odour masked by deodorant; falsehood, the antithesis of what is real, lies around us every day like pungent cologne, almost scary to look at directly in the eye but even more terrifying to remain completely blind to it. But to take this away leaves a gaping hole of uncertainty, held in the knowledge that some things can't ever really be changed. After all, I would rather be abandoned for the person I really am than loved by someone who doesn't know me at all. I took one last look at the Heathrow departures board, the fluorescent yellow destinations flickering down. Now all that remained was me.

I couldn't get my train ticket out of my pocket and I felt like a failure. The queues were backing up behind me creating a scrum at the mouth of the Piccadilly line. In my short absence, Heathrow tube station had become a mass of angry commuters. As I pushed my way towards the front of the crowd and slammed my card against the yellow pad, the doors shot open and I was through. I wheeled my carry case to the top of the escalator and made a brave hop onto the moving stairs. I waited dutifully behind a family, who stood to the left, beneath a few disdainful glances from onlookers. Didn't they know that this was for speedies – perhaps they didn't they know the rules? I patiently waited, adjourned to the sidelines. Tolerant.

After all, I was in no hurry. The past year had been a little tumultuous, a major transition down a slippery slope, but I'd managed. And so life had thrown a different ball than the one I presumed to catch, but I was still breathing. Although my beige rain mac was now a little stained, my hair hanging loosely around my ears, I sat on the platform and waited for the next train, four minutes… and counting…

An hour later, I turned the key in the flat that still felt like home, opening the door to the familiar waft of Amber's perfume: a sign that she was out, at a party or somewhere. In a familiar motion I threw my keys onto the table in the hallway and wheeled my only case into my familiar bedroom. I stepped into the bathroom, turning on the shower to full power, taking off my clothes, standing naked beneath the falling water. I leaned against the wall steadying myself with my hand as the water cascaded over my face. What I thought was a tear fell on to my cheek, but it cleverly disguised itself as water.

As I sat on the edge of my bed in Amber's white bath towel,

my dripping wet hair slicked to my back, I looked around at my room: my candles and magazines still adorned the bookcase, clothes hung in the wardrobe that I hadn't thought to pack. But there, on my floral pink bedspread, I made a silent promise to myself: this time there would be no days in the flat wearing only my pyjamas, no thinking sad thoughts, images blazing through my head, no crying, no self-pity, no regret.

Instead I focused on the practicalities and opened the door to my wardrobe. As I stood in front of the rail – sparse and limited – it occurred to me that although it was only clothing, these garments were the touchstones of my life so far. I flicked through the rail and stopped at the dress I wore when I first met Charlie, the outfit I bought for my first day at work, my white-shirted uniform, my black work shoes from my job at Guido's; a catalogue of memories, a catalogue of clothes that only I had lived in. I leaned over and folded an errant T-shirt up and put it to one side. What remained? Not much, as it turned out. I took a sip of water from the bedside table and turned off the light. I closed my eyes and pictured the situation: single again, yes, and technically alone, but as far from lonely as one could possibly be.

The next morning I stood outside the red brick building of *Route* magazine, secretly hoping I could go unnoticed and just step back into the shoes of the girl who used to work there. I walked through the glass entrance and saw Vin in the lift, just as the doors were closing. He pressed the button firmly and waited for me to step in. Maybe there was something about his face or the honesty in the way he smiled at me but I could feel my eyes welling as soon as I looked at him. I swallowed it and stood next to him, tightly holding my portfolio bag as we rose to the fourth floor.

'I need you to take a portrait of Rebecca in the courtyard before lunchtime.'

I nodded. 'Of course.'

We exited the lift together and walked passed his office. He veered off as I continued through to my own.

I sat down at my desk and pulled my pictures from my bag, sticking each one back up in its usual spot. I looked down at my phone at a message received from Charlie. That got me. It read:

I still love you.

I inhaled deeply before typing out a reply:

I love you too, always did, always will.

I pressed send, picked up my notebook and before I could think anymore, made my way down to the courtyard. Of course I knew that the feeling would somehow dilute over time. Things always came to pass, just like the seasons: spring, summer, autumn and winter.

I lifted up the camera as Rebecca stood confidently next to a rosebush in the courtyard, her eyes looking directly into my lens as I raised my camera.

Click.

And I would learn to care again. Learn to give a damn about

the small stuff, the things that seem so trivial to me now: text people back, make the date. Learn to fight. Fight so hard for what you want that it suddenly becomes true…

Click.

In a city so relentless and heartbreaking as London, it is crazy for anyone to want to stay, but I can never leave. And we'll always exist within it. In ghost-infested attics of my mind, the very thought of him: in the buildings, the streets, the people, the stars. But now I take the part of observer.

Click.

Chapter Twenty-Seven – Love, and Other Things to Live For

Here is a story of the rebels and queens
Make-up and break-ups and all in between
Stealing a look from a man at the bar – did
it, but didn't want to go that far

And here in a land of flirting and sass
Helped along by the stuff in the glass
Knowing the facts that you know to be true
Stuck to your roots and transgressions like glue.

A promise, a gift will be handed to you.
Just don't show your feelings no matter what you do –

Don't show your feelings no matter what you do.

So here life now stands on a wing and a prayer
Travelling the world over, both here and there
Taking the hand of those either side
With honesty and courage and nothing to hide.

Aiming high though we may hit the floor...

Guided only by Love, and Other Things to Live For.

Acknowledgements

I wanted to share my gratitude to my family: the
Dohertys and the Hopleys – this book is a part
of me and therefore it is a part of you too.

To all the team at HQ at Harper Collins:
Lisa Milton, who believed that this could be
more than just an idea and provided me with a
platform on which to share it; you helped me find
my voice and gave me the confidence to use it.

My editors, Anna Baggaley and Clio Cornish,
for their persistent hard work and dedication
in bringing order to a chaotic mind – your
patience and positivity knows no bounds.

Juliet Mushens – my one-woman army agent,
soundboard and trusted ear. Thank you for standing
by me at every turn. From the moment I arrived in
your office with a folder full of notes to having the
unprecedented foresight to see that through to a novel.
I don't know how you do what you do, but thank you.

My heartfelt gratitude to Susanne and Brando
Boniver, for lending me a castle in the skies of
Rome within which this book was written.

And to all my close friends, colleagues and random strangers
who encouraged me in times of self-doubt by uttering
the simple yet invaluable words: *just keep on going...*

Website: www.louiseleverett.com
Instagram: @louiseleverett

ONE PLACE. MANY STORIES

Bold, innovative and
empowering publishing.

FOLLOW US ON:

@HQStories